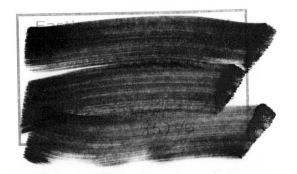

# THE TEMPLAR
# MAGICIAN

Also by P. C. Doherty

# THE TEMPLAR MAGICIAN

# MAGICIAN

P. C. Doherty

MINOTAUR BOOKS ✖ NEW YORK

THE TEMPLAR MAGICIAN. Copyright © 2009 by Paul Doherty. All rights reserved. Printed in the United States of America. For information, address St. Martin's Press, 175 Fifth Avenue, New York, N.Y. 10010.

www.minotaurbooks.com

ISBN 978-0-312-67502-8

First published in Great Britain by HEADLINE PUBLISHING GROUP, an Hachette UK Company

First U.S. Edition: November 2011

10  9  8  7  6  5  4  3  2  1

In loving memory of our wonderful Mum
Kathleen Elizabeth Kenny
Carmel, Brigid, Siobhan, Rosaleen, Michael and
Kathleen
We were blessed to have you as our Mum
May you rest in peace
God Bless

# Historical Note

By 1152, the great Frankish lords had occupied Outremer (Palestine) for over fifty years, since the leaders of the First Crusade had stormed the walls of Jerusalem and captured the Holy City. In that time, it had become a Frankish outpost of the West. The great lords had elected a king, Baldwin III, and were busy dividing Outremer into spheres of influence, each baron jostling for power, occupying towns, cities and ports. The Templar order, founded by Hugh de Payens within a decade of taking Jerusalem, had also expanded its influence. The Templars were now an international movement, patronised by the great and the good, hallowed by the papacy and made into the professional fighting arm of the West. They had their own headquarters in Jerusalem, and were already expanding their power, taking over or building castles and fortresses throughout Outremer. The order was also busy establishing and spreading its roots in Europe, be it France, England, Germany or Spain. The Templars represented the ideals of the Western knight, the paladin who offered his sword for the love of Christ and the defence of Holy Mother Church.

They also acquired great wealth, and the combination of riches, power and status made them intrigue and negotiate with the best as they strove to consolidate and expand even further. Hugh de Payens allegedly visited England and saw the prospects of further advancement of his order there. By 1150, the Temple had set up its headquarters in London and owned manor houses throughout the kingdom. Nevertheless, the expansion of the order meant that successive Grand Masters were eager for recruits, and the Temple attracted not only idealists and romantics but also those who had a great deal to hide.

Nowhere was this more true than England. The invasion of the Normans in 1066 had created a fighting elite intent on acquiring land and wealth. Norman influence stretched to the Welsh and Scottish marches, and the constant jostling of Norman warlords meant that there was a pressing need for the English king to be a strong military ruler. William the Conqueror and his two sons, William Rufus and Henry I, proved to be most adept at this. However, when Henry died without a male heir (his son William having drowned in the *White Ship* disaster), the English crown became the object of intense rivalry between Mathilda, Henry's daughter, and her cousin, Stephen of Blois. England descended into civil war so bitter and violent that men said it was the age when God and his saints slept. Both sides recruited the worst mercenaries from abroad as well as rogue knights from the English shires, eager for plunder, ruthless in its pursuit. The war, which lasted between 1135 and 1154, grew even more savage and brutal when Mathilda's son Henry Fitzempress took up the cause of his mother, determined to settle for nothing but the crown itself. The opponents manoeuvred for position even as they secretly recognised that an end to the war and the possibility of a lasting peace could only come about if one of the sides was totally destroyed . . .

The quotations at the head of each chapter in Part One are from William of Tyre's chronicle *A History of Deeds Done Beyond the Seas*. Those in Part Two are from the chronicle *Gesta Stephani – The Deeds of Stephen*. An author's note at the end provides an accurate context for many of the events described in this novel.

# Main Historical Characters

## OUTREMER

Baldwin III:            King of Jerusalem

Raymond:               Count of Tripoli

Melisande:             Count Raymond's wife

## THE CHURCH

Eugenius III:          Pope, Bishop of Rome

Theodore:              Archbishop of
                       Canterbury

Henry Murdac:          Archbishop of York;
                       fervent supporter of
                       King Stephen

Thomas à Becket:       cleric and royal clerk;
                       later Archbishop of
                       Canterbury

Bernard of Clairvaux:  one of the founders of
                       the Cistercian order;
                       an international figure,
                       preacher and politician;
                       an ardent supporter of
                       the new Templar order

## ENGLAND

| | |
|---|---|
| William the Norman, or the Conqueror: | King of England, 1087 |
| William II, or Rufus: | son of the Conqueror; King of England, 1087–1100; mysteriously killed whilst hunting in the New Forest |
| Henry I: | Rufus's brother; King of England, 1100–35 |
| Prince William: | Henry I's son and heir; drowned when the *White Ship* capsized and sank |
| Mathilda: | Henry's daughter, Empress; married Henry, the Holy Roman Emperor, then Geoffrey, Count of Anjou |
| Stephen of Blois: | grandson of the Conqueror through the latter's daughter Adela; King of England, 1135–54 |

| | |
|---|---|
| Eustace: | Stephen's son and heir |
| William: | Stephen's second son |
| Henry Fitzempress, or the Angevin: | son of the Empress Mathilda, through whom he claimed the English crown; King of England, 1154–89, founder of the Plantagenet dynasty |
| Geoffrey de Mandeville: | Earl of Essex; a leading protagonist in the civil war; killed in battle. Certain chronicles have given him a very sinister reputation |
| Simon de Senlis: | Earl of Northampton; one of King Stephen's most loyal supporters |

## TEMPLARS

| | |
|---|---|
| Hugh de Payens: | founder of the Templar order, 1099–1100 |

Bertrand (de) Tremelai:     Grand Master of the
                            Templar order, 1152

Andrew (de) Montebard:      Grand Master of the
                            Templar order, 1153

Jacques de Molay:           last Grand Master of
                            the Templar order;
                            executed by Philip IV
                            of France, 1313

Boso (de) Baiocis:          possible master of the
                            English Temple,
                            c. 1153


## FRANCE

Philip IV, or 'Le Bel':     Capetian King of
                            France, d. 1314; the
                            architect of the
                            destruction of the
                            Templar order, 1307–13

## SCOTLAND

Robert the Bruce:                         King of Scotland; drove
out the English armies
of Edward I and
Edward II; provided a
sanctuary for Templars
after the dissolution of
their order

# Prologue

Melrose Abbey, Scotland

Autumn 1314

The monk lifted his head and listened to the peal of bells roll through the abbey buildings. A funeral was being prepared. The dirige psalms were being sung, the plainchant drifting on the evening breeze. Soon the solemn peal of bells would begin again. If it was a woman being buried, two peals; for a man, three; for a cleric, as many as the minor orders he had received.

1

'*Have you even been shown the Gates of Death? Or met the Janitors of the Shadowlands?*'

Brother Benedict turned swiftly. He stared at the old woman. She was dressed in the blackest widow's weeds and sat on the high-backed chair close to his cot bed with its plaid-patterned drape.

'Mistress.' The young Benedictine monk smiled apologetically. 'I was distracted. I really did not expect you until tomorrow, Lammas Eve . . .'

'But I came today.' The old woman gripped her walking cane by its carved handle. 'I have studied the manuscripts.' She sighed, and rose to her feet, eyes no longer on the Benedictine but on the arrow-loop window behind him. The day was darkening, the weak sunlight fading. Next to the window hung a Little Mary, a wooden carving of the Virgin Mother and her Divine Child.

'The Gates of Death?' Brother Benedict whispered. 'The Janitors of the Shadowlands?'

'Magic, Brother!' the woman whispered.

'Brother Guibert, our precentor, claims he met a warlock who talked of a monastery that sank into the ground then rose like Christ on Easter Day.'

'No, no.' The old woman shook her head. She tapped the chancery coffer beside her, then walked over to where the monk sat on his scribe chair. 'Brother Benedict.' She grasped an arm of the chair and stared hard at the young monk. 'You write, at my request and that of His Grace Robert de Bruce, King of Scotland, the history of our order, the Templars. Yes?' She gazed fiercely at him, her light-blue eyes betraying the passion that burned like a firebrand within her. 'Our order,' she repeated, 'the Templars, founded by our great and saintly ancestor Hugh de Payens, now destroyed by Philip, the Stone King of France. He burned Jacques de Molay on a small island in the Seine. Our Grand Master was lashed to a beam with cords and chains, beside him Geoffrey de Charnay. Both men, Brother Benedict, protested to the very end against the allegations of black magic, sorcery and witchcraft levelled by the Stone King's lawyers. They testified to the piety, saintliness and innocence of the Templars. Ah well.' She paused. 'Later, secret adherents of our order, those who'd survived brutish, black betrayal, torture and gruesome imprisonment, swam the Seine and collected in their teeth the holy but charred remains of these valiant warriors. Yet,' the old woman, who rejoiced in the family name of de Payens, grasped the ivory handle of her walking stick, 'such innocence wasn't always so. Here, in these islands . . .' Her voice faltered.

The young monk glanced up in expectation.

'Madam, such hellish accusations, levelled often against the Templars, have always been lies.'

'Is that so?' the old woman whispered. 'Listen now. Our order was founded by the great Hugh de Payens in Outremer. It was blessed by Bernard de Clairvaux, hallowed by popes, favoured by the princes of this world. Little wonder the Templars waxed fat and powerful, but in the end, monk, dreams die, visions fade. *Ab initio*, from the very beginning, there were those who immersed themselves in the hunt for sacred relics and the power these might bring. Worse,' she hissed, 'some even turned to dark imaginings, calling on the shadow host, conjuring up demons garbed in the livery of hell's flames. They hired witches who collected the poison herbs of Thessaly. They set up a nursery of sorcery, tainted our order like the poisonous yew tree with its roots deep in the grave-yard, digging down into dead men's tombs and draining from them malignant vapours to poison the air. Oh yes.' The old woman tapped the manuscripts stacked on top of the flat lid of an iron-bound coffer. 'Brother, study these here. Do so carefully. Write as you did last time; base yourself on the manuscripts, weave your web and tell your tale.' She moved across to the lancet window, staring out at the evening mist moving like a gauze veil over the Melrose countryside. 'Conjure up the past.' Her voice became strident. 'Robins and nightingales do not live long in cages, nor does the truth when it's kept captive. Read all these manuscripts, Brother, and you'll meet the Lord Satan, as you would in a crystal or a burning sapphire, bright with the glow of hell's fire.'

# PART ONE

## TRIPOLI: OUTREMER
## AUTUMN 1152

# Chapter 1

Count Raymond was struck down by the
swords of the Assassins at the entrance
to the gate.

'A time of turbulence, of visions, portents and warnings! Heaven glowers at us because we have lost our way! Our souls, with their open ulcers, will go to hell on crutches. Around us, nothing but hollow graves, rotten and rotting corpses. Water may soak the earth. Blood soaks the heavens and calls on God's justice to flash out like lightning. The sins committed in close and secret chambers will be paraded along the spacious pavements and squares of hell, where the rack, the gallows and the torture wheels stand black against the eternal flames of God's wrath. I urge you to repent! We have taken Jerusalem, but we have lost our way.'

The preacher, garbed in filthy animal skins, lifted his staff and pointed up at the sheer blue sky, which curved above the gleaming white city of Tripoli, overlooking the Middle Sea.

'Repent!' he yelled in one last attempt to provoke his listeners. 'Repent, before the doom gates open and disgorge the power of hell.'

Edmund de Payens, knight of the Templar order, leaned across in a creak of leather and touched his English comrade Philip Mayele on the wrist.

'Are you frightened, Philip? Fearful of what is to come?'

The Englishman's long, swarthy, lined face broke into a grin. He clawed at the greying hair that straggled down to the white cloak around his shoulders. He scratched his beard and moustache, his brown eyes gleaming with cynicism.

'Edmund, you are a soft soul, to be driven by many a black storm before you harden. Look around you. Life is as it was, as it will be and ever shall be.' He laughed abruptly at Edmund's frown over such mockery of the 'Glory Be'.

De Payens quickly remembered his resolution, after he'd last been shriven, not to be so pompous and quick to take offence. He forced a grin and nodded, curling the reins of his horse around his mittened fingers.

He and Mayele were moving slowly along the Street of Aleppo down to the city gates of Tripoli. They were escorting Count Raymond, the Frankish lord of the city, who was about to leave to be reconciled with his estranged wife, Melisande, in Jerusalem. De Payens closed his eyes against the bustle of the crowds. In truth, he wanted to be back with his brethren, his fellow warrior-monks. Yet, he opened his eyes and glanced quickly at Mayele, not all the brothers were dream-followers or visionaries. Hadn't Mayele been excommunicated with bell, book and candle for killing a priest in Coggeshalle, a town in that mist-hung island of England on the edge of the world?

'*Cruciferi, à bas, à bas!*' The cry of derision was hurled in Provençal, a guttural shout by a Turk. It shook Edmund from his reverie, and he became aware of the crowd pressing around him. Ahead of them, Raymond of Tripoli's lightly armed Turcopole mercenaries were pushing their way through the throng, their lamellar cuirasses gleaming in the strengthening sun. Edmund searched the faces on either side, but no one dared catch his eye. Anyone could have hurled such an insult. Most of the men had their heads hidden by white turbans, their faces half veiled by the end of the cloth pulled across nose and mouth against the dust-bearing wind and the swirling black horde of flies. De Payens remained uneasy. A dust haze billowed. The stench of camel and horse dung thickened the air. All around rose the cries of the various traders. Here in Tripoli, Jew and Muslim, Catholic and Orthodox,

Frank and Turk rubbed shoulders uneasily in the tunnelled darkness of the alleyways, in the noisy bazaars and the sun-scorched squares. Tripoli was the meeting place of different faiths and cultures, kept calm by the mailed fist of the old count riding behind them with his escort of clerks and men-at-arms. Above their heads, Raymond's gorgeous blue and yellow banners, displaying the silver cedars of Lebanon, floated in the late-morning breeze.

'Stay calm, Templar!' The count's powerful voice forced de Payens to twist round in the saddle. The Templar nodded politely at Raymond even as he regretted not wearing his mail hauberk and chausses; nothing but lightweight boots, quilted jerkin and hose beneath the white Templar mantle sewn with its red cross. On his back was slung a concave shield, around his waist a simple leather sword belt with scabbards for sword and dagger. Was this enough protection if such hurled invective gave way to violence? De Payens twisted his neck against the bubbles of sweat beneath his long hair. He clutched the reins between his quilted mittens and murmured the Templar prayer: '*Non nobis, Domine, non nobis, sed nomini tuo da gloriam*' – not to us, oh Lord, not unto us, but unto yourself give glory.

He must remember he was a Poor Knight of the Temple, dedicated to poverty, obedience and chastity. He had sworn to follow the Templar cross in unblemished fealty to his Grand Master, which was why he and Mayele were here. For the last few months they'd been garrisoned at Chastel Blanc, a Templar fortress to the south of Tripoli. From there they'd been summoned to escort Count Raymond down into Jerusalem. Edmund was impatient. He was glad to be free of the grim routine of Chastel Blanc, eager to see Jerusalem again, but he quickly remembered how this mission was his prime duty. He was bound by oath. The Templars had been founded to patrol the highways of Outremer, Palestine, the land of Le Bon Seigneur. Jesus Christ, God incarnate, had walked, slept, eaten, talked to his friends, preached, died and risen again on this very soil. Nevertheless, de Payens felt a disquieting anxiety clawing at his heart and dulling his brain. Tripoli was noisy and frenetic, a sea of shifting colours, constant dust haze, strengthening heat and marauding flies. His body was soaked in sweat, his horse restless. The crowd on either side could house enemies as well as friends.

'Stay awake.' Mayele leaned over in a gust of sweat and ale. 'Stay awake, Edmund, for ye know not the day nor the hour; it will come like a thief in the night!'

De Payens blinked away the beads of perspiration and licked his sand-and salt-caked lips. The heat was closing in around him like a thick blanket. He must not, as he often did in such circumstances, dream about his grandparents' house, its whitewashed coolness among the cypress and olive groves of northern Lebanon. He stirred restlessly in his saddle, tapped the hilt of his sword, slid his dagger in and out. The procession was now swinging its way down the main thoroughfare towards the great walled gate, above which the banners of Tripoli flapped between the gibbets ranged along the turreted walkway. Each scaffold bore a cadaver hanging by its neck, a proclamation pinned to its chest. This had become the gruesome feeding ground for kites, buzzards and vultures, their blood-splattered wings wafting away the black swarm of flies dancing against the light.

The noise grew deafening. Horses and donkeys brayed at the sweet smell of water. The clatter of pots and pans, the dull booming of kettle drums, the chatter in a myriad of tongues as traders called and beckoned was constant. The crowd broke like a shoal of multicoloured fish around the sea of stalls. A woman caught Edmund's eye. Her raven-black hair fringed a broad, smooth forehead, with arched brows over lustrous eyes. The bottom half of her face was hidden by a bead-laced gauze veil, which only enhanced her mysterious beauty. She smiled at him. Edmund felt his interest quicken, then he glanced away as if distracted by a group of Jews in their long dark shubas, who slipped out of a side street to mingle with long-haired Maronites from Syria and dark-skinned Copts from the fabled land south of the Nile. From a nearby church floated the faint hum of plainchant and the spicy fragrance of incense.

The singing grew louder as Greek priests made their way through the crowd, blessing the rabble of dirty children as they bore their precious icons and statues, all arrayed in costly garments and flashing precious stones, to some shrine or chapel. Behind these a line of camels, heavily burdened and swaying like carracks on the sea, battled against the throng, their drivers and guides screaming for room.

De Payens did his best to ignore all these. They were now close to the gates, where Count Raymond's mercenaries were marshalled, soft Provençal voices mingling with the guttural tongue of Swabia. Nearby, carpenters and blacksmiths created a raucous clatter of axe, hammer and sword. Trumpets rang. Cymbals clashed. Kettle drums rolled in greeting. The mercenaries arranged themselves into ranks to greet their seigneur, as the sun reached its zenith on a day about to crack and crumble into a welter of killing and bloodshed.

De Payens startled as a flock of pigeons swooped low above him. Mayele swore loudly. Edmund turned in his saddle. A group of Maronite priests garbed in dark brown robes, braided black hair hiding their faces, had appeared, holding petitions for Count Raymond. The Lord of Tripoli gestured at them to approach. The Maronites hastened on, like a pack of hounds, hot and keen on the scent. They closed in around the Frankish lord and his principal knight, screaming their blood lust. Assassins! The count and his henchman became slightly separated; their escort surged forward. De Payens and Mayele turned their horses in alarm – too late! The assassins had dropped all pretence, the white scraps of parchment fluttering away like butterflies. They drew long curved daggers decorated with red ribbon; these cut the air, gashing and slicing the count, all unprotected in his hose, cotehardie, cloak and soft boots. He and his henchman had no time even to mutter the Miserere, let alone draw sword or dagger. The assassins circled them, knives tearing and gouging, blood spurting out like wine from a skin. The daggers rose and fell like flailing rods. De Payens drew his own sword. Mayele, yelling the Templar war cry, *'Beauséant! Beauséant!'* lashed out at the crowd milling about them. Their horses skittered, alarmed at the tang of fresh blood, this sudden violence. The count was now falling, drooping down over his horse's neck. Still the knives scythed the air in glittering arcs. Two of the assassins broke away and sped towards de Payens. The Templar urged his horse forward, crashing into the pair, his sword hacking and twisting as he shouted prayers, curses and battle cries. The blood frenzy overwhelmed him, the song of his sword, the sheer exuberance of the clash, with more assassins now swarming around him. They had finished with the count and were intent on joining their comrades in killing this hated Templar. De Payens' battle fury became a red mist. He turned his horse, its sharpened hooves lashing out, and the assassins promptly broke and fled into the crowd.

Count Raymond's constables, now recovering from their shock, were eager for blood. They did not pursue the assassins but like Mayele struck at anyone within sword reach. They swept into the terrified crowd like reapers, cutting, gashing and smashing with mace, axe and

14

sword. Some of the bystanders fought back; the massacre spread like some demonic black cloud. The garrison from the gatehouse walls, blood-hungry mercenaries, needed no second urging.

'Let the ravens and vultures feast!' Mayele screamed as he swept into a group of merchants and camel traders.

De Payens, now free of his battle lust, stared around in horror. Count Raymond's corpse and that of his henchman, both swimming in blood, were being carried away wrapped in their cloaks. On either side of the thoroughfare the killing swirled swift and sudden like a breeze across the sands. Archers on the wall and the gateways darkened the sky, showering the fleeing crowd with a hail of bolts and arrows. Swords red to the hilt glittered and flashed. The dust-choked cobbles became drenched with blood pouring from severed limbs. Decapitated heads rolled like dirty bushweed across the ground. The white walls of buildings grew splattered with splashes of scarlet as if a gory rain was pelting down. Children screamed in terror. Plumes of black smoke curled up against the blue sky. The mayhem was spreading deep into the city. People fled into houses and churches.

Edmund heard a hideous cry carry across the bailey before the gateway. Two Syrian girls were struggling in the greedy grasp of Swabian mercenaries, their great two-headed axes lying on the ground beside them. The Swabians were stripping the sobbing girls and pushing them from one to another. The girls screamed; one of them pointed at the blood-encrusted corpse of a man lying beside them. Edmund roared in anger. He fought to settle his fretting horse, but it was too late. The mercenaries had either tired of their game or recognised the danger. They stood aside as one of their company swiftly plucked up his axe and cleanly severed the heads of both girls. The rest turned to face de Payens. He abruptly reined in and stared horror-struck as the two corpses, blood pouring from their severed necks, collapsed; their heads, shrouded by clouds of hair, bounced and rolled across the cobbles.

De Payens turned away in disgust. Sword drawn, he urged his horse towards the steps of a crumbling church, its doors flung open to allow in the flight of citizens, and rode up the steps, forcing aside the fugitives. The flickering darkness was heavy with the scent of myrrh, aloes and incense, the blackness broken by flaring torches and the glow of candles burning before icons and statues. At the far end stood the sanctuary altar, hidden by a heavy dark cloth with a silver pyx embroidered in the centre. The nave of the church was swiftly filling with refugees of every faith and none. Families clung to each other in terror, children whimpering. A Greek priest carrying a gold cross, accompanied by acolytes and a thurifer, processed out through the sacristy door. The priest bellowed that all who were not *cruciferi*, cross-bearers, should leave at once. Behind him shuffled mercenaries garbed in mailed hauberks, dirty boots scuffing the floor, kite-shaped shields slung on their backs, swords and daggers drawn in fierce expectation.

'Leave!' bellowed the priest as his escort clattered their arms. 'Infidels, heretics, schismatics! There is no sanctuary for you here!'

His proclamations were greeted with fresh moans. De Payens urged his horse forward into a pool of light thrown by one of the clerestory windows high in the wall. The sun's rays caught his white cloak, emphasising the red cross stitched on its right shoulder.

'No one need leave here, Domine,' he declared in the lingua franca. The priest spluttered, fingering the cross around his neck. His escort, greedy for blood, plunder and rape, grumbled menacingly, but a Templar knight, sword drawn, his horse's withers wet with blood, was objection enough. The priest bowed and, snapping at his dog soldiers, swept back into the sacristy.

De Payens took up guard at the open doors of the church. All were admitted, flooding into the nave, fear-crazed and shocked. Any pursuers were turned away by the grim sentry, his cloak wrapped about him, the blade of his bloodied sword resting against his shoulder. He sat as if hewn out of granite, staring across the great bailey carpeted with corpses, blood gleaming and twinkling in the sunlight. Flies swarmed in black hordes. Vultures and buzzards, wings flapping, floated down to their banquet. Yellow pi dogs, ribs sticking out, moved from corpse to corpse, nosing at the clothes, eager to tear at the flesh. These scattered only at the appearance of looters and corpse-plunderers, sneaking across, greedy-eyed, for any precious item. A merchant, grateful for his escape, offered the grim Templar some sesame seed cake and a pitcher of water. De Payens ate and drank as he stared out, his mind pitching like a galley on a stormy sea. He felt cold, dead. Was it for this that he had entered the great order, vowed to serve God, Christ and St Mary and obey the master of the Temple?

To calm himself, de Payens remembered his dawn mass of ordination and investiture. How he had received the mantle of the order, the woollen waist cord that signified chastity, the soft cap symbolising obedience, all sealed by the master's kiss of peace. No more than two years ago, though it now seemed like an age! He'd arrived in the Temple forecourt in Jerusalem dressed in his best clothes. There he'd been met by Templar serjeants and escorted across the Great Pavement, where the Knights Templar had their lodgings. They had gone along porticoes, colonnades and vaulted passageways lit by dim lamps, the stone slab floor echoing every footfall. After he'd been blessed and incensed in an antechamber, he had been led into the great chapter house, where the Templars waited; their white mantles displaying the red cross, soft silk caps on their heads, gauntleted hands resting on the hilts of drawn swords. Under terrible oaths in that cavernous chamber, cold and dark, the pricks of light from the juddering oil lamps shifting the shadows, de Payens had sworn that he was of knightly cast, of legitimate birth and in good health. That he was a faithful adherent of the Catholic faith according to the Latin rite of Rome, that he was not married and was free of all such commitments. There, in the brooding gloom, close to the stables where Solomon once stabled his horses, a mere walk from where the Saviour had preached and driven out the money-sellers, the great oaths of the White Knights rolled out. Bertrand Tremelai, the Grand Master, proclaimed the challenge in a powerful voice:

'You must totally renounce your own will. You must admit to that of another. You must fast when you are hungry. Thirst when you wish to drink. Keep strict vigil even when tired.'

To all of these de Payens had replied:

'Yes, Domine, if God so pleases.'

It seemed like a whisper in contrast. After he had sworn the oath, the investiture had taken place as the massed ranks of the Templars chanted the psalm: 'Behold how good it is for brothers to live in union and harmony.'

Once invested, he'd been escorted into the refectory to receive the congratulations of his grandparents, Theodore the Greek, with his lazy smile and soft ways, and his redoubtable grandmother Eleanor, sister of the great Hugh de Payens, founder of the order. Then they had returned to Lebanon, while he had remained in Jerusalem to undergo the grim discipline and training to be a Poor Knight of Christ.

De Payens had been relegated to the meanest lodgings within the courtyard of the Temple. Obedience was a harsh fact, not a choice, rigorous hardship the theme for every day and night. He slept in his clothes on a bed that was no more than a carpet strewn across the floor, on one side a lighted candle, on the other his weapons ready for use, his sleep constantly broken by calls to sing Divine Office. Meagre meals taken in silence were his only sustenance. Harsh sword and lance practice in the glaring heat of the noonday devil was a daily requirement. Hunting, hawking and women were strictly denied, severe punishments imposed for any infringement of the rule: forty days of fasting for striking a comrade. Those in disgrace had to squat on the floor with the dogs to eat their food, and must not attempt to drive the dogs off.

Once training was finished, he had been sent on patrol along dusty roads that wound through eerie gorges or across sandy scorched wastes dotted with oases, their precious water bubbling up under the bending trunks of sycamore, terebinth and date palm. He had served as an escort for pilgrims who landed on the coast eager to journey inland to kneel in the shadow of the Holy Sepulchre. He had guarded merchants with their baggage of hemp sacks, leather cases, wicker baskets and chests, all heaped on the bare backs of sweaty porters; as well as important couriers, dignitaries and officials. During such missions he had clashed with the bearded, harsh-faced men of the desert who came swirling out of the dust with their green banners and ululating battle cries. Along with other Templars, he hunted for these same men out in the arid desert, where the sun beat down as merciless as a battle mace, searching for the encampments of the desert-crawlers, as they called them, with their orange pavilions, attacking and killing, seeking out their chieftains in their turbans, velvet robes and silver girdles. Women and children had fallen, tumbling beneath the hooves of his charging destrier. During one such attack he had captured a young woman who had escaped and fled deep into the wasteland. She had begged for her life, pressing her body up against his, breasts ripe and full pushed into his hands, slim waist soft against his mail shirt, eyes and lips promising everything. He had turned away, stumbling in fear from such temptation, and when he looked back, she was gone.

The encounter had changed de Payens. He'd been plagued by phantasms, succubi of the night, with soft perfumed flesh and alluring eyes, the prospect of a sinuous body twisting beneath him, of silky tendrils of hair wafting his face. In contrition he had prostrated himself in chapter, confessed his thoughts and been condemned to black bread and brackish water. He'd crept to the cross in the Templar chapel and done penance out on some sea of rock in the blinding heat of the desert. More importantly, he lost his appetite for blood: not the fury of battle, sword against sword, but for those who could offer no defence. He'd conjured up the fabulous stories about the paladins of old, whose deeds he had learned from the indomitable Eleanor. Hadn't she whispered how the great Hugh had established the order to defend the weak and the defenceless, be it Christian or Turk? She had lectured him on the futility of killing with all the cold finality of death brooding over the haunting landscape of the battlefield. She had taught him his horn book and his prayer wheel by quoting poetry about the aftermath of slaughter. How did those lines go?

'Many a spear, dawn cold to the touch, we wave them high but the poet's harp won't raise the fallen warriors, whilst the buzzards, winging sombrely over the plain, will bear tidings to the vulture, how he plucked and ate, how he and the jackal made short work of the dead . . .'

'Domine, Domine!'

De Payens felt a hand on his thigh. He glanced down at the wide-eyed woman, her stricken face, her iron-grey hair charred and singed.

'Domine.' Her lips hardly moved. She pointed to the church door. 'We own a wine shop with a small vineyard behind it. The soldiers came. They took my husband and put him beneath the wine press and turned it until his head cracked like a nut, blood and brains seeping out to mingle with our wine. Domine, why did they do that?'

'Demons!' De Payens stroked her brow gently. 'Demons incarnate. The world is thronged with them.' He ushered the woman away, aware of how the noise in the church was settling, then returned to his guard and wondered what to do. A scorched, tattered figure came stumbling across the bailey, screaming:

'Christ and His Holy Sepulchre!'

De Payens waved him forward. The man staggered up the steps and crouched just within the doorway, gulping like a thirsty dog from a pannier of water a woman brought. When he had slaked his thirst, he peered up at de Payens.

'God curse you all,' he muttered. 'Parts of the city are burning. They claim that assassins sent by the Old Man of the Mountain are responsible.'

'Why?' de Payens asked.

'God knows!' The man rose and stumbled towards him. He grasped the horse's bridle, frenetic eyes glaring up at the Templar.

'The city is knee deep in dismembered corpses, the ground is sticky and jellied with blood. Men like you—'

De Payens moved quickly, turning his horse even as his sword blocked the swift lunge by the knife hidden in the man's right hand. The weapon went clattering along the floor. Women screamed in terror; men sprang to their feet, shouting warnings. De Payens hooked the tip of his sword under the man's chin, forcing him back into the light. His assailant didn't beg; the close-set eyes in that nut-brown face never wavered.

'How did you know?' he whispered.

'You are right-handed, but you used your left for the bridle.' De Payens searched the man's face: intelligent, purposeful, with a snub nose, full mouth and firm chin. 'Why?' he asked.

'Killers!' the man replied. 'Killers bound for hell for this day's work. You must all confront the Gates of Death and meet the Janitors of the Shadowlands.'

'A quotation from the Book of Job,' de Payens retorted. 'You are a scholar, a clerk?'

'A physician who has seen enough of killing to glut himself for many a lifetime.'

De Payens lowered his sword.

'Then pick up your dagger and get behind me. I am no demon, not yet at least.'

The man slid past him into the darkness of the church. De Payens tensed, straining his ear for any sound of a fresh attack. Instead the man came to stand beside him, sheathing his dagger as he whispered:

'A terror of the twilight, blinded and bloated with blood, stalks the city in his livery of lion skins. Behind him trail the shackles of death. Whole legions he takes . . .'

De Payens stared down at him.

'You sound more like a priest than a physician.'

Screams carried across the great bailey. Three figures rounded the corner, running towards the church, hastening like shadows under the sun, tripping over corpses, glancing fearfully over their shoulders. They had almost reached the steps of the church when their pursuer appeared, garbed in white, head shrouded in a hood. Mayele! He trotted his horse across the bailey, then paused. He glimpsed Edmund, but made no sign of recognition. Instead, he coolly raised his Saracen horn bow, notched, loosed, then notched again. Each arrow sped like a curse, swift and fatal. Two of the men twisted as the shafts took them deep in the back; the third, a clutch of jewellery in his fist, was halfway up the steps, but Mayele was a deadly archer. The shaft sliced the fleeing man in the back of the neck, its barb breaking and shattering his soft sweaty throat. He collapsed in a gargle of blood as Mayele serenely guided his horse across the square, then reined in, grinning up at de Payens.

'They were infidels, corpse-plunderers.'

'What proof?'

Mayele pointed to the third man.

'He had stolen a pyx.'

'It's not a pyx.' De Payens gestured with his sword. 'It's jewellery. He was fleeing for sanctuary, innocent, Philip, as are so many who have died today.'

'Innocent, guilty?' Mayele hooked the bow over the horn of his saddle. 'Who can judge but God? Let him decide . . .'

# Chapter 2

It is rare that an enterprise, bad in inception
and perverse in purpose, has a good ending.

Edmund de Payens, clad only in his loincloth, squatted
near the door of the great refectory in the Templar house
built on the corner of the Great Pavement at the heart
of the old Temple enclosure in Jerusalem. He scratched
the sweat coursing down his chest, wafting away the
flies, trying to ignore the great wolfhounds eager to
snatch his bread. He clutched his goblet, brimming with
wine, and glared furiously at Mayele, who was similarly
attired. Both were undergoing punishment for the chaos

in Tripoli. The massacre there had ended when the standard-bearer of Baldwin III, King of Jerusalem, had processed solemnly through the city with trumpeters and heralds, demanding a cessation to the killing or immediate forfeiture of life and limb. The gallows were soon festooned with the corpses of those who had disobeyed. Decapitations, amputations and castrations had enforced the decree, and a royal standard had been placed outside the church. De Payens and Mayele had departed for the castle, only to be immediately arrested on the specific command of the Grand Master, Bertrand Tremelai, who ordered both Templars to be stripped, chained and brought back in disgrace. They'd spent two weeks in the Temple dungeons, only to be released for further punishment and humiliation.

Edmund greedily drank the watered wine. He tried to catch Mayele's eye, but his comrade was too busy finishing his food before the wolfhounds did. Edmund glanced up the hall at the dais beneath the great Templar banner, a black cross on a sheet of sheer samite. Bertrand Tremelai sat there with his seneschals, clerks and other officers of the order. In truth, Edmund reflected, he did not like Tremelai, a cockerel of a man, proud and arrogant, with the spirit of wrath in his nostrils; a soul who neither feared God nor revered man. Red-haired, hot-tempered and choleric, Tremelai had lashed de Payens and Mayele with his contemptuous words, accusing them of failing to protect Count Raymond, of not capturing or destroying the assassins.

In the presence of the full chapter, the Grand Master had condemned them to this. Now he sat feasting on the dais, drinking from a pure glass goblet, the best protection against poison, whilst de Payens and Mayele squatted on the floor amongst the dogs. Edmund wondered if he should bark, then grinned quietly to himself. He squinted at Mayele, who sat with his back against the wall, chewing on a piece of gristle, a half-smile on his face. Mayele caught his glance and spat out the piece of meat for the waiting hound.

'Edmund de Payens,' he whispered, 'noble member of a noble family.' His voice was tinted with sarcasm, but de Payens did not object. Mayele was his brother-knight, a strange, bloodthirsty man with apparently no sense of fear. During the chapter meeting where they had been judged and punished, he had loudly protested his innocence, arguing hotly with Dominus Tremelai, shouting that the Grand Master would do better to find the reason for Count Raymond's murder and demand a full investigation by the papal legate into the incident. Tremelai had shouted back before ordering them both to strip and lie prostrate before the chapter. De Payens had done so; Mayele objected, so he'd been seized, stripped and beaten with a sharp cane. The purple welts and bruises had now faded, the fresh skin neatly growing back, but Mayele had not forgiven or forgotten either the beating or the fresh humiliation.

'*Pax et bonum*, brother.' Mayele leaned over. He grasped

de Payens' goblet, sipped from it and handed it back. 'This will not last long. Our brothers have intervened for us. No less a person than your great friend and patron William Trussell has pleaded on our behalf.'

De Payens nodded in agreement. Trussell was a legend, an Englishman who had joined Hugh de Payens after the *cruciferi* had stormed and taken Jerusalem some fifty-three years ago. A man well past his seventy-fifth year, a veteran treated as a hero, cared for and trusted by the order.

'Ah, good day, Brother Baker, Brother Thurifer, Brother Smith, Brother Cook.' Mayele's sarcastic greeting rang through the hall as the lesser serjeants of the order trooped in for their main serving of the day.

His taunting refrain must have reached the Grand Master, for shortly afterwards burly serjeants appeared. The two men were dragged to their feet and pushed out along a vaulted passageway on to the pavement, then across to the house of correction beneath the old mosque. De Payens winced as his naked feet touched the hot paving stones. The light blinded him, whilst the sun was as hot as a roaring fire. Mayele tried to make light of his discomfort by dancing a jig, much to his guards' amusement. While they tried to restrain his companion, de Payens shielded his eyes and peered across at the view that rose above the Temple walls: the towers and belfries of the Church of the Holy Sepulchre. Here, de Payens reflected, in the heart of Jerusalem, whilst the army of the *cruciferi* had rampaged like hungry wolves through the streets of the Holy City, Hugh de Payens and his companions had reached the Great Pavement and raced across to the Dome of the Rock, down into the darkness beneath, where the great Solomon had built his stables. According to legend, Hugh and his brethren, the first group of Poor Knights of the White Mantle, had found treasure greater than any gold, silver or gorgeous rubies. Relics, artefacts from the time of Christ! The crown of thorns thrust on to the sacred head; the nails that had pierced his hands and feet; the shroud in which his corpse had been wrapped, and the cloth thrown over the Saviour's face, which allegedly still bore a miraculous imprint.

'Sir!' The serjeants now held Mayele fast. The scribe in charge beckoned de Payens to follow.

They went down steep steps into the cold darkness and along a vaulted passageway: it reeked of oil and pitch, the walls on either side glistening as if drenched with water. A door to a dungeon was opened, and de Payens and Mayele were pushed inside to squat down on straw-filled palliasses.

'When,' de Payens asked, 'will this end?'

'Soon.' Mayele crawled across, took the lamp and put it between them.

'And why?' de Payens asked. 'Why was Count Raymond murdered?'

'Rumour runs like mice in a hay barn,' Mayele murmured. 'What was the count but another great lord snatching territory, dividing Outremer like a loaf of bread? A squabble of barons.' Mayele laughed at his own joke. 'Fat lords supported by their even fatter priests.'

'So who murdered him, and why?'

'They say the hashish-devourers, the Assassins, a secret cult of Islam under their master, the Old Man of the Mountain. They are hated by the Franks and loathed by the Turks. Rumour holds them responsible. They and their leaders live high in mountain eyries, dealing out death. Come, Edmund,' Mayele's voice turned soft, 'you must have heard the legends? How when the Old Man goes out he is preceded by a herald bearing a huge Danish axe, its long haft enclosed in silver, to which braided knots are fastened. As he goes, the herald proclaims: "Turn out of the way of he who has in his hands the fate of kings".'

Mayele's voice thrilled through the shadows, unsettling de Payens even further.

'But why Count Raymond? Why should the Assassins kill him?'

'God knows.'

'And why were we brought from Chastel Blanc to act as his escort?'

'Only God and our Grand Master know that, Edmund. We've been away from Jerusalem for a year, locked up in the fastness of Lebanon.'

'Not you,' de Payens retorted, moving on the uncomfortable palliasse. 'You were the Chastel messenger to Jerusalem and elsewhere.' He paused at the sound of a braying horn, followed by the distant tolling of bells, marking a fresh hour in the horarium of the brethren.

'Time limps,' Mayele murmured, 'like a thief. In the light of day, Edmund, all will be revealed. Yes, I was a Templar messenger. I collected all the gossip and chatter from the brothers, winnowing the wheat from the chaff. Did you know Walkyn, one of our brethren, an Englishman?'

De Payens shook his head.

'Expelled from the order!'

'On what charge?'

'Some say witchcraft, dabbling in the black arts, conjuring up the demons of the dark angel. I don't know the full truth. Rumour has it that he was arrested, tried secretly and found guilty. He was supposed to be sent back to England in chains. Another Englishman, Richard Berrington, was delegated to escort him. You know Berrington?'

De Payens shook his head.

'Anyway,' Mayele sighed, 'Walkyn may have escaped. Berrington has certainly disappeared, so the gossips say.'

'Perhaps the Grand Master wishes that we would do the same.'

Mayele laughed and shook his head.

'No, brother, not that.'

'What happened?' De Payens returned to the question haunting him. 'What truly happened in Tripoli? Why were we there? Why did they kill Count Raymond?'

Mayele didn't answer. The sound of footsteps echoed in the passageway. The door was unlocked and swung open, and a serjeant beckoned to them to rise and follow.

Bertrand Tremelai was waiting for them in his octagonal chamber in the Temple manse, a ground-floor room decorated with brilliantly hued tapestries. The first described the fall of Jerusalem some fifty years earlier. The second related the story of the Templars from their founding to their patronage by St Bernard of Clairvaux. The third described the order's adoption by the papacy and the issuing of the decree *Milites Dei et Militia Dei – Soldiers of God, Army of God*. The Pope was shown flanked by St Peter and St Paul, with the title of the decree, which took the Templars fully under papal authority, inscribed on a silver tongue of parchment issuing out of the Pope's mouth.

Tremelai sat enthroned beneath these glories behind a broad desk of polished cassia. In the far corner two scribes copied documents, whilst a third poured hot wax on manuscripts before sealing them with the Temple seal displaying two poor knights sharing the same horse, suggesting both comradeship and humility. There was little of such virtue in the Grand Master's choleric red face or his luxurious chamber with its opulent furnishings, lambswool rugs and beeswax candles. Tremelai thrust himself back in his chair and jabbed a finger at de Payens and Mayele.

'You will be readmitted to our ranks in chapter tomorrow. In preparation for which . . .' He raised a hand, flapping his fingers. One of the clerks rose, collected two cloaks from a wall peg and hurried across. De Payens and Mayele donned these and sat on the stools provided. 'In preparation for which,' Tremelai repeated, 'you will read the great Bernard's work, *De Laude Novae Militiae – In Praise of the New Knighthood.*'

'I've read it,' Mayele retorted.

'Then read it again.'

'Domine,' de Payens chose his words carefully, 'what happened in Tripoli?'

'Count Raymond was murdered by the Assassins, the Naziris, Islamic heretics lurking with their so-called prince, the Old Man of the Mountain. As for why?' Tremelai pulled a face. 'The count raided a caravanserai under their protection.' He glared fiercely at de Payens, his watery blue eyes bulging, red beard bristling, chin jutting out aggressively, as if ready to refute any contradiction.

You are lying, de Payens swiftly concluded. You're blustering, but why?

'More importantly,' Tremelai continued, shifting his gaze, 'Count Raymond was under the protection of the Temple. The Old Man of the Mountain must be checked, brought to book, made to pay reparation, accept the power of the Temple. You two will lead an embassy into the mountains.' He stilled de Payens' objection with his hand. 'You'll take six serjeants and a clerk. You'll demand both an apology and compensation.'

'And what happens,' Mayele snarled, 'if he sends our heads back to you pickled and dried in a basket?'

'He will not do that,' Tremelai soothed. 'I have already received his written assurances. You will be received honourably.'

'Does he deny the charge?' de Payens asked.

'He denies nothing, he offers nothing.'

'The murderers,' Mayele insisted. 'Their corpses were found?'

'No.' Tremelai shook his head. 'In the bloodbath, heads and limbs were severed, bodies mangled.' The Grand Master shrugged.

'So why were the Assassins blamed?' de Payens insisted.

'Naziris,' Mayele interrupted. 'That's their true name, heretics!'

'They are killers, murderers and marauders,' de Payens countered. 'Even so, what proof do we have that they were involved?'

'True, their corpses weren't found,' Tremelai replied. 'But one of their medallions was, a token they leave on the corpses of their victims.' He gestured at the clerk, who handed across a circle of copper about six inches across, the rim fretted with strong symbols, in its centre a striking viper. De Payens and Mayele studied this, then handed it back even as the clerk produced two long curved daggers, their handles of ivory decorated with blood-red ribbons. De Payens recalled similar ones in the hands of those brown-garbed assassins racing towards the count.

'These too were found,' Tremelai barked. 'Proof

enough – at least for the moment. Now . . .' He paused. 'I said that you will travel with six serjeants and a clerk. The latter has chosen himself.' He snapped his fingers and whispered to one of the scribes, who hurried out, then returned ushering a figure garbed in the dark robe of a serjeant of the order. The stranger kept to the shadows behind the Grand Master's desk. De Payens had to strain his eyes to make out a figure and face he thought he recognised.

'I believe you have met.' Tremelai gestured the man forward into the full light. De Payens startled in recognition. It was the physician who had tried to stab him in the church after the massacre. The man's dark hair, moustache and beard were now neatly clipped, the swarthy skin oiled, the deep-set eyes calmer, the face more tranquil than the violent mask de Payens had glimpsed. The new arrival sketched a bow and spread his hands.

'Thierry Parmenio, Domini,' he murmured, 'physician, wanderer, perpetual pilgrim.'

'Whom I should have hanged out of hand,' bellowed Tremelai, though his tone was surprisingly good-humoured, like that of a man who had drunk deep and well. De Payens glimpsed the poison-proof glass goblet, brimming with wine, standing amongst the curled manuscripts littering the desk.

The Grand Master's guest came forward, hand extended. De Payens rose and clasped it.

'My apologies, Domine, my apologies.' Parmenio's grip

was warm and strong. 'Let me explain.' He rested against the Grand Master's desk and turned to Mayele, who rose, staring narrow-eyed at the newcomer, then shrugged and clasped the extended hand. Parmenio gave a loud sigh and gestured at de Payens.

'I was in Tripoli because I had to be,' he began. 'Business with King Baldwin. I am, sirs, both physician and clerk, trained in the cathedral school of Genoa, later an avid scholar at Salerno. I have the deepest distaste for violence. I witnessed the horror, the rapacity of Count Raymond's mercenaries. I thought that you, Edmund, were one of them.'

'Garbed in Templar dress?' Mayele sneered.

'In my shock, I did not recognise that,' Parmenio answered tactfully, eyes still smiling at de Payens. 'Just another killer, I thought. Only later did I realise who you were, what you had done and what great scarlet sin I had nearly committed. I hastened to be confessed, shrived and pardoned by the Grand Master. I offered to do penance, to rectify what I had done. So,' he spread his hands again, 'for a while I have donned the robes of a serjeant of your order, and will go with you into the mountains.'

'Why, sir?' de Payens asked.

Parmenio's grin widened. 'You look at me as if my neck was garlanded with dead men's fingers. I am not a cullion, no wandering beggar, but a bachelor of learning, eager to pour balm on a wound . . .'

De Payens left the Grand Master's chamber bemused

37

and startled. Mayele clapped him on the back and laughingly dismissed Parmenio as a glib, glossy-throated Genoese. De Payens shook his head, but Mayele just scoffed, adding that there was little they could do about it. The Grand Master had declared that they were to leave the day after tomorrow, so there was much to arrange. Together they went to the draper's office to draw fresh linen, cloaks, hauberks, cooking pans, drinking cups and all the impedimenta they would require for the journey. Clerks of the scriptorium, chancery and muniment room provided charts. Grooms and ostlers prepared the sure-footed garrons and sumpter ponies they would need. The six serjeants had also been chosen: wiry, tough Provençals, surly but skilled, hand-picked by the Grand Master. De Payens realised that their allegiance would be solely to Tremelai, not to the Templars they escorted. Parmenio joined them, all affable, a fount of amusing stories, anecdotes and tales, chattering about his previous travels, the marvels he had witnessed, the people he had met. Mayele remained wary of him, while de Payens, still intrigued about what had happened in Tripoli, eagerly seized the opportunity to escape from his companions and visit the old Englishman William Trussell.

The honoured veteran had been given a spacious chamber overlooking the Temple pavement, its great open windows providing a breathtaking view of the city and the Mount of Olives beyond. The polished cedar-wood used to lay the floor and provide the furnishings gleamed with its own polished fragrance. Tapestries decorated the walls; embroidered mats covered the floor. The ceiling was concave, and from its centre hung a Catherine wheel with numerous lamps embedded in its rim; this could be lowered and the wicks lit when darkness fell. Bowls of fruit – oranges, figs and apples – were laid out along the flat-topped chests. In the corners stood baskets of fresh flowers, rock rose, bell flowers and hollyhocks, their lovely smells mixing with the sweet aromas of balsam, cassia and myrrh placed in little sacks and pressed against any small hole in the walls. Trussell's furry tabby cat, Tortosa, sprawled like an emperor on a quilted stool. Trussell himself was sitting in a high-backed chair, peering down at a lectionary placed to catch the light pouring through the great open window behind him.

The old Englishman rose as de Payens entered. He was a tall, angular man with stooped shoulders and the long arms of a born swordsman. His undressed grey hair fell to his shoulders; his face reminded de Payens of the colour of weathered manuscript. He clasped de Payens' outstretched hand and fussily waved him to a stool next to the chair. They exchanged pleasantries, whilst de Payens quietly studied his host. Trussell was a veteran much favoured by the order, a hero who had stormed the walls of Jerusalem and fought his way through the ranks of seasoned Egyptian soldiers who had been the bulwark of the city's defenders. He'd cut a path through these and decapitated the witches the

Egyptian governor had placed behind them: evil harridans, their faces full of hate, their foul mouths spitting curses. In his time, Trussell had met all the heroes of the order: Hugh de Payens, Geoffrey de St Omer, Eleanor de Payens and her redoubtable husband Theodore the Greek. It was Theodore and Eleanor who had raised Edmund, and ever since he could remember, he had visited Trussell, who had filled his mind with all the daring, noble deeds of the Temple. Now, however, the old man was weakening, his mighty frame racked by fevers and ulcers that never healed. Sometimes his mind wandered; his eyes could assume a glassy look, his face hang slack, though he seemed alert and active enough now. He pointed down at the manuscript he'd been reading.

'Fulcher of Chartres, his description of the expedition to Jerusalem. Very good, Edmund.' He recollected himself, rolled up the manuscript, then glanced sheepishly at de Payens.

'I am sorry to hear about what happened in Tripoli. How you were blamed. Tremelai is a fool, arrogant and devious . . .'

He was about to go on, then struck his breast.

'*Mea culpa*, I have sinned. I should not speak so about our Grand Master. Edmund, you will not denounce me in chapter?'

De Payens leaned forward and gently cupped the old man's face in his hands.

'Magister, Domine, I thank you for your kind intervention, but I am confused. Why was Raymond of Tripoli assassinated? What is happening here in the order? You must also have heard how Philip Mayele and I are bound for the Old Man of the Mountain.'

Trussell nodded, and his face assumed a sorrowful look. He touched the roll of manuscript with a vein-streaked hand and glanced across at one of the tapestries.

'I see visions, you know. In the dead of night, dreams come. Ships sail into the west,' his voice fell to a whisper, 'black sails billowing, masts bending as violent winds drive them swiftly over the deep. It will come, Edmund, the vengeance, Jerusalem besieged. The cross will go, and the visions of the *cruciferi* will become no more than the dreams of shadow-riders.' He lifted a hand to fend off de Payens' startled exclamation.

'I dream,' he continued, 'of how, along the roads to the west, the horses clatter, taking their sombre message across the sleepy, golden, autumn-tinged fields.' He looked up. 'They'll gather at crossroads, before the great doors of cathedrals and the wooden planks of hamlet chapels. They will assemble in the meagre rush-light of taverns or the fire glow of castle hearths, the chilling darkness full of moans at our stupid sins of pride and avarice. Listen, Edmund: the standards of the Antichrist will be raised, the banners of Satan will fly above this city once hallowed by Christ's presence and sanctified by his blood. A storm is coming, and it's not to be checked by half-finished prayers or feverish chatter.' He smiled to himself. 'I write my own chronicle about life here in

41

Outremer. We have won the land, taken the city, but look around. Our king, Baldwin III, is steeped in intrigue. The great lords divide the Holy Land into counties, cities and shires. They squabble and intrigue whilst fresh threats gather. The house of the Temple is no different. Tremelai is ambitious, ruthless, but not far-seeing. We have our roots here, but they stretch back to France, Burgundy and the Rhineland. Tremelai wants more. He has talked about sending envoys to England to intervene in the civil war between King Stephen and his cousin Henry Fitzempress, the Angevin. He wants to put down roots there, grasp a place close to the Crown.' Trussell paused, blinking, and dabbed at the silver froth between his lips. '*Omnia mutanda* – all things must change. Look at me, Edmund. I once ate rats' heads outside Antioch, before Bohemond stormed its gates. I ate rats and chewed foot leather and harness. Now every day I am allowed three kinds of soups in honour of the Trinity.'

'And Tripoli?' de Payens asked.

Trussell shook his head. 'Something is missing,' he murmured. 'God knows why you were there. I don't know, Edmund, I truly don't.' He paused. 'Sinister forces threaten our order.'

'Magister?'

'Here in the Temple house of Jerusalem, they talk about how Henry Walkyn, one of our company, has been arrested and expelled.' He glanced quickly around, then over de Payens' shoulder, as if some eavesdropper might lurk at the door. 'Witchcraft and sorcery!' he hissed.

'Nonsense!' de Payens murmured.

'Not so, not so.' Trussell drew closer. 'We have found relics here. They are still hidden away. Then there's the secret knowledge. For fifty years our order has mingled with the mystics of Islam and studied the Kabbalah of the Jews. All the secrets of the kingdom lurk here. You say nonsense – I agree, but beyond these walls, Satan lays siege. Ah yes, the Lord Satan!' Trussell grew more alert, leaning back as he chanted: '"His brows are full, his face is flat, with owlish eyes and the nose of a cat, his wolfish mouth gapes open, showing wild boar's teeth, bloody and sharp." A children's verse, Edmund, but Satan still prowls here, as he does the desert wastes. Oh yes, I have seen him,' his fingers flew to his lips, 'a small black shape clinging to the cliff face. He scuttles insect-like, eyes gleaming green in the daylight, burrowing like a maggot into the hearts of men.'

'Magister, Magister, please!' De Payens chewed his lip. Were Trussell's wits turning fey, riddled with dreams?

'Look around, Edmund.' Trussell peered at him. 'We now recruit from as far east as Iberia and as far north as the icy wastes of Norway and Sweden. We Templars are as powerful as the Benedictines or the Cistercians. We are under the direct authority of the Pope. We own the heart of the Temple, castles at Acre, Gaza and Chastel Blanc. We possess the great treasures of our faith, yet many of us want more, and because of that, do we really reflect on whom we attract into our ranks? Men who have murdered, committed heinous sacrilege; sanctuary men, wolfsheads in their own countries. Tremelai has a great deal to answer for. He is so greedy . . .'

'And here in Jerusalem?' De Payens desperately tried to bring the conversation back to his own concerns.

'Tremelai reaps what he sows. Gossipers and whisperers say that there are covens, secret fraternities within the brotherhood dedicated to this or that, yet that might all be ale-bench gossip. We are under siege, and the belfries of hell, crowded with our enemies, edge closer.' Trussell clenched a fist. 'Dark souls are already in our order!'

'Magister, what are you saying?'

'You've heard about Walkyn being expelled from the order on suspicion of witchcraft?'

'Yes, Mayele whispered about that.'

'Ah, Mayele!' Trussell smiled cynically, then paused and glanced over his shoulder, as if he felt a cold breeze from the window behind him. Then he turned back and touched Edmund on the knee. 'Listen to this!' He licked his lips. 'Corpses were found around the Temple area and out in the Valley of Hinnom, others amongst the trees on the Mount of Olives. Young girls, their bodies hideously brutalised and their blood drained. Now, our so-called Holy City teems with ribalds and all the human scavengers from around the Middle Sea. Witches and warlocks are as plentiful here as lice on a dog. Most are mountebanks and tricksters, charlatans preying on other people's fears. One, however, Erictho, is a true demon-worshipper, a witch whose very breath pollutes the air. A sorcerer of whom even the rock vipers would be wary. Anyway,' Trussell wiped his mouth on the back of his hand, 'Erictho was held responsible for many crimes. She was accused of draining corpses of moisture, of gnawing nails from dead hands, clawing through the nooses of hanged men, biting off their swollen tongues. More importantly, she was accused of being involved in these murders, hungry, thirsty for human blood for her sacrifices.' He paused. 'Edmund, you think my wits are wandering? I will tell you the full story, then you can understand my anxiety. Jerusalem is riddled with sorcerers and warlocks, but serious allegations have been levelled that demon-worshippers also lurk here in the Temple.' He held a hand up to fend off de Payens' exclamation. 'It's true! Our Grand Master and some of our leaders know about this. Objections have been raised by both the governor of the city and the Patriarch of Jerusalem about such filthy practices. Demands have been made that something be done. Now, have you ever met the two Englishmen, Walkyn and Richard Berrington?'

'No, but Mayele has mentioned their names.'

'Oh yes, he would.' Trussell gnawed the corner of his lip. 'Well, Walkyn gained a reputation for visiting the brothels and flesh houses. Apparently he found his vow of chastity difficult to keep. Here, Edmund, is an example of some of the men we are now recruiting. I suspect Walkyn had no more fidelity to his vows than Tortosa, my alleycat. Now, what concerned our master were reports from his legion of spies that Erictho had been glimpsed slipping into the Temple precincts. According to these reports, she dresses like a witch, a wig about her head, her face all painted, swathed in a robe fashioned out of crow's feathers. Tremelai had no choice but to keep his own house under close scrutiny. Walkyn's nocturnal expeditions to visit the ladies of the town were noted, but then fresh allegations were levelled at him that he was actually consorting with devil's worshippers. I don't know the true details, but Walkyn was arrested and his chamber searched. Evidence was found that he may have been involved in the same coven as Erictho.' Trussell took a deep breath. 'You know how the Temple works, Edmund. A secret inquiry was held. Walkyn was found guilty, but Tremelai did not want him punished here in Jerusalem. Instead he turned to a senior English knight, Richard Berrington. Berrington's task, along with two serjeants, was to take Walkyn back to England, where he could be questioned thoroughly and imprisoned for life, or even executed. Everything was kept secret. A few weeks ago, Berrington and the two serjeants took Walkyn under chains from the city. Tremelai also summoned the English master from London, Boso Baiocis, to answer certain questions. Tremelai does nothing right.' Trussell rubbed the side of his face. 'Perhaps he should have provided a stronger escort, but to cut to the chase, it appears that Walkyn escaped.'

'How?'

Trussell shook his head. 'We don't know, but he may have fled to Tripoli.'

'Oh no!' Edmund gasped. 'Could a malefactor like Walkyn have had a hand in what happened there?'

'Gossip alleges that the Assassins may not have been involved but a rogue Templar might have been, which explains why Tremelai is so eager in his pursuit of the Assassins. He wants to lay the blame for Count Raymond's death at their door. Now, we have no proof of what truly happened or who was responsible. Walkyn? The Old Man of the Mountain? Or was it some other group we know nothing about? Our spies in Tripoli also report that Count Raymond's murder may simply have been an excuse for the city to be plundered. Already the lists are coming in.' Trussell spread his hands. 'It would appear that certain merchant houses were pillaged within a short while of the count's death. But in the end, Edmund, if you want to know what truly happened in Tripoli, I can't really say.'

'And this Berrington?'

'Tremelai is deeply concerned. Berrington was a leading knight, a man of good reputation. He came here and joined the order, bringing his fair sister, the Lady Isabella. She lodges in the Benedictine convent close to Herod's Gate. Berrington seems to have disappeared.

Tremelai believes that he and the two serjeants were murdered by Walkyn, assisted by the coven in Jerusalem. There has been no sign of him, no report.'

'And Erictho?'

'Oh, our malignant witch! She has apparently disappeared from the face of the earth. Tremelai is secretly worried but at the same time rather pleased about that. More importantly, the hideous murders have ceased. Tremelai is using his spies and his army of informants to discover where Walkyn could have fled and what has happened to Berrington.'

'And you, William, what do you think?'

'I wish I could tell you, Edmund. Some allege that Count Raymond became nervous, that he heard rumours about something nefarious being plotted in his city and asked the Temple for protection.'

'Did he?'

Trussell's eyes refused to meet Edmund's. 'I don't know,' the old Englishman grumbled. 'I sit here in the vespers of my life, chomping on my gums. I don't know the truth of it all. *Nihil manet sub sole*, the psalmist says – nothing lasts under the sun, and,' he added half in a whisper, '*dixi in excessu omnes mendaces* – I said in my anger that all men are liars.' He stretched out and grasped Edmund's hands. 'Anyway, enough of rumour. Tremelai the bully has now realised that what happened in Tripoli is a real mystery. No one knows why Count Raymond was foully murdered. In the end, do not be too harsh on Tremelai. He chose you for Tripoli

48

because he respects you. You are a de Payens, a mark of honour and respect for Lord Raymond.'

'And Mayele, what do you know of him?'

Trussell smiled with his lips only. 'Very little, but Tremelai has high hopes for you, Edmund. The blessed Hugh journeyed to England to establish the Temple there, a mere foothold. Tremelai wishes to develop that. He and his council are thinking of sending you to England, even though the country is being torn apart. King Henry I died without a male heir; his daughter, Mathilda the Empress, claimed the throne only to be challenged by her cousin, Stephen of Blois. He in turn has been opposed by Mathilda's son Henry Fitzempress, or Henry the Angevin, as they call him. That island now resounds with the clash of swords and,' he added, 'has done so for the last eighteen years.' He sat back in his chair, wafting his hand as he peered at Edmund. 'May God always be with you. I have spoken enough.'

De Payens made his farewells and left the chamber. He went along the gallery and down the stairs, so lost in his own thoughts that he was startled when a hand touched his arm. He turned quickly and gazed at the vision of beauty staring intently back at him. The woman was of medium height, dressed in the blue robes of a Benedictine novice, a white wimple framing her face. She was threading a set of ivory ave beads through her fingers.

'Madam.' De Payens stood back and bowed.

'I am sorry for startling you, but I want . . .'

'Madam, there is no need to apologise.' De Payens was struck by the lucid beauty of the woman, her fair skin and violet-blue eyes. Was she laughing at him, teasing or just smiling?

'Madam, what do you want with me?'

'My brother, Richard Berrington, is a knight of the order. You must have heard of him?'

'Madam, I certainly have. I am sorry about your sad loss. I know he was escorting a prisoner, who escaped, whilst your brother has now disappeared. Perhaps . . .'

'I live for perhaps . . . Domine de Payens.' She took a step closer.

The Templar caught her faint scent, the trace of an exquisite perfume. He stood fascinated by that face, the woman's delicate movements as she moved the beads, those lovely eyes searching his.

'I beg your pardon, sir,' again the smile, 'but I come to the Temple daily to learn news about my brother. I've heard that you and another knight, Philip Mayele, are to leave Jerusalem on some errand for the Grand Master. I just wondered if you could keep eye and ear open for any news of my brother's whereabouts.' She stepped closer and grasped de Payens' hand. Her skin was soft, smooth as silk. She stood on tiptoe and abruptly kissed him on the cheek, then stepped back, fingers to her lips as if to stifle a smile. 'That is the only payment I can give you, Templar, but please, remember Richard Berrington! Anything you learn, anything you discover. I'm sure my brother is still alive.'

De Payens nodded. He stretched out his hand, clasped hers between his, then kissed the tips of her fingers.

'Madam, it will be my pleasure. I shall do what I can.' He stepped back, bowed and left.

# Chapter 3

Neither Christians nor Turks know whence
their name, Assassins, is derived.

Edmund de Payens, Philip Mayele, Thierry Parmenio
and their six serjeants left the Temple precincts the
following day. They'd all visited the shriving pew before
the Pity displayed in the Lady Chapel. Each had knelt
on the prie-dieu and stared at the carved dead face
of their tortured Saviour, his corpse taken down from
the cross and laid across the lap of his sorrowful
mother. De Payens had whispered his litany of petty
offences, including thoughts about Isabella Berrington.

He received absolution and went to stand in the church porch, where he lit tapers before a painting of St Christopher, a powerful protector against sudden, violent death. The others joined him, and they were met there by Tremelai, who carried a sealed chancery pouch containing letters to the Assassin leader in his mountain eyrie of Hedad, which lay to the east of the Templar castle of Chastel Blanc. Maps and charts were handed over to Parmenio, who'd act as their guide as well as their interpreter. Mass was then celebrated, the singing bread distributed, the Pax Tecum shared and the Eucharist taken. Once the Ite Missa was sung, they gathered on the Great Pavement. The afternoon sun was still strong, glistening off the Temple buildings in a sheen of light. Tremelai, his marshals and his seneschals bestowed their blessings. De Payens and his companions mounted, a black and white Templar gonfalon handed over as their official standard. Above them a horn blared, followed by blood-tingling trumpet blasts along the walls of the inner courtyard. De Payens lowered the gonfalon, a stiffened pennant, three times in honour of the Trinity, and they left the Temple enclosure through the Beautiful Gate, which led down into the city.

De Payens, the memories of that savage attack at Tripoli still fresh, was very wary. He was always struck by the contrasts of Jerusalem. The city was supposed to be a house of prayer, yet it was hard to imagine this as he and his companions, lost in their own thoughts, moved from blazing sunshine into the near darkness of narrow, filthy streets and vaulted bazaars lit only by flickering oil lamps and the dull glow of acrid-smelling candles. Sunshine pierced the rents in the clothes stretched out between the adjoining flat rooftops. Occasionally they'd approach a crossroads bathed in sunlight, then plunge back into the blackness, reeking of excrement, cooking smells, musty clothes, sweaty bodies and the hideous stench of cheap oil being burned and burned again. The walls on either side glittered as if the rough rock exuded its own sweat. Voices shouted, screamed and prayed. A variety of tongues babbled above the clattering chaos from the tawdry markets. The crowd thinned and thronged as they moved deeper into the city along the Streets of Chains to the main thorough-fare leading down to Herod's Gate in the west of the city.

De Payens recalled Trussell's dark thoughts about what had happened in Jerusalem, a city that certainly attracted all and sundry, a fact de Payens reminded himself of as he guided his horse through the crowds of Armenians, fat and well pursed; fierce-looking warriors from the dry lands across the Jordan; crafty-eyed ragged tribesmen from the arid stretches around the Dead Sea; Bedouins, Arabs and Christians, hostile and wary, their scarred, hardened faces betraying many a battle wound. De Payens' attention was also caught by the beauty of the women: fair-haired, rosy-cheeked Christians; swarthy-faced Greeks, their skins brightly tattooed; Bedouins garbed in black, except for the fringed opening around the eyes. Men and women of every nation and tongue swarmed into Jerusalem, seeking salvation or profit, usually both. Whores wheedled through opened windows. Pimps and flesh purveyors offered all kinds of secret delights deep in the shadows behind them. Relic-sellers, faces flushed with false excitement, announced yet another find. Cooks and their apprentices darted from behind their stalls with skewers of roasted meat, mixed with vegetables and coated with a heavy spice to disguise the putrid taste. Water-sellers touted pewter cups of cool, miraculous water from the pool of Siloam.

No one dared approach the Templars. De Payens, carrying the gonfalon, had little need to clear his path. The very sight of their insignia, the knights garbed in the robes of their order, was inducement enough. Traders, pedlars, pimps, prostitutes, wandering scholars, even the scrawny pi dogs scattered into the darkening gaps between the houses or the mouths of ribbon-thin alleyways. De Payens heard a strange humming and glanced up. A woman was standing on the roof of a house with the light behind her so that she appeared as a stark dark shape. He glimpsed thick wild hair, the sombre rags she wore puffed up like the feathers of a crow. De Payens narrowed his eyes, shifting in the saddle. He glimpsed a white-daubed face, a necklace of bones, and gauntleted hands. She raised these as if about to intone some demonic prayer, and he fumbled for the ave beads wrapped around his sword hilt, but when he glanced up again, the hideous apparition had disappeared. The witch Erictho? he wondered. Surely not. He gripped his reins and stared around. It was best not to think of that, not now!

They left the dingy markets and bazaars, moving into the more opulent quarter of the city, where lovely mansions stood behind ornate gates. They crossed small squares with bubbling fountains, shady sycamores, and terebinth and palm trees. Songbirds trilled from gilded cages fastened to gateposts, and the air grew subtly sweet with the fragrance of flowery cactus and other plants. Eventually they reached Herod's Gate, and were waved on through by dust-covered sentries, out on to the long road stretching north to Ramallah and Nablus. The late-January heat was not as oppressive here as in the city; even the sandy breezes felt fresh after the acrid odours of the streets. For a while de Payens rode in silence, staring at the distant hillsides covered with deep-blue flowering mandrake, whilst closer to the trackway, pale violet and yellow irises flourished.

The road was busy with travellers, pack ponies and camel lines. Pedlars and traders pushed their barrows and handcarts or urged on oxen fastened to cumbersome wagons. Soldiers, their livery covered in dust, slouched on shaggy garrans. Pilgrims moved in throngs under makeshift banners and rough-hewn wooden crosses. Beggars importuned for alms. Enterprising villagers came out of a line of pine trees to offer platters of bread and beakers of water or crushed juice. Above them all circled the ever-vigilant buzzards and vultures, thick wings feathering the air, whilst rock pigeons, aware of the danger above, darted from cover to cover across the road.

De Payens knew the route. They'd follow the Jordan valley, thick with olive groves, where the crickets sang their constant hymn, not even interrupted by the great tawny foxes slipping through in their hunt for vermin or the occasional unwary bird. As they journeyed on, they broke free of the crowds, following a route laid out by Parmenio, who seemed to know every twist and corner of the land. At first, conversation was desultory, until they spent their first night camped out in a wadi. In the far distance, thunder rumbled and jagged lightning flashed across the sky, but the rain never reached them. The Provençals set up camp, collecting dried dung and whatever bracken they could find. Soon a merry fire crackled. Meats were cooked, bread warmed, wineskins circulated. De Payens sang the Benedicite, and they ate, even as they began to talk about the desert and all its haunting, ghostly legends. Naturally, on that and successive evenings, the conversation then turned to gossip about recent events in Jerusalem. One of the Provençals alluded to a tale about witches concocting potions from the froth of mad dogs, the hump of a man-eating hyena and the eyes of an eagle, but de Payens discovered precious little more about the corpses of the young women found around the city. Tremelai seemed to have succeeded in suppressing the whispers, although the Provençals, who seemed to know about the rumours, fiercely rejected any allegation against the Temple. No mention was ever made of Walkyn and Berrington.

In the mornings, just before dawn, they would continue their journey up through Galilee, past the lake where Christ had fished and walked amongst the plants and bushes now bereft of their summer's glory. They paused there for a while, watching the ducks and the ringed grey plovers dart and sweep above them. At Parmenio's insistence they moved on. Sometimes they stayed in villages, flea-ridden and poor; occasionally at some Templar castle or outpost. Finally they reached their own garrison at Chastel Blanc, high up in the mountains, a stark, lonely place with its oval perimeter walls and soaring keep, which contained both the chapel and the main water supply. The castellan was only too pleased to meet former members of his garrison and gather what news he could. He listened as they described their mission, and pulled a face in surprise, but granted their list of fresh stores and personally escorted them out on to the final stage of their journey.

Once the castellan had left them, Parmenio came into his own, leading them up through lonely rocky passes and culverts, steep ravines and sandy gulleys. There was little soil; nothing grew except hardy shrubs and a scattering of flowers such as lavender and cactus plants. No plough- or meadowland; just sheer rock, a few trees and bushes, with the occasional waterhole in the shade of some sun-bleached culvert. At night they sheltered under rocky outcrops, the silence cut by eerie howling and snuffling as the predators emerged. They grew accustomed to the spine-tingling wafting of hunting owls, which hovered for a brief while in the glare of their fire before floating like ghosts back into the blackness. Occasionally they'd catch a glow of light as if from some distant lantern-horn. Parmenio explained how the mountains were the haunt not only of demons and lost souls but hermits and anchorites, wild men seeking God in the high places. He also added that they were undoubtedly being watched by scouts, the followers of Shaikh Al-Jebal, the Old Man of the Mountain.

On their third evening out from Chastel Blanc, they sheltered in a mountain cave, a fire flickering before them. The sky was brilliant with stars and washed by the silver light of a full moon. Mayele murmured how in a few months it would be the spring equinox, the feast of Easter. De Payens, half listening to the chatter of the Provençals behind him, glanced sharply at his comrade. He had first met Mayele at Chastel Blanc. They'd been given the same chamber to share, so they'd become sword brothers, placed next to each other in the battle line with the sworn duty to protect one another. That would have been about twelve months ago. As Edmund became more accustomed to the barrack life of the Templars, he'd found Mayele reasonable enough, though rather secretive, a good fighter with a love of battle; a cold heart with an iron will. The execution of what Mayele described as the three looters in Tripoli confirmed that. During their punishment at Jerusalem, the Englishman had grown less taciturn, whispering jokes about Tremelai and other Templar leaders, an amusing stream of observations and remarks. He was a brother who attended the litany of the hours and the services as if they were part of a drill, though he laughingly dismissed himself as neither religious nor devout, hardly a cross-creeper, as he described it. De Payens had concluded that this might be due to the sacrilege Mayele had committed in England, the slaying of a cleric, which had provoked instant excommunication. On one occasion Mayele had even described what had happened: how he'd slain the cleric in an argument, then fled to a church, grasping the corner of its altar and pleading sanctuary. Eventually, after forty days, he'd been allowed to leave, taken refuge in London and accepted the penance imposed by the bishop for his sins, of being enrolled in the Templar order. Mayele was, de Payens reasoned, hardly a man to be reflecting on the feast of Easter or its preparation through the Lenten fast.

'You are pining for Easter, Philip?' he teased. 'Why now? Why here?'

'You may not know this . . .' Mayele leaned forward, stirring the fire with his dagger, digging at the dried dung and kindling, which burst into fiery sparks. He paused at the mournful yip of a jackal, followed by the raucous screech of a night bird. 'Tremelai talked of sending us both to England, Edmund. We have a small-holding there in London, near the royal palace of Westminster.' For the first time de Payens could recall, Mayele's voice turned wistful. 'It would be good to be in England at springtime, well away from the dust and the heat, the dirt devils and the flies. Coolness,' his voice grew soft, 'a wet, green darkness with clear air.' He paused and stared at Parmenio, who squatted with one hand across his face. De Payens hid his surprise; he was sure he'd caught a gesture by the Genoese, a swift movement of fingers as if signalling to Mayele. Parmenio, sharp-eyed, caught de Payens' look and grinned.

'I am warning him to be prudent,' he whispered, the fire bathing his clever face. He indicated with his head. 'Those Provençals are not the dumb mules they pretend. They are hand-picked, with a better knowledge of tongues than we think. They are Tremelai's spies.'

'And you, Parmenio?' de Payens asked. 'Are you a spy? That story about reparation for your assault on me . . .'

Mayele, head down, laughed softly. Parmenio clicked his tongue and sat listening to sounds from the darkness: the scuttling of night creatures and the swift chatter of darting bats. The night air was turning bitterly cold; the heat from the sun-scorched rocks had faded. Parmenio threw more bracken on to the flames.

'Edmund, I am a physician, a trader in simples and potions. I move like a shadow across God's earth. I also collect and barter information for the rulers of this

61

world. Yes, I have worked for the Temple before, Tremelai knows that, but Tripoli was different. I saw mercenaries dash the heads of babies against stones, after raping and killing their mothers. I was truly angry that day, but,' he gave a crooked smile, 'I admired what you did. I also learned that I had attacked not only a Templar, but a scion of the powerful de Payens family. The Temple would never have let that rest.' He spread his hands. 'Hence my approach. Tremelai was only too pleased to use me, especially now.' As if he wished to change the subject, Parmenio pointed through the darkness at the glow from some distant oil lamp. 'I wonder,' he breathed, 'what Tremelai has written in those letters. What he intends to happen at Hedad.'

'More importantly,' de Payens scratched his bearded chin, 'what can we expect from Shaikh Al-Jebal? You've never been here before, Parmenio?'

'Yes and no. I've learned a little about the Assassins.'

'Which is?' Mayele demanded.

'The prophet Muhammad's followers are divided between those who accept what they call the true descent from one son-in-law, Ali, and others who claim legitimacy through another son-in-law. This division has been deepening since the Prophet's death. In the civil wars that followed, other sects flourished, including the Naziris, or Hashishonyi, the hashish-eaters, founded by Hassan Eben Sabbah. He surrounded himself with Fedawis, the Devoted Ones. This sect not only broke away from the main body of believers, but declared war

62

on them. They seized rocky outcrops on which they built their castles. The Fedawis have their own distinctive dress, being garbed in pure white with blood-red sashes and slippers. Each carries a pair of long curved knives. According to legend they are fed on hemp and opium mingled with wine. Over the centuries their emissaries have been dispatched to murder their opponents sometimes openly, other times disguised as camel men, water-carriers, beggars, priests. A few of the men we passed on the road,' Parmenio stretched his hands towards the flames, 'might have been Fedawis.'

'But we are safe?' Mayele leaned over and patted the leather panniers carrying the chancery pouches.

'We have our safe conducts,' Parmenio agreed, pausing at a strange howling that echoed from below, followed by the scream of some animal caught by a hunter. The horrid growls and screeching faded away.

'Once the Old Man of the Mountain or his representative guarantees your safety,' continued Parmenio, 'you are assured. Indeed, they follow a very strict code of hospitality to all who seek them out. For the rest, the Old Man sows fear. The Assassins have a mordant, black sense of humour. Once they have chosen their victim, they often send him a flat sesame seed cake on a snake medallion as a warning of what is to come. The victim wakes to find the cake and the medallion beside their bed, two curved daggers, adorned with red ribbons, pushed into the ground beside them. Over the years, the influence and power of the Old Man and his Fedawis have spread. They defend themselves in their lonely mountain fortresses. Hewn out of stone, impregnable and sheer, such castles can be held by a few men even if besieged by armies of thousands.'

'True,' Mayele murmured. 'How could any invading army feed itself in country like this?'

'Of course,' Parmenio agreed. 'And so the legend was born. Every malcontent from around the Middle Sea to the borders of Samarkand hastens to join he who rejoices in his title of Shaikh Al-Jebal, Old Man of the Mountain. Their most precious castle is the eagle's nest at Alamut in Persia. According to legend, on the summit of that sheer mountain the Old Man built a paradise, a walled garden laid out with the richest soil and watered by underground springs. A veritable Eden, with trees of every kind, pools of pure water, marble fountains bubbling the finest wines, garden beds fertile with the most exotic plants and exuding the rarest perfumes. All around stand pavilions and arbours, their outsides covered in flowers, carpeted and hung with silk inside. The paths of this paradise have been tiled by craftsmen in colours that catch the sun. Songbirds trill from golden cages. Peacocks, resplendent in their thousand-eyed plumage, strut against lush, cool greenness. The garden is entered by a gate of pure gold studded with gems. The Fedawis are taken there to drink drugged wine and be waited on by the most beautiful, sensuous maidens . . .' Parmenio paused, and laughed self-consciously as his own mouth watered at the prospect.

De Payens glanced quickly at Mayele, who had retreated deeper into the shadows. He could only glimpse the lower half of that bearded, lined, cynical face. He shivered, and stretched his hands out to the fire. Parmenio's story stirred his own secret sinful dreams about the veiled beauties he'd glimpsed in the streets and marketplaces, as well as the young woman he'd seized on that raid, pressing up against him, whispering how she would do anything for life . . .

'Continue,' he murmured.

'Above the garden gate,' Parmenio whispered, 'is a proclamation, etched in silver and studded with diamonds.' He paused. 'It runs as follows: "Appointed by God, the Master of the World breaks the chains of all, let everyone praise his name." Anyway,' he shrugged, 'the Fedawis emerge from their drugged sleep rested and refreshed. They are assured that if they carry out their master's orders, what they've just experienced will be theirs for all eternity. As for the truth of all this,' he pulled a face, 'legend perhaps, rumour, other people's dreams, but the Assassins are a fact. They are vultures clustered on their rocky summits watching for prey in the valleys below. The very shadow of their wings strike terror.'

'And now our Grand Master wishes us to do business with them?' de Payens asked.

'Why not?' Parmenio's tone became taunting. 'They say the Templars and the Assassins have much in common.'

'Never!'

'Edmund, they do indeed have much in common: their own rule, obedience to their master, a kingdom within a kingdom, dedication to war, their own vision. Ah well.' Parmenio sighed as he got to his feet. 'Tomorrow, I am sure we will meet them.'

The next morning, they left the cave and began their ascent to Hedad. They had to dismount and lead their horses and pack ponies. At first the air was so bitterly cold, de Payens thought it would crack the rocks. A mist closed in like an army of wraiths, deadening all sounds and muffling their hearing. Occasionally a bird would shriek, a piercing, harsh call. One of the Provençals thought it was not a bird but the warning call of a sentry. Another maintained it could be a lost soul. Then the sun rose fast and strong and the mist disappeared to reveal a landscape of ragged cliffs, stunted trees and wiry gorse. They rounded a bend and stopped. Over a huge boulder near the trackway were blood-stained clothes, neatly laid out as if to dry in the sun. Further along hung a naked corpse, fastened securely to the rock face. The man, a Turk, had been shot by arrows. The cadaver was ripe, and already the carrion-eaters had been busy. Even as the Templars passed, kites and buzzards floated down to the rock, flashing their blood-tinged feathers, impatient to continue the feast.

'A warning,' Parmenio whispered.

They passed other grisly sights: skins and skulls pushed into crevices, now nesting places for birds and

66

lizards; more bloodstained garments and gibbeted corpses. They reached a narrow pass through a needle-thin culvert, the rocks on either side rising sheer above them, and went through on to a plateau, green and gorse-covered, which stretched away to the craggy summit of Hedad and the castle of the Assassins. The Old Man's masons had been most cunning. They had used a broad, jutting ridge just beneath the summit to build their fortress, a long line of crenellated walls, soaring donjons and towers. Any besieging army would find it impossible to take. The bare, windswept countryside would provide little food or fodder, whilst the rock face of the castle rose sheer on all sides. The main fortified gateway was separated from the plateau by a deep gorge, a long gash through the earth that could only be crossed by a swaying rope bridge, which could be easily cut or rolled back in any attack. Even if a hostile force managed to cross that, the fortifications beyond were impressive. The gateway was flanked by towers of polished square stone blocks; each tower was at least a hundred feet high and ten feet wide. On either side of these stretched a vaulting curtain wall, crenellated and fortified, interspersed with narrower towers. De Payens and his companions stared in astonishment at this fearsome house of war, black and threatening against the lightening blue sky, a mass of hard stone, an eagle's eyrie to protect those within from attack. De Payens studied the fortifications. Impossible to take, he concluded: Hedad could be held by a hundred men. In many ways the fortress reminded him of Templar castles built in similar desolate places.

'Empty,' Mayele observed. 'It's like a castle of the dead!' De Payens studied the fortifications. Mayele was right. Hedad looked deserted, forsaken. No fires flared along the ramparts. No lantern glow, no fluttering banners or pennants. No glint of armour or movement of watchmen. They mounted their horses and moved slowly towards the bridge. The ominous silence was abruptly riven by the clatter of chains as the drawbridge fell. They reined in. A horseman thundered out through the gateway. He was dressed in a flowing white robe with a broad red sash around his waist, and his long black hair streamed in the breeze as, without any hesitation, he galloped across the rope bridge and headed directly towards them. The small but agile Arab courser's galloping hooves pounded the earth like the threatening roll of kettle drums. De Payens turned his own horse, hand going to the hilt of his sword, but the rider reined in close before them, his dark, bearded face breaking into a grin. As he bowed, he gave a brilliant display of horsemanship, his mount rearing and turning until at a quiet word it stopped still. The rider gently stroked its grey, sweat-soaked neck, then pointed to de Payens and his companions, speaking quickly in the lingua franca of Outremer.

'Templars, Genoese, sirs, whatever you call yourselves. You are most welcome. I am Uthama, captain of the guard. On behalf of my father, I welcome you to Hedad.'

'A captain without a guard?' said Mayele. 'Without a sword or shield?'

'Magister Mayele, my sword, my shield, my buckler and my defence stand right behind you.'

De Payens turned abruptly. A line of horsemen clad in blue cloaks, their heads and faces masked by chain-mail hoods, had come silently up behind them. A long, threatening line of men, their horn bows notched, the arrows pointed directly at the Templars. De Payens turned, pulled back his own hood and rode towards Uthama, hand extended.

'Friend,' he smiled, 'I thank you for your warm reception.'

'And friend you are.' Uthama clasped the Templar's hand firmly. 'Here in the mountains, as in the desert, there are no strangers, only friend or foe. But come, my father waits.'

They followed Uthama back across the rope bridge over the narrow but sheer-falling gorge. They were grateful to reach the rocky shale path leading up under the arched gateway into the central bailey, dominated by a lofty four-square keep. De Payens hid his surprise; it was not the dusty yard he had expected, but a sea of lush green grass that stretched either side to outer courts. Uthama led them through to the bailey on the left. It reminded de Payens of a prosperous village, with its thatched houses, stables, granaries and smithies. Again a rich stretch of lush grass, wells and fountains, a small waterwheel, gardens and herb plots, a busy, harmonious place. Now that they had arrived, fires that had been banked and doused were rekindled, their smoke billowing up against the sky. The Templars dismounted, their horses taken away by servants, who bowed and grinned in a display of white teeth. The Provençals were led to their lodgings at the far side of the enclosure, where, Uthama assured them, they would have soft beds and good food. He then snapped his fingers at his escort and whispered to one of them. The man hurried off. Uthama turned back to his guests, openly amused at their surprise.

'What did you expect, Magister Edmund? A band of cut-throats, of vagabond robbers from the slums?'

'We passed corpses.'

'Not as many as I see when I enter Jerusalem or Tripoli,' Uthama retorted. 'Come, my father waits.'

'Your father is Shaikh Al-Jebal?'

'Yes and no,' Uthama laughed. 'Our Grand Master shelters in Alamut; my father, Nisam, is his caliph in these mountains, though he can, if he wishes, use his lord's titles.'

He led them back into the central bailey and across into the great keep. De Payens was surprised. Frankish donjons were cold and bleak, squalid places of war. This was different. The windows were broad and cunningly placed to catch the sunlight at every hour of the day. The floor was a mosaic of hard tiles laid closely together, each displaying intricate geometrical patterns in a variety of colours. Brilliant cloths softened the walls.

Baskets of crushed flowers and strewn grains of delicate spices perfumed air already cleansed and sweetened by myrrh sprinkled over caskets of burning charcoal.

In a large antechamber, supervised by Uthama and his escort, they took off their outer clothes, leather boots and gauntlets. Mayele wanted to keep his sword, but de Payens shook his head, whilst Uthama murmured that such weapons would not be necessary. Platters of unleavened bread and goblets of wine were brought. All three Templars ate and drank, knowing that once they had done so, their safety was assured. Afterwards they washed their hands and faces in rosewater, drying themselves on soft woollen napkins. Robes and slippers were offered. Uthama, his face all serene, quietly whispered a prayer in Arabic and anointed each of their foreheads with a sweet-smelling chrism. He then stood back and bowed without any trace of sarcasm.

'Come.' He led them up some stairs, their stone flags covered with soft material, a polished wooden rail driven into the wall serving as an aid. They passed enclaves, stairwells, and narrow apertures, in each of which stood a blue-garbed guard, his face hidden by a chain-mail mask; all were armed with a silver shield boasting a crimson boss and a curved sabre in a scarlet scabbard.

The audience chamber Uthama led them into was truly remarkable. It glistened like a treasure house; the carved wooden beams of the ceiling were inlaid with gold, silver, malachite and precious jewels. Great windows, open to the sun, were covered by pure white gauze veils, which allowed in air and light but not the flies, insects or dirt. The walls were covered in carvings of exotic birds with silver enamel feathers, large rubies serving as their eyes. The floor was of the finest cedar of Lebanon, polished and ingrained with scent, covered here and there with the most luxuriant turkey rugs. The furniture was of delicate gleaming acacia; around the walls were ranged deep divans stacked with plump, gold-fringed cushions.

The main seating area was cordoned off by a double curtain of gold-edged cordovan leather intricately studded with silver twine. This was pulled back, and the three Templars were ushered to cushions placed before small square tables. Heaped bowls of fruit, platters of sweet bread and filigreed goblets brimming with wine stood next to exquisite chalices of Venetian glass crammed with slowly melting sherbet. On the other side sat Nisam, flanked by his Fedawis, dressed in sheer white gowns, red cords around their waists. Dark-faced, long-haired warriors, they stared unblinkingly as their guests bowed and squatted down.

'In the name of the Compassionate,' Nisam's lips hardly moved, but his voice was strong and carrying, 'I greet you, travellers, friends, honoured guests.' He was white-haired, his beard and moustache neatly clipped; he had a round, genial face with smiling eyes and full red lips. He was dressed in a silver gown with a gold-brocaded blood-red cape over his shoulders. He smiled at de Payens and suggested that they should all eat and drink. Uthama placed the leather panniers containing the chancery pouches beside de Payens.

'Eat and drink,' Uthama whispered. 'My father will say when you should hand your letters over.'

De Payens obeyed. The Fedawis grew more relaxed, chattering amongst themselves. Nisam ate slowly. Now and again he smiled at Uthama, then at de Payens. The Templar tasted the wine. It was delicious, undoubtedly the best grape of Gascony or Burgundy. Eventually Nisam leaned over and asked about their journey and the news from Jerusalem. He was courteous, and in the flow of gossip that followed, he showed himself well apprised of what was happening elsewhere. At last he gestured that the chancery pouches be handed to him. De Payens did so slightly uneasily. Nisam's stare was now cold and calculating, as if he recalled some grievance or grudge. Uthama whispered that they should withdraw. Once out of the antechamber, Mayele demanded to know when a reply would be made. De Payens just stared out of the window, still concerned at that hostile glance from Nisam. Beneath the courtesies and the lavish hospitality, this was a place of intrigue, a house of blood. Uthama was busy talking to the other two Templars, though when de Payens joined them, the young Assassin gave him that gracious smile.

'All will be well,' he declared, then insisted on showing them personally to their chambers on the floor above.

Mayele and Parmenio were given one to share. De Payens had his own, small, comfortable and well furnished. They ensured their baggage was brought up, then visited the Provençals, who, like any soldiers, had quickly made themselves at home, sitting outside, boots off, backs against the wall, enjoying the sun and fresh air whilst sharing a jug of wine. At Mayele's question, Uthama replied that in his view, the drinking of wine was not an infringement of the Prophet's teaching. He then asked his guests to forget their mission and join him on a tour of the castle. De Payens suspected this was to be a show of strength. In the end, both he and his companions were deeply impressed. Hedad was a fortress built on a sheer ridge, its formidable walls and towers dominating every approach. Fresh water was brought in from underground streams and springs, enough to soak the spacious gardens as well as the private paradise that lay behind the wall of one of the outer baileys. The fortress was well stocked with arms, mangonels, catapults and all the other impedimenta needed to counter a siege. Smithies, forges and the infirmary as well as stables and storehouses were in good order. Parmenio questioned Uthama about Nisam's deep knowledge of affairs beyond his castle walls. The Assassin clapped his hands in glee and took them to the pigeon cotes, where he explained how these 'horses of the air' carried messages in small cylinders attached to their legs. Both de Payens and his companions knew about this device for collecting information and were full of questions. Uthama simply shrugged and explained that the homing instincts of the birds would carry them to their destination.

'Of course,' he tapped the side of his nose, 'that means that we must own places in the plains that they know, secret places, but,' he lifted his hands, 'apart from that, and the danger of marauding hawks, the birds fly true and straight. Let me inform you,' he stood, hands on hip, face all rueful, 'King Baldwin III has unfurled his standards and proclaimed war. He has summoned all Franks to the siege of Ascalon. Oh yes,' he continued, enjoying their surprise, 'Ascalon, the Bride of Syria, the southern key to Jerusalem, the port for Egypt, is under siege.'

'You seem pleased,' de Payens said.

'Of course. If Ascalon falls, the *mulahid*,' Uthama used the Islamic term of abuse for heretics, 'the *mulahid* of Egypt will be weakened.'

'Your father . . .' De Payens steered Uthama away from Mayele and Parmenio's heated discussion of what they'd learned.

'What about my father, Templar?'

'He looks at me as if he knows me. Not as a friend.'

'As an enemy?' Uthama breathed. 'And so you should be. As you Franks say, *usque ad mortem* – to the death.' He drew his dagger, swift and menacing.

The rasp alerted Mayele and Parmenio, who hurried over. De Payens stepped back, but Uthama handed the dagger to him.

'Look, Templar, stare into the blade, see your face!'

De Payens did so: the polished steel served as a mirror, slightly twisting his features.

'The eyes,' Uthama turned to acknowledge Mayele and Parmenio, 'deep set, light green. The black hair, streaked with grey. The face dark, harsh and bearded, the furrows in the cheeks. A warrior, perhaps an ascetic, a man not sure of himself. My father may see all that, but most of all he sees the face of de Payens, his mortal enemy.'

The Templar lowered the dagger, then swiftly turned it so the Assassin could grasp the hilt. Uthama resheathed the blade and stepped forward.

'Didn't you know, Templar? Your great-uncle, Hugh de Payens, your grandfather, Theodore the Greek? They once hunted my father through these mountains. They failed, but they killed his two brothers. A blood feud exists between us. Didn't your Grand Master, Bertrand Tremelai, warn you?' Uthama's face was now unsmiling. 'Apparently not, since you do not even know the story!'

# Chapter 4

The brethren of the Temple held certain
fortresses adjacent to the lands of the Assassins.

'So will I, despite your safe conduct,' de Payens retorted
fiercely, trying to hide the fear curdling within him, 'now
be murdered, my naked corpse fastened to a rock?'

Uthama stared at him solemnly, then burst out
laughing, head going down, slapping his thighs.

'You think that?' he gasped, his face turning abruptly
solemn.

De Payens wondered if this man's wits were wandering.

'You think that?' Uthama shouted, grasping de Payens'

arm. 'You are safe here. I shall show you who is fastened to rocks.' He yelled orders at his guards, and one of them hastened away as Uthama almost dragged de Payens out on to the steps of the keep. The day was drawing on, the sky dulling. The garrison was now busy, as the first evening coolness made itself felt. All paused at the appearance of Uthama and the Templars. Retainers scurried about. One brought Uthama a powerful horn bow and a quiver of arrows. The Assassin issued a stream of orders as he slung the quiver over his shoulder. Notching an arrow, he stood on the edge of the top step. From behind the keep his retainers pushed a man, his wrist and ankles chained. Plucked from the dungeons, he was covered in dirt and wet straw, but he still yelled a tirade of abuse at Uthama. The Assassin retorted in kind and pointed to the gateway. The prisoner laughed and did a mocking little jig. The chains were loosened. De Payens sensed what was about to happen. The prisoner was being given a chance. The manacles were released, and the prisoner broke into a run, deliberately swerving from side to side. Uthama brought up the curved bow, pulling back the twine cord. The barbed arrow, with its eagle-feathered flight, was loosed. De Payens thought he'd missed, but Uthama's accuracy was chilling. The arrow struck the fleeing man just beneath the neck, flinging him forward. He crashed to the ground, rose, then staggered a few paces before the second arrow drove deep into his back. He lifted his hands as if in prayer and collapsed once again. The rest of the garrison went back to their business as Uthama loped down the steps. He raced across, dagger drawn, pulled the man's head back by the hair and sliced his throat. The blood splashed out, a deepening red pool darkening the earth. Uthama wiped his knife clean on the man's corpse and strode back. He smiled up at de Payens.

'Templar, he'll be exposed on the rock! A murderer sent here by the Princes of the Plain to kill my father. You've not come to do that, have you?'

De Payens simply stared back. He recognised Uthama's soul, no different from Mayele's or his own, a killer here in this house of blood.

Over the next few days, de Payens and his companions discussed what they'd learned: the attack on Ascalon; the blood feud between Nisam and his own family; the failure of the Grand Master to inform them of this.

'So you never knew about the blood feud?' Mayele insisted.

'No!' de Payens retorted. 'Both my parents died when I was no higher than a flower. Grandfather Theodore and the Lady Eleanor lectured me day and night about the glories of the Temple. Only God knows what Uncle actually did. Tremelai must know, yet never once has he referred to a blood feud with the leader of the Assassins.' He paused. 'And neither has Trussell, who has advised me so much. Is it just a coincidence that I'm here . . . ?' De Payens deliberately didn't finish his sentence, but stared around his chamber, where they'd met for the evening meal. They had been four days in

79

Hedad, and still Nisam hadn't asked to see them again. Uthama remained their ever-smiling, generous host, but de Payens was distinctly uncomfortable in his presence. The Assassin was a blood-lover, a violent man who would be very much at home in the retinue of some great Frankish lord or the Temple barracks. De Payens glanced across at Mayele, carefully chewing on highly spiced shreds of lamb; Parmenio, staring moodily into his wine cup. Since their arrival, the Genoese had taken to wandering the fortress, adopting the guise of the curious traveller eager to learn. He had become more open with Mayele, who in turn began to reveal a little more about his past, especially his fighting in the civil war between King Stephen and Henry Fitzempress.

'I was in the comitatus of Geoffrey de Mandeville, Earl of Essex,' he declared, when he and de Payens climbed to the top of the keep to admire the view. 'A grim war leader, Edmund. We fought in the cold, dark fens of East Anglia. We seized the Abbey of Ramsey and fortified it. Oh, the priests issued excommunication against us, damning us in our eating, our shitting, our sleeping and our waking! A time of bitter war.' He paused.

'And what happened?'

'We were besieging a castle at Burwell on the Essex coast. Earl Geoffrey took an arrow to the head, a minor wound, but it became infected and grew malignant. He died listing his sins, but the Church refused to grant him holy burial. The Templars heard of this. They

80

graciously collected the earl's corpse and took it to their house in London near the Bishop of Lincoln's Inn. Again the Church refused burial, because Mandeville had died *in peccatis* – in his sins – so the Templars hung his coffin from a yew tree in their cemetery.' Mayele laughed sharply. 'So he's in God's Acre but not buried in it! Ah well,' he continued, 'my sins are just as numerous, and deep as scarlet. The Templars were the only ones to show charity, so . . .' He leaned against the crenellations, allowing the mountain breeze to sweep his rugged, fierce face. 'When penance was imposed, I became a postulant in the order and was dispatched to Outremer.' He turned and grasped Edmund by the shoulder. 'But enough of the past! Let us deal with the present. Master Uthama gave us a display of archery; let us return the compliment.'

They went down to the exercise yard behind the keep, where the Fedawis and the blue-liveried guards practised their arms. Mayele insisted on his own display. He called for his horse and provided a brilliant tourney: the joust, the charge; sword- and dagger-play at close quarters, as well as archery and javelin casting. De Payens, used to watching the cream of his order clash on the jousting field, was deeply impressed, as were Uthama and his retinue. Mayele was a superb horseman; knight and steed become one, swift and relentless. He guided his horse with his knees whilst grasping shield, lance, mace or sword. Some of the Fedawis volunteered to act as his opponents. Mayele then showed the terrible

81

beauty of a knight in combat, twisting and turning, using his horse to break his opponents whilst he lunged with blade and kite-shaped shield to scatter, isolate then deal with the enemy. When he had finished, Uthama himself led the hymn of praise. Mayele simply shrugged, winked at de Payens and made the droll observation that he and his host would hopefully never meet in combat.

Mayele's cunning demonstration of how the Templars were also warriors was not lost on the Fedawis: it eased the tension caused by Uthama's brutal display of power and brought the three men closer together. Parmenio confided to his companions what he'd learned about the castle; how he had studied every postern door and sally port just in case they had to leave earlier than their hosts expected. De Payens remained suspicious that Parmenio was also searching for something else, something he wouldn't mention. Nevertheless, he realised it was important to maintain good relations with his comrades. Every morning they met the Provençals, and in the evening the three would gather again to discuss the events of the day or listen to Mayele's stories about his campaigns in the gloomy fens of eastern England. Perhaps it was boredom, the realisation of how futile it was to speculate about Tremelai's secret plans or the hints that the Grand Master was thinking of sending them to England, but de Payens became eager to learn more about the civil war raging there. Mayele needed little encouragement. He described how Stephen and his son Eustace were locked in mortal combat with the Angevin Henry Fitzempress; how the latter, young, ruthless and bounding with energy, was determined to seize the English throne and crush the great barons whose bitter rivalries prolonged the war. Edmund suspected that Mayele's loyalty lay with Henry Fitzempress, as his old master, Geoffrey de Mandeville, had been King Stephen's resolute opponent. In the end, however, as on every evening, the conversation returned to the reasons for being in Hedad, and Tremelai's secret intentions. Since leaving Tripoli, de Payens had accepted it as gospel truth that the Assassins had been involved in Count Raymond's murder. He believed that the Grand Master had his own secret evidence to prove it. Such a conviction was soon vigorously shaken.

Uthama eventually summoned them to appear before his father and his advisers. Once the usual courtesies were observed, Nisam leaned over, pointing at de Payens. He spoke slowly in the lingua franca, emphasising his points on his fingers.

'You understand,' his gaze took in Mayele and Parmenio, 'that we had nothing to do with Raymond of Tripoli's murder? True, true,' he nodded, 'we did have our difficulties with the count, our misunderstandings, but we sent him no warning – did we?'

De Payens could only agree.

'And you found no corpses?'

Again de Payens and his companions nodded in assent.

'But we were there.' Mayele spoke up. 'We heard the cries. We saw the daggers decorated with your red ribbons. Two of these were found, as was one of your medallions.'

'And any fool can cry to God!' came the cutting reply. 'Daggers, red ribbons and copper medallions can be bought in any bazaar or market. Just because a woman has strumpet eyes doesn't make her a whore.' Nisam breathed in deeply. 'What proof do you have?' he insisted. 'Indeed, if we were involved, we Assassins as you call us, why not Templars?'

'Impossible,' de Payens countered. 'We were sent to guard him.'

'And you failed.' Nisam smiled. 'Master Edmund, I ask you to reflect carefully. What do you remember?'

De Payens quietly conceded the point. He had not really reflected on those few heartbeats of time: the killers surging forward in their long robes, the knifemen rushing towards him, the bloody, dusty swirl, Count Raymond drooping from his horse, the daggers rising and falling.

'Not the Temple!' he whispered, as Mayele loudly voiced his own objections.

'Masters,' Nisam lifted his goblet of sherbet in solemn toast, 'I did not say the Temple, but Templars. Has not one of your company been expelled? We are aware of a great scandal in Jerusalem, hideous murders, allegations of witchcraft, how some Templars were paying service to the dark lords of the air.' He smiled at their silence and pointed to the gorgeous fresco of a bird on the wall to his left. 'The Peacock of Gabriel,' he explained, 'has a thousand eyes; he sees everything.'

'And you, lord, have a thousand pigeons,' de Payens retorted.

Nisam put his cup down and joined in the laughter of his comrades, clapping his hands in appreciation. 'Very good, very good, Master Edmund; you are waking from your dream. We know what goes on in the Temple precincts and in the sacred city itself. More precisely,' he chewed on his lip, 'we know all about the expulsion of Walkyn, and Berrington's disappearance. I know this not only because of Gabriel's Peacock, oh no,' he stared solemnly at de Payens, 'but because Walkyn came here. He asked for my help. I refused. Is it possible he had a hand in the count's murder?'

'He asked for your help?' Mayele interrupted. 'For what?'

'Magister,' Nisam retorted, 'we are no different from one of your monasteries or Templar houses. We are not mountain cut-throats. You've seen how we live in our own community. True, we execute those who wish to do us harm. However, don't your lords and abbots have the power of the axe, noose and tumbril, the authority to execute outlaws on their gallows? Many come here seeking help. Our code of hospitality is most strict. Such guests are welcome. Your brother knight was no different. Indeed, where else could he go? Your order had turned its face against him.'

'What did he want?' de Payens asked quickly. 'What did he say?'

'He was a beggar,' Uthama spoke up, 'ragged, dirty and hunted. He made no pretence. He needed food, money and clothing. We were obliged to help. He explained how he'd been expelled from the order for unspecified crimes. He did not tell us what, but protested his innocence. He was determined to reach Tripoli, seek help and take ship back to his own country. He mentioned a port, Dov . . .' He stumbled on the word.

'Dover,' Mayele offered.

'Dover,' Uthama agreed. 'Walkyn was no threat to us. Why should we have Templar blood on our hands? We gave him what we could, provided him with an escort down to the plains, so . . .' Uthama rocked himself backwards and forwards. 'Could such a man have killed Count Raymond? Did he ask for the count's help, only to be refused? So he decided to take revenge? Master Mayele, we have seen your prowess with arms. Wasn't your former brother a swordsman, a warrior?'

'There was more than one assassin,' de Payens declared.

'True,' Nisam agreed, 'but in the cities of the plains, murderers flock like flies on a turd. They call themselves scorpion men, or some other title, for the same sinful crime. Did your former brother join these? No matter.' Nisam's voice turned more decisive. He glanced at his Fedawi, who sat alongside him, close-faced, eyes watchful. 'In the end,' he declared, 'we had no hand in the murder of Count Raymond. We had no motive, no reason; there is no evidence. However . . .' He drew from beneath the cushion beside him the empty chancery pouches of the Grand Master. He handed these to de Payens, followed by an exquisite casket fashioned out of cedarwood and ribbed with jewelled enamel strips. The domed lid was clasped shut with three locks and sealed along the rim with greenish-blue wax. A small leather pouch containing the keys was also handed over. The casket weighed heavy; de Payens concluded it must contain either coins or precious stones. He gave it to Mayele; the keys he slipped into his own wallet.

'A gift for your Grand Master. The coffer contains my response. Masters,' Nisam spread his hands, his eyes holding de Payens' gaze, 'you shall not look upon my face again.' He grinned. 'At least, not here. Rest and refresh yourselves. In two days you must depart. My son Uthama will see you safely down to the plains.'

The meeting ended. De Payens, Mayele and Parmenio murmured their thanks, then returned to their own quarters, where they engaged in fierce and rather fruit-less debate about what had truly happened to Berrington and Walkyn and, once again, about how much the Grand Master knew. De Payens muttered his excuses and withdrew to his own chamber to reflect upon what Nisam had said, trying to recall all the details of that attack on Count Raymond. The Assassins leader was correct: apart from the blood-curdling cries, the medallion and the red-ribboned daggers, there was no real evidence that the Fedawi had been involved. So why had the Grand Master decided that they had? Sitting on the edge of his bed, he startled at the soft knock on his door. He thought it would be Mayele, but Uthama stood there with two of his escort.

'Come,' whispered the Assassin. 'My father wishes to speak to you alone.'

De Payens had no choice but to follow him out of the keep, turning left into the outer bailey. Uthama led him across to the walled enclosure. He tapped the gate; it opened, and de Payens was ushered into the paradise. The gate shut with a click behind him. No Uthama, no guards; at least none he could see. On either side rose a boxed hedge. He took a step forward, boots crunching on the white pebbled path.

'Come, Templar, awaken! Do not be afraid.' Nisam's voice carried powerfully.

De Payens walked forward and reached the end of the path. He stared around. The garden was truly exquisite, a perfect square bounded on three sides by trees and bushes of every kind: sycamore, terebinth, myrtle, pine and palm, dark ilex, rhododendron, and hibiscus with its dull red blossoms. A rich green lawn stretched in front of him. In the centre was a fountain intricately carved in the shape of a peacock, inlaid with gold, silver, gems and coloured glass, all blended together to catch the light then reflect it in a blaze of glory. Through the peacock's mouth bubbled the purest water, splashing into a gilt-edged bowl beneath. To the right of the fountain stood a tent-shaped pavilion of polished cedar, with coloured glass windows. Nisam was waiting on the steps leading up to it, garbed in a red gown, one hand clutching a jewelled goblet. He beckoned at de Payens. The Templar took off his boots and, rather self-consciously, crossed the lawn and ascended the steps into the sweet-smelling pavilion. The inside walls were studded with miniature tiles of electrum, gold and silver, each with its own exotic designs. The floor was carpeted with the finest rugs from Persia. On each side of the entrance, large round drums, neatly perforated, gave off a richly fragrant warmth. Nisam gestured to the heap of cushions in the centre. Once de Payens had taken his seat, Nisam sat to his right at the end of a long polished table on which glittered goblets, platters and bowls.

'The finest wines and fruits.' Nisam filled the goblet in front of de Payens so that the wine winked at the jewel-chased rim. He then lifted his own in toast. De Payens responded, sipping so carefully Nisam grinned. 'Drink, Templar, drink deep of both wine and life.'

The wine was delicious, as was the soft sugar bread and sliced fruit Nisam insisted on serving to de Payens. The Templar ate and drank, relishing the exquisite tastes. A sense of deep comfort and peace swept through him as he stared at the Peacock of Gabriel pouring out its life-giving water.

'Drink,' Nisam urged again.

De Payens did as he was told, fascinated by the way the peacock was now moving in all its gorgeous splendour. He felt his eyes grow heavy, his body nestling in the alluring warmth of a comfortable bed, swathed in the blankets that Lady Eleanor was pulling close about him. Other memories returned. He was drifting in that small boat Grandfather Theodore had built, *The Cog of War*, he called it. Then he was in Tripoli, turning his horse, moving to meet those darting assassins, whilst from a tree close by hung a coffin swinging gently on ropes lashed to the branches.

'Templar, Magister!'

De Payens startled. He was back in the pavilion, staring out at the fountain.

'You have been sleeping, Templar, dreaming. I suspect that that is what you have been doing for most of your life: dreaming about being the perfect paladin, or of following in the footsteps of your great and illustrious ancestor Sir Hugh.'

'With whom you had a blood feud.' De Payens shook himself. He felt refreshed, strengthened and slightly resentful at Nisam's implied criticism.

'Magister,' Nisam smiled, 'I mean no offence. I am trying to help. I do not want you to sleepwalk to your death.'

'What do you mean?' De Payens grew fully alert.

'Look around you, Edmund. The world you live in is not that painted by your grandmother, the formidable Eleanor. Beware of illusions. The house of the Temple

90

is no longer comprised of poor knights vowed to poverty, dedicated to protecting pilgrims. The Temple now owns cities, towns, castles and estates. They have a fleet of ships. A Templar can travel from here to the ends of Christendom and beyond and still meet fellow Templars. Your order has power, wealth and influence.'

'The blood feud?' de Payens insisted.

'I shall come to that by and by. Your Grand Master, Bertrand Tremelai, is a great lord with bounding ambition. He intends to spread his roots deep,' Nisam pulled a face, 'and to become a church within a church, a kingdom within a kingdom. He dreams of imperium: an empire, a power to rival anything in the West. What I told you earlier about the Templar who came here,' he shrugged, 'I did not tell the truth.' He pursed his lips. 'I trust you, but not your companions. Mayele is a dark soul, Parmenio a host of secrets who scurries around my fortress like a rat seeking food. He searches for something; what, I do not know. Of course,' he breathed out noisily, 'he might even suspect the truth.'

'Which is?'

'Walkyn certainly came to Hedad, but he was no ragged beggar. He had shaved his head and face and was dressed in Arab clothes. When my son escorted him out of the mountains, he was sure that Walkyn intended to meet other people. Walkyn did not come to beg for food or alms. He came to ask for my help in assassinating Count Raymond of Tripoli.'

'What?'

91

'He argued that since the count had attacked caravans coming to Hedad and plundered them, I should have a grievance against him. He talked of revenge, and invited me to carry that out.'

'And you refused?'

'Of course I did.' Nisam chuckled. 'Not because I had any love for Count Raymond – indeed, we did have debts to settle with him – but we Assassins, as you call us, make our own decisions. We choose our own victims. We do not allow others to dictate what we do.'

De Payens stared hard at this cunning old man.

'Why didn't you kill Walkyn? After all, he was a Templar. You have no love for us.'

'Why do you persist in thinking that we are a gang of cut-throats? Walkyn came here with hands outstretched in peace. He ate our bread, drank our wine; he was a guest, a merchant with a business proposition. He was protected by our strict code. I admit, we were intrigued. I asked him why. He said, to cause chaos, create mayhem, but also that he had his own private reasons. After he left Hedad,' Nisam sipped from his goblet, 'we decided to watch what would happen. When I met you and your companions, I raised the possibility that a Templar may have been involved in Count Raymond's murder. Now you know why, and not just because of Walkyn's request. My pigeons, my horses of the air, nest in Tripoli. There were rumours before the count was killed, as well as afterwards, that a Templar, or at least a Frankish knight, may have been involved. Indeed, the thought crossed my mind that perhaps you and Mayele were accomplices of Walkyn, at least until I met you, but, Edmund, you are an honourable soul. You must also be wondering,' he toasted de Payens with his cup, 'why your Grand Master sent you here. I mean the blood feud between our two families. Do not be harsh on Tremelai! Perhaps he sent you not only because you witnessed Count Raymond's murder, but because he knows the full truth about our blood feud, as does your great friend William Trussell.'

'And that truth is?'

'Ah.' Nisam closed his eyes. 'Years ago, when I was a warrior, your great-uncle and your grandfather led raids up into these mountains. During one of these, my brothers were killed in hand combat with Lord Hugh. True, a hero's death, but blood is still blood. Six months later, Lord Hugh, cunning as a serpent, came again. The winter snow thawed and he launched an ambuscade against a caravan bringing provisions from Ascalon. My wife, the mother of Uthama, was part of that caravan. She was captured. Lord Hugh, however, treated her with every respect. He sent her and her escort safely back to me with a message that the house of the Temple did not wage war on women and children.' He opened his eyes. 'So, Templar, where does that leave me? I shall tell you what you are, Edmund de Payens. You are a dreamer in a darkened room. You live in an illusion.

You do not realise what is happening in your order. You should open your eyes, draw your knife and keep your back to the wall.' He plucked a piece of parchment from beneath a cushion and passed it over. 'Take this, and may your god go with you. My debt has been paid.'

# Chapter 5

The enemy, for our undoing, suspended the
bodies of the slain by ropes from the ramparts.

Ascalon, which rejoiced in its grandiose titles, 'The Bride
of Syria', 'Southern Door to Jerusalem' and 'Gateway to
the Sea Lanes of the East', was under siege. At the heart
of the magnificent city rose a mosque, its columns of
gleaming black marble supporting cavernous stone. It
was approached by a lofty colonnaded walk of white
limestone with archways and a floor of shimmering
marble. The walls around the inner courtyard were
exquisitely decorated with mosaics of gold and silver.

Fountains of pure water splashed into basins where visitors could slake their thirst. In the shadowy corners of this inner sanctum, the Turkish governor's Mamelukes, fierce warriors clad in black and silver cloaks, watched the pilgrims throng to worship. All came here: desert wanderers in their camel-skin robes; Turkomen in dark hides; Nubians in flaming crimson; sombre mercenaries with shields slung across their backs; leather-clad kadis shuffling under their parasols; merchants in gaudily striped robes; fly-infested beggars, their spindly legs dependent on their staves, their bellies swollen, wooden begging bowls slung around their necks. Veiled women slipped by like ghosts. Holy men squatted in the shade. Prophets, courtesans and couriers, the arrogant and the woebegone, all flocked to Ascalon before travelling on to Frankish-held Jerusalem, to visit the Dome of the Rock, gather in the Cavern of Souls and worship in the Holy Place of Ascent. Now they were trapped, as were the men and women of the bazaars, where the carpets of Persia were stacked high next to bales of hemp, vases of olive oil, chests of spices and caskets of pearls. All had been caught up in the siege: the Jews in their blue robes, as well as the Armenians and Venetians, who had to wear a noose around their necks to distinguish them as foreigners.

The governor of Ascalon had been astounded. The Franks had abruptly stirred themselves, emerging from their bleak fortresses, a stream of men under their coloured standards, all flocking to the banners of

Baldwin III, who was determined to take this vital sea port. The spies and scouts of the governor, riding the swiftest mounts of Arabia, had galloped in swirling clouds of dust up through the great Gate of Jerusalem with the dire news. The *cruciferi*, the cross-bearers, were on the march again! The hideous mailed cavalry of the Franks was gathering, readying itself to deliver a thundering charge to sweep away any opposition. Hordes of archers, long columns of trudging men-at-arms, hobelars and infantry followed. Behind these trundled a heavy siege train, mangonels, catapults, battering rams and war carts crammed with pitch, tar and firebrands.

Ascalon was to be ringed, battered, breached and torched. Worse, the house of the Temple, those vengeful warrior-monks in their long loose robes of white samite, stole caps on heads now shaven for war, faces masked by rough beards, had joined the siege. Grand Master Tremelai had summoned his veterans, and had emerged as the fiercest of Baldwin's supporters. The Templars had pitched camp, their dark hide tents grouped tidily around the sacred enclosure containing the blue pavilion of the Grand Master and the scarlet and gold chapel tent, which held the altar and a host of sacred relics. Ascalon was to be stormed. Dominus Tremelai had insisted on this. He'd answered the summons of King Baldwin, stripping the Holy City of virtually every fighting member of his order, as he had the great castles and outposts throughout Outremer. The Templars pressed the siege. Ascalon was blocked, sealed in, and its garrison had no choice but to raise the black banner of war from its towers and walls. The governor had issued his defiance of the *cruciferi* to rolling kettle drums, clashing cymbals and booming gongs. Already the ground between the city walls and the outlying pickets of the *cruciferi* was littered with corpses rotting in the heat. A relentlessly scorching sun burned the cream and grey stonework of Ascalon, as it did the tents of the besiegers. The *cruciferi* hoped for a swift, savage resolution. Ascalon, however, proved stubborn. The besiegers chafed under the ferocious heat, their irritation worsened by a persistent desert wind that wafted in its own feverish restlessness.

Edmund de Payens had also joined the siege. He sat in the shade of a hide awning over the entrance to the tent he shared with Mayele and Parmenio. He was dressed in a simple white linen gown, beside him a pouch of water from a nearby spring as he moodily watched a straggle of skinny black goats being tended back to their pens. A dust haze hung yellow in the air, muffling sound and coating everything with a fine shimmer of sand. De Payens snatched up the waterskin and took a gulp as he recalled his meeting with Tremelai. The Grand Master had received them deep in his blue tent. He'd almost snatched the sealed pouches sent from the Assassins before listening intently as de Payens and his companions delivered their report. The Grand Master's glistening red face had creased into a smile when he opened the casket and glimpsed the precious stones heaped there. Pleased, yet quietly angry, de Payens concluded, as if their mission to Hedad had not accomplished everything the Grand Master had wished. During the meeting, Tremelai had refused to look him directly in the eye, but seemed distracted by the letter Nisam had dictated. De Payens had kept a close watch on both his companions. They did not know about his secret meeting with Nisam, whilst he had urged them not to reveal what they had discovered at Hedad about Walkyn or the blood feud between the Assassins and the de Payens family. Both Mayele and Parmenio had agreed to this.

Once they had delivered the report, all three were dismissed, given this tent and ordered to be ready for the next assault. That had been five days ago. Rumours were now rife that an all-out attack was imminent. De Payens, Mayele and Parmenio had been ordered to join an advance party shortly after the ninth hour, when the day's heat began to cool. De Payens unlaced the pouch on a cord around his neck, and took out the parchment Nisam had given him. He studied the neatly transcribed numbers, the message hidden in a secret cipher he could not break, at least not yet. He scratched the sweat on his cheek and curbed his irritation as a page, dirty and dishevelled, screamed at a pup he'd befriended. Then he put away the parchment and stared at the shifting yellow haze, his stomach unsettled, bubbling with agitation. He'd been in the camp for almost a week, yet he remained anxious. He accepted that the comfortable horarium he had woven for himself, the hours of the day intertwined with his duties as a Templar, was now rent like some tapestry drenched with water. Tremelai had to be questioned, but how? To whom could he turn? On his arrival at the camp, he had learned about the sudden death of Trussell. The great hero had contracted a fever and died within a day. De Payens, his mind teeming with suspicion, wondered if the Englishman's death was by natural causes.

'It's time!'

De Payens glanced up, shadowing his eyes. Parmenio and Mayele stood staring down at him.

'It's time.' Mayele patted him on the shoulder.

De Payens joined them deep in the tent. He put on his mail chausses and hauberk, looped his war belt over his shoulder, put on his conical helmet and picked up his kite-shaped shield. He rinsed his mouth with a gulp of water as he waited for Mayele and Parmenio. Once ready, he muttered a prayer for protection, then all three left the tent and entered the main camp.

The afternoon haze hung more thickly here. They passed a huge cart tipped to the front, its handles being used as a makeshift gallows for two felons caught, tried and hanged that morning. The stench of the rotting corpses had already attracted camp dogs, which were only kept away by an old man, toothless and bleary-eyed, who sat on an overturned basket waving a club. On the other side of the cart, a black-garbed Benedictine monk crouched on the ground, hearing confessions. A group of camp women in their tawdry finery swirled by, shouting and singing. The rich smell of horse manure mingled with the sweaty odour of thousands of unwashed bodies and the strange fragrances from the cooking pots. The three men avoided the glaring heat of the forges and smithies, picking their way carefully around the refuse and impedimenta of the camp. A dream, de Payens thought, a nightmare full of eerie scenes: a man and a woman coupling noisily under the awning of a tent; a preacher standing on a broken tub singing a psalm; relic-sellers offering medals as sure protection in battle; great lords on their gaudily caparisoned destriers trotting by, hawks on their wrists, lurchers yapping noisily around them. A muffled, misty, grotesque world.

De Payens was already bathed in sweat; his sword arm felt heavy. Behind him, Mayele and Parmenio were chattering. They called out to him, but he ignored them. Other figures garbed for war were also making their way to the edge of the camp, climbing the slight rise crowned with sharpened stakes, most of these decorated with the severed heads of executed prisoners. De Payens tried to ignore the dryness of his throat and lips. He followed the path between the stakes along which the waiting mangonels, trebuchets, battering rams, catapults and towers would be dragged for an all-out assault on the city. He stopped for a moment and studied these terrifying engines of war, their keepers busy about them, greasing axles, strengthening ropes, loading the nearby carts with pots of fire, rocks, bundles of hemp and cloth tarred and ready for burning. Ox hides from the siege towers were being stretched out across the ground to be drenched in vinegar, the only protection against the devastating Greek fire the defenders of Ascalon would use.

'It will happen soon,' Mayele observed, 'a full assault on the city.' He came alongside de Payens. 'Perhaps tomorrow, or the day after. Tremelai is insisting on that.'

De Payens grunted in agreement. They breasted the rise and went down the steep slope towards the grim walls of Ascalon. The area stretching up to these was bleak and grisly as any dream of hell. The yellowing rocky ground was littered with stinking corpses and the tattered remains of battle. Hordes of vultures, hyenas and the occasional slinking fox or jackal came to feast at night. An empty, soul-harrowing stretch of earth dominated by the battlements of the city, festooned with banners, armour twinkling in the sunlight. Black trails of smoke curled up against the sky, a sure sign that the governor and his troops were preparing the defences against sudden attack.

'One of the five cities of the Philistines,' Parmenio declared, 'a city of the plains, steeped in blood, constantly fought over, seized, captured and recaptured.'

On either side of the Jerusalem Gate, now bricked up, rose lofty, massive towers. Common rumour amongst the troops claimed that despite its formidable appearance, the gate had been weakened and forced. De Payens stared through the heat haze. Templar engineers were busy constructing a giant siege tower, the wood being supplied from the masts of ships. Gossip had it that the tower was now ready and this present foray was to spy out the terrain in preparation for the all-out assault. De Payens joined the rest as they gathered together with engineers and stonemasons behind the great pavise, a lofty barrier on wooden wheels under the blue and gold standard of King Baldwin. About sixty men from various retinues had assembled under the command of a royal knight whose shield boasted a silver griffin on an azure background. A veteran of many sieges, the knight swiftly explained how they would approach the Jerusalem Gate as closely as possible. They were to try and discover the number of siege engines mounted on the walls and check how many guard posts lurked amongst the rocky outcrops that peppered the land between the besiegers and the city. De Payens breathed in, wetting his mouth, pinching his nose at the sandy breeze. He peered through an eyelet of the pavise. The ground ahead seemed empty, the only movement being the great winged vultures sweeping backwards and forwards. He murmured in agreement at the royal knight's hissed warnings about a possible ambush. The buzzards and vultures kept well clear of the outcrops that dominated the approach to the city gates.

'Be careful.' Mayele spoke up. 'The mounds are fortified.' He punched the pavise with his fist. 'I hope this holds true.'

'*Deus Vult!*' the royal knight shouted. '*Deus Vult!*' The

cry was taken up as they all leaned against the pavise, its creaking wheels screeching. De Payens pushed with the rest, ignoring the heat, the curling dust that laced nose and mouth. He glanced over his shoulder. Crossbowmen, Templar serjeants, were following, slightly edged away on the flanks, to watch both the walls and those mounds. Behind the archers, a horde of mounted knights massed ready to charge. De Payens wondered why he and the rest had been chosen for this duty, but then dismissed the thought. Others had also borne the brunt of the siege. He whispered verses from a psalm about walking through the valley of darkness. The pavise reached the bottom of the slope in a rattling clatter, inching its way forward, bumping over rocks and holes. One of de Payens' companions cursed as his boot became entangled in the rotting remains of a corpse, its bones snapping and cracking under the crashing wheels of the pavise. A serjeant shouted a warning. De Payens peered through the eyelet again. Thick smoke now billowed from the ramparts. Again the warning shout. A whooshing sound split the air, followed by a fire storm of burning pots, flaming tar bundles and oil-drenched boulders. These smashed on to the ground in sheets of fire and dancing sparks. A wall of fiery heat raced towards the pavise, making the men behind it cough and splutter. More missiles followed. Most fell short or on to the flanks. One of them shot over the pavise, crashing into the line of crossbowmen, turning three of them into living torches who screamed and danced in terror until other arbalestiers cut them down as an act of mercy.

The pavise rolled forward again. Another hail of fire. One of the tar bundles hit the side of the pavise, scorching a man's face, rippling his skin, turning his eyes to water. He sank to his knees, screaming for relief. The royal knight urged them to push faster so as to distract the aim of the watchers on the battlements. They were now approaching the first mounds. Warning cries rang out as those hidden behind the rocky outcrops sprang out, racing towards the pavise. De Payens and the rest staggered away, pulling out their swords to meet the enemy. The crossbowmen hurried forward, knelt and loosed a volley. Some attackers fell; the rest swirled around the pavise. De Payens moved to meet an assailant, a Turk, robes billowing, face and head almost hidden by his spiked helmet with its chain-mail lacings. Armed with a studded spear and rounded shield, the Turk moved to de Payens' right, lunging crosswise. He missed. De Payens crashed into him, using both shield and sword to batter the man against the pavise. A sweeping blow to his attacker's face, then he sprang away. Other attackers were being beaten off. The dust swirled. Kettle drums rolled from the battlements, to be answered by the call of Frankish trumpets. De Payens leaned his face against the wooden boards. He turned, and as he did so, a crossbow quarrel struck just above where his head had been.

He glanced around. The battlefield fury was dying,

the enemy retreating; nothing but cloying dust. The royal knight roared out orders and the pavise moved forward. The mounds were now deserted, their defenders fleeing back to a postern gate high in one of the towers flanking the Jerusalem Gate. Some reached the lowered ladder; others were caught by the Frankish horse, to be trampled down before being clubbed or speared. Once again screams, yells, battle cries and the scrape of steel shattered the air. Trumpets from the camps sounded the recall. The leather-clad engineers and stonemasons, their heads protected by sallets, had approached as close to the gates as they could. Now, apparently, they had the information they needed. The pavise was pulled back even as de Payens tried to control his terror and panic, so intense he felt as if his throat was closing up. He could not confess his fear. The stark realisation of how the crossbow bolt might have shattered his skull had all but drained his courage. On the one hand he was certain he'd been deliberately marked, but by whom? The Turks did not carry crossbows, whilst he had been in the centre of the pavise. The enemy had appeared only on the flanks before swiftly retreating; none had broken through to the rear. And yet, de Payens blinked away the sweat, his mysterious assailant had waited for him to move away, aiming slightly too high. Why?

'No accident,' he murmured.

'What was that?'

De Payens glanced to his right. Mayele, grasping the bar of the pavise, was staring quizzically at him. There was no sign of Parmenio. De Payens shook his head. 'The snares of the tomb surround me,' he whispered, 'the deep pit of death yawns.' This was not the life he'd yearned for. Nisam was right. Everything was an illusion, a phantasm: no white-robed paladins on swift destriers, no chanting of the psalms during the cool grey light of dawn, no true friendship or camaraderie. This was more a valley of death, a glade of pits and traps he had to pass through. De Payens was determined he would.

They reached the bottom of the ramp leading to the camp. A hot breeze licked up the dust. Cries of help for the wounded rang out; stretcher-bearers ran forward gathering these up, dragging them back like battered sacks. Three serjeants brought wicker baskets containing the severed heads of the enemy; these were thrust on the tips of the forest of stakes to the wailing of bagpipes and yells of defiance towards the walls of Ascalon. Men lowered their breeches and performed obscene dances, taunting the city defenders. The enemy gave their bleak response. A mighty roll of kettle drums echoed across the gory remains of battle. A black banner was hoisted. Figures moved along the parapet and a cluster of naked bodies were flung over to jerk and dance as the nooses tightened around their necks. The Franks replied. Prisoners were hustled forward, struggling, and stripped and impaled alive on stakes. Blood spurted amidst soul-raging screams. Buzzards and vultures swooped low, only to drift away to wait for the carrion.

De Payens scrambled to his feet and staggered back into the stinking camp. When he reached his tent, he pulled back the flap and collapsed on the pile of sacks and blankets that served as a bed. Images, memories and thoughts swept his soul like a blizzard of sand: turning to meet those assassins back in Tripoli; Nisam's cynical gaze; the secrecy of Tremelai, the Grand Master's sly, watchful smirks. He felt the small pouch around his neck containing the cipher Nisam had given him. He found it impossible to translate the Arabic numbers, but he suspected their secret. Had Tremelai, knowing of the blood feud between the Assassins and the de Payens family, deliberately sent him to Hedad to be killed? Had he also been marked down for slaughter in Tripoli? But why?

He was awakened from his sweat-soaked sleep by an anxious Parmenio. De Payens peered at the tent flap: the light was dying; the evening breeze provided a welcoming coolness. Outside echoed the creak of ropes, the rumble of wheels, the screech of axles, shouts and cries, the harsh crack of a whip.

'What is the matter?'

'The siege tower is ready.' Parmenio paused at the blare of trumpets. 'Edmund, the Grand Master has summoned us. An all-out assault on the Jerusalem Gate is imminent. Everyone is summoned to the standards.'

Cursing and muttering, de Payens pulled himself up. Still dressed in his mail, he was sore, sweat-drenched, parched with thirst, his lips sticky, his tongue slightly swollen. He grabbed a waterskin, splashed his face and drenched his mouth. Mayele came in. Both knights fumbled around for sword, helmet, shield and dagger, then followed Parmenio out, the Genoese looking slightly ridiculous in the pot helmet squeezed on to his head. They gathered before the armour stand and altar outside the Grand Master's gold-fringed tent. Tremelai stood in a cart from which fluttered the order's sacred standards. He bellowed for silence. Serjeants imposed order. The great six-storey siege tower, open at the back, its other three sides draped with vinegar-drenched ox-hides, lumbered to a halt. Looking around, de Payens also noticed the siege sheds, trebuchets and catapults; behind these stood the carts of war, crammed with pots of tar, bundles of hay, wool, rope and wood-shavings ready to be fired. The smell of oil and pitch thickened the air. Parmenio was right: this was going to be a great assault during the cool of the evening. Tremelai confirmed this, explaining how all the Franks' great siege engines, monsters dubbed with names such as 'Bad Neighbour', 'God's Vengeance' and 'The Fires of Hell', had been entrusted to the Templars. They would force a breach in or around the Jerusalem Gate, and establish a holding line whilst the rest of the Frankish army poured in. A weakness in the fortifications had been observed; they would concentrate on that.

Tremelai's speech was greeted with a roar of approval, followed by the blare of trumpets. The order's black and white banners and pennants were solemnly unfurled and blessed, the incense smoke rising in thick grey

109

clouds. A hymn was sung, ending with the order's great battle paean to God: '*Non nobis, Domine, non nobis.*' War horns brayed. The Templar host formed a broad, deep phalanx with archers out on the flanks. They began their march, trudging across what de Payens privately called 'The Land of Deep Shadow'. He still felt weak after that first attack, his body aching, his belly frothing like a cauldron. On either side, Mayele and Parmenio were lost in their own thoughts. They paused for a moment to drink water and loosen weapons in scabbards. Then they were ready. The great engines of war breasted the rise in a fearful clatter and rolled towards the walls of Ascalon.

De Payens glimpsed the shimmering glare of the enemy awaiting them. Smoke poured up from the fires boiling the tar, oil and other incendiary materials. The tops of catapults and mangonels could also be seen, black against the sky. The coolness of the evening breeze was now offset by the swirling sand stirred up as the Templar host made its way towards the Jerusalem Gate. They were protected by the great siege tower trundling ahead. Orders were shouted. The keen-eyed reported how the defenders had thrown thick rolls of cordage and rope over the walls as protection against the tower. De Payens gripped his sword and shield as the final orders were issued. The attack would be a feint. Tremelai had chosen the narrow postern door in the tower flanking the Jerusalem Gate as his real target. The attack earlier in the day had provided information that the door was weakened and could be forced. De Payens tried to distract himself with more peaceful memories: of walking with Theodore through the woods of Lebanon, his grandfather describing the various trees and shrubs, marvelling at the majesty of the myrtle or the strength of the oak.

A scream shook him from his reverie. The siege tower and other engines of war were now close to the walls. The evening sky was seared by flashes of flames, trails of smoke and an ominous orange glow as the defenders launched a fire storm at the approaching enemy. There was the screech of cord, the whoosh of projectiles, and boulders, hay, tar and linen bundles smashed around them, as if the fires of hell had broken through the crust of the earth. Men died in a myriad of grisly ways, scalded, burned or struck by arrows, boulders or flying metal. The screams, shouts and battle cries conjured up the burning landscape of hell. In de Payens' eyes, they were no longer men but creatures of the dark massing in their mailed might, ready to force, plunder and kill.

The Frankish engines of war crept closer, and they loosed volley after volley to sweep the parapets above them. At last the siege tower reached the gate, crashing against the thick curtain of protective cordage. Templars climbed the ladders within the tower, ready to reinforce those fighting on the two top platforms. De Payens and his companions, however, stayed outside; protected by the tower, they could only witness the horrors of the attack. Men reeled away, drenched in oil, engulfed by

111

fire, which melted their bodies so that mail and flesh became one. Soldiers, blinded by bags of lime, staggered back to be struck by arrows or stones. Bodies fell as if from the heavens to bounce on the ground. Ladders were tipped or ravaged by bursts of crackling Greek fire. A stifling blackness descended. Smoke curled about. Mayele was cursing Tremelai's stupidity even as engineers brought up a battering ram alongside the siege tower to hammer the wall to the right of the postern gate. The gate had been blocked from the inside, but a weakness had been found in the masonry alongside, some flaw in its construction. Tremelai, helmet off, bellowed that those on the third storey pound the postern gate, whilst the battering ram under its shield-shaped roof thundered against the wall. The attack was now spreading to both sides of the Jerusalem Gate. The distracted defenders did not know which way to turn, and still Tremelai shouted his orders. De Payens, sheltering in the shadows, could only watch, tense and fearful at the death and destruction swirling about him.

'*Deus Vult! Deus Vult!*' The war cry greeted a thunderous rumble of stone and masonry. The wall next to the postern gate had been holed and breached, and there was a great fall of masonry, followed by a gust of thick dust, which thinned to reveal a gap about three yards high and the same across. Tremelai came running back, helmet now on, his sword scything the air, and pointed at the waiting Templars, screaming at them to follow. De Payens was pushed and shoved around the tower as he and the rest, their shields raised against the missiles raining from the walls, rushed towards the waiting ladders and clambered up into the gaping black hole, where dust and smoke billowed like a fog, flinging themselves in, gasping and panting. Waterskins were produced and quickly emptied, then they were up, shields to the front, swords out, a mailed mass of about forty men edging along a paved passageway, its murky darkness lit only by flickering lamps and cresset torches.

'We came through a chamber!' Parmenio gasped. 'We must be in a passageway leading out of the tower. We . . .'

The rest of his words were drowned, as a host of men appeared as if out of nowhere to block their way. The Templars, giving vent to their fury and fear, burst forward in a savage melee of stabbing and clubbing. Men clutching wounds fell screaming to their knees. The ground grew slippery with blood. Then they were through, out of the tower, gasping the cool night air. They hastened down steps, spreading across the cobbled area stretching down to the alleyways leading into the city. An ominous rumble echoed behind them. Parmenio clutched de Payens' arm. The Templar tried to shake him off. He was still blood-crazed from that ferocious clash in the passageway, where his sword had hacked flesh, the hot blood of his enemies spurting against his skin; haunted by fierce dark faces, whirling steel, the stench of gore and sweat, the pervasive odour of burning.

'Edmund, Edmund, here!'

They had now reached the bottom of the steps.

The Templars were forming an arc, ready to advance. De Payens heard his name being shouted, but Parmenio was pulling at him, pushing him across the cobbles. De Payens stumbled away. He did not know why, but he had caught Parmenio's sense of dread. They reached the mouth of an alleyway. A cool breeze swept along it, chilling his sweat. Parmenio was tugging at his shield.

'Edmund, Edmund, for the love of God, take it off.'

De Payens let his shield fall; his sword slipped from his hand. He took off his helmet and, like a sleepwalker, stripped off his hauberk even as Parmenio's hissed warnings alerted him to danger. He stared across the cobbled expanse. The other Templars, about thirty in number, had drawn together, shields locked, no longer an arc but a circle. Parmenio's whispers calmed his battle-crazed mind. They were alone, cut off. De Payens recalled that second rumble of masonry. The walls had collapsed further, sealing off the breach; the Templars outside could no longer help. The distant sounds of battle carried. The attack would be beaten off, and then the Turks would deal with the enemy within.

De Payens watched in horror. The Grand Master and his lieutenants who had led the foray realised they were trapped: they could not go back, whilst further advance was futile. The small phalanx tightened even further, a ring of steel, shields locked. There were shouts and cries. De Payens made to go forward.

'Foolish!' Parmenio whispered. 'Foolish,' he repeated, 'another death for nothing!' He grasped de Payens, pulling him back, and the two men stood watching. Ominous speckles of light appeared. Torches were thrown, shadows shifted. The city garrison, surprised by the savage turn of events, could not believe what had happened. The breeze carried the fading sounds of the grand assault. The Franks outside the walls were retreating. More torches were lit and hurled at the waiting Templars. De Payens leaned against the filth-strewn wall as a powerful Frankish voice intoned the *De Profundis* – 'Out of the depths, O Lord, I have cried to thee. O Lord, hear my voice.'

More torches were flung. The singing became intense, the sheer power of men hurling their defiance back in the face of certain death. Templars would never surrender. They would ask for no quarter and be offered none. Arrows whipped through the air as the shadows moved. The shafts clattered against shields, the war cry *'Deus Vult!'* rang out and the phalanx retreated, shields still locked, up the steps, back towards the tower. Now a river of men poured out of the darkness, racing up the steps, hurling themselves against the phalanx in a whirl of steel and strident war cries. The shield hedge remained unbroken; the Turks in their spiked helmets and heavy cloaks were beaten off. More torches were hurled, followed by a fresh assault. In the light of the darting flames de Payens, cold-eyed and tense, glimpsed blood dripping down the steps. A gap was made in the shield wall, but again the attackers withdrew. Templar corpses littered the top steps. No more cries or psalms;

just a watchful silence. The attackers swept in afresh. A great war cry echoed as the shield hedge was finally broken. The Templars were dispersed, one man against many in solitary fights to the death. The attack faltered; the enemy retreated. Archers sped forward, horn bows strung; one volley after another was loosed, whilst the master archers chose individual targets. Templars fell, weapons slipping from their hands. Another horde of men rushed up the steps with axe and club, sword and dagger, then at last it was over.

The Turks searched amongst the corpses. The occasional glint of steel flashed, followed by a coughing sound as they finished off the wounded. Tremelai's lifeless body was hauled up, stripped and hung from an iron bracket fixed on to a wall. The exultant Turks danced in glee as they realised that they had trapped and killed the Grand Master of the Temple. Trumpets sounded. City dignitaries in red and white robes hurried across the bailey to inspect the dead. Orders were given. Torches were placed beneath Tremelai's hanging corpse. De Payens glimpsed the straggling red hair of his once proud lord, his dirty-white cadaver streaked with blood from the gaping wounds in his head, neck and stomach. The rest of the corpses were now stripped and gibbeted, the Templars' clothes and armour piled together in a basket.

'They'll hang those from the battlements.' Parmenio's breath was hot against de Payens' face. 'And they'll do the same to the corpses.'

De Payens flinched as the point of the Genoese's dagger dug into the soft part of his throat.

'Master Edmund,' Parmenio whispered, 'this is not the time for brave and noble charges. We've had enough of those for tonight, and see what has happened. Do not be a fool. If you reveal yourself we shall both die, slowly, so come.'

De Payens followed Parmenio deep into the darkness, then paused and turned. He could not go, not yet; he had to watch. The bodies of the dead Templars, now stripped naked, were being lashed with ropes, ready to be dragged through the city. Already the trumpeters were proclaiming the news along streets fastened shut against the attack. Ascalon was coming to life, even in that stinking alleyway. Lamps were being lit, windows unshuttered, doors opened. Parmenio scooped up de Payens' cloak, helmet and armour, and thrust them into a midden heap, kicking the dirt over them. A voice called, strident and querulous. Parmenio answered in the same language, then, grabbing de Payens by the arm, pushed him into the blackness.

For the next few days they lived as beggars. Parmenio told de Payens to act the mute as they sheltered amongst Ascalon's swarming legions of poor, who lurked in the shadows during the day and slunk out at night. Parmenio, a master of tongues, acted the part, whining and wheedling. He begged or stole bread, rotting fruit, a pannikin of water and on one occasion a bulging wineskin. No one bothered them. Dirty and dishevelled, they were simply two of the despised. Moreover, the city thrilled with the news of how the attack had been repulsed, the Grand Master of the Temple killed, his corpse and those of his company gibbeted naked over the walls. The citizens rejoiced that all who had entered the walls had died.

De Payens felt as if he was in a dream. Any shame at not dying with Tremelai soon disappeared. In truth, he reflected, the Grand Master had acted maliciously towards him, whilst the foray into the city had been hasty and ill planned. He wondered what had happened to Mayele. Parmenio informed him that his brother knight had been behind them; he'd either been killed in the attack or fortunate enough to retreat. Such conversations were carried out in hushed tones in the corners of filthy recesses. For the rest, they had to survive. Parmenio continued to be adept at begging; a consummate actor, he could weasel scraps of food and present himself and his companion as two more beggars in a city of beggars. He also listened carefully to the chatter of the bazaars and tawdry markets. How the Templar corpses had been dragged through the city at the tails of horses before being gibbeted on the battlements. Such humiliation, however, had only made the Franks more obdurate. They were now pressing the siege harder. Even more dangerous, they had beaten off a fleet sent from Egypt carrying much-needed supplies for Ascalon.

"'Put not your trust in Pharaoh,'" Parmenio quoted from the psalms, "'nor his horses, nor his power." Listen,

Edmund, we must remain hidden here. Act as we do now until the siege ends, either way.'

Parmenio insisted that they keep to the poorest quarter of the city. It was like a vision of purgatory: black-mouthed alleyways snaking between crumbling houses; trackways crammed with ordure; hot, dusty tunnels of reeking stench. No rest, no shelter, each mouthful of food and water gratefully acknowledged. De Payens recovered from his shock and grew more vigilant. Parmenio he now trusted. If he'd wanted to, the Genoese could have killed him a hundred ways. Instead, he ensured the Templar ate and drank carefully, even sharing his takings after being hired as a temporary porter in the oil bazaar. At the same time he comforted de Payens, insisting that Tremelai had brought his own death on himself. They continued to live like scavengers, mixing easily with a myriad of races; as Parmenio remarked, 'Who really looks at the poor, especially at a time such as this?'

The siege was now being pressed with a fury. The Franks brought forward their trebuchets, siege towers and catapults and unleashed a veritable storm against the city walls. Fresh fears swept the bazaars. The intense, constant volleys were clearing the parapets. The dead had to be dragged away and stacked on funeral pyres; the flames and smoke curling up from these became a constant, sickening reminder of the terror lurking beyond the walls.

The mood of the city changed. The grumble of the

bazaar became a constant moan that swept through Ascalon. The citizens were losing all appetite for battle. They wanted to sue for terms. Fearful of a revolt in the city, and deeply alarmed at the Franks edging their war machines even closer, the governor hoisted boughs of greenery over the battlements and asked for a truce. The volleys immediately ceased; a welcome relief, as the last hail of boulders had crushed more than forty men. Later that day, heralds proclaimed the jubilant news. The Franks would accept the conditional surrender of Ascalon!

# Chapter 6

By declaring however his innocence to the
Master of the Assassins . . .

Edmund de Payens, bathed and clothed in clean robes,
stared around the whitewashed walls of the council
chamber of the former governor of Ascalon. The latter,
his household and all who wanted to follow were now
journeying south, being given free and honourable
passage into Egypt. Ascalon and all it held was now a
fief of Baldwin III. Royal banners floated from its towers
and battlements. The king's men patrolled the streets.
Frankish knights lorded it in the city palaces, whilst

the central mosque had already been stripped in preparation for its rededication as a church to St Paul the Apostle. Once the surrender had taken place, de Payens and Parmenio had made themselves known to the new rulers. The house of the Temple had welcomed them like prodigals returned, hailing them as heroes and insisting that Parmenio, time and again, describe Tremelai's last stand, now viewed as heroic as any feat of arms by Roland and Oliver, Charlemagne's great paladins.

De Payens and Parmenio had been housed in this spacious mansion close to the spice market, where they were reunited with Mayele. Cynical and mocking as ever, the Englishman explained, supported by the eloquent testimony of three serjeants, how they were about to enter the breach when the second fall of masonry sealed the entrance. De Payens believed him. His brother knight was no coward. Mayele was scathing about Tremelai, who'd led so many to destruction, and made no attempt to hide his glee at the Grand Master's death. He explained how the Templar command was now in disarray, with a Burgundian, Andrew Montebard, a close kinsman of the great Bernard of Clairvaux, being hastily elected as temporary Grand Master. De Payens stared around the brilliant white chamber. In truth, he was confused. He did not know what was happening. They'd been brought here, praised and commended, but at the same time kept as prisoners, not allowed to leave or mix with their brothers. Mayele also reported how

Temple clerks and couriers kept coming and going around the mansion. Now, after eight days, de Payens had been summoned to sit at this oval cedar table, Mayele on his left, Parmenio on his right.

Edmund stirred as the door opened. Montebard and the English master, Boso Baiocis, entered, escorted by two guards, and took their seats at the far end of the table. The Grand Master clicked his fingers; the guards withdrew, as did most of his retinue except for one clerk, his lanky hair framing a thin, cadaverous face, who held a cushion. At the Grand Master's signal, the clerk solemnly processed down the chamber like a priest crossing a sanctuary and placed the cushion before de Payens. It bore an icon. At first glance it looked common enough to be found in any Greek church. It depicted the ravaged face of the crucified Saviour; a man in agony, hair sweat-soaked and bloodstained, eyes half shut, mouth open in silent protest at the agonies inflicted on him, his brow crowned by sharp thorns. De Payens stared at this most sacred relic, suppressing a shiver. He had heard rumours about this being the true likeness of the crucified Christ, an image solemnly venerated by senior commanders of the order. In clear tones Montebard instructed him to touch the icon and take an oath that what he heard here would be *secretissime* – most secret. De Payens obeyed. Mayele and Parmenio were also sworn, and the clerk withdrew. Montebard, fingers steepled, stared down at de Payens. Now and again his glance would shift to Parmenio or Mayele.

He opened his mouth to speak, but paused, then bowed his head as if praying for guidance. De Payens was sure he heard the Grand Master whisper the words *'Veni Creatus Spiritus'* – 'Come Holy Spirit'.

'It's best.' Montebard lifted his head. 'Yes, it's best that you hear the truth yourself.' He shouted at the door, and the clerk scurried back in. Montebard whispered to him, and he hurried out again. Footsteps were heard in the corridor, and a man was ushered into the chamber: tall, garbed in flowing Temple robes, his face and head completely shaven and glistening with oil.

'Devil's tits!' Mayele whispered. 'Richard Berrington!'

De Payens started in surprise as Berrington bowed to the Grand Master and Boso Baiocis, then took the proffered seat to the right of the table. He smiled at de Payens and nodded knowingly at Mayele. De Payens' first reaction was that there was little or no family resemblance between this harsh-featured Templar and his sister, La Belle Isabelle, whom de Payens had met in Jerusalem. Richard Berrington was hard-faced and sloe-eyed, with high cheekbones, thin lips and a jutting chin. A warrior, de Payens concluded, a dangerous man, lean, muscular, swift in all his movements. He reminded de Payens of a wolf.

'Brothers, Domine.' Berrington bowed once again towards the top of the table. 'It is good for brothers to dwell in unity.' He intoned the usual courtesy greeting of the Templars.

'Tell us.' Montebard's harsh voice was a stark contrast

to the soft tones of Berrington. 'Tell us, brother, what happened, what you know.' The Grand Master rubbed his face in his hands. 'I have scrutinised the Chancery records. I have already heard you speak. It's best if you tell your brothers.'

Berrington stared hard at Parmenio, then glanced pointedly back down the table at Montebard.

'He can be trusted, Richard. He has sworn the oath.'

'In this he is one of us,' Boso Baiocis grated. The English master had, until now, sat as if carved out of wood. A small man with a barrel stomach, he had protuberant eyes, and his thinning grey hair hung down in wisps, though his beard and moustache were a luxurious white. De Payens had met him earlier. Boso seemed an anxious man, eyes constantly darting, lower lip all a-tremble. He was fussy, uncertain as to why he'd been summoned from London to meet the Grand Master now killed in that bloody affray within the walls at Ascalon.

Whilst Berrington murmured his thanks to Boso, de Payens glanced quickly at his companions. Mayele sat head down, fingers splayed hard against the table top. Parmenio was staring at Berrington, who was waiting to speak.

'From the beginning,' Montebard declared. 'Richard, we're all brothers around the cross, but to some of us you are a stranger.'

'I was born,' Berrington began, 'in Bruer in Lincolnshire, the second son of a manor lord. I served in the retinues of various barons, including Mandeville, Earl of Essex, before deciding to travel to Outremer. My sister,' he smiled at de Payens, 'agreed to accompany me. In Jerusalem I joined the Templar order. Dominus Tremelai was my novice master. As you may know, I served in several castles and garrisons before he brought me back to Jerusalem. I was declared a veteran knight. I served under his banners in many forays.' He paused, licking his lips.

Montebard got to his feet. He brought across a flagon of water and a cup, which Berrington filled then sipped neatly from.

'You mention your sister,' de Payens interrupted. 'The Lady Isabella; yes, I have met her. Was she not lonely in Jerusalem?'

'No, brother.' Berrington shook his head. 'She stayed with other ladies in the Benedictine convent near Herod's Gate. Dominus Tremelai was most kind. He even offered her a small house to the north of the city. She had her own inheritance, whilst I made sure she lacked for nothing.'

'Late last summer?' Montebard demanded, glaring at de Payens as if he resented the interruption.

'Late last summer,' Berrington continued, 'hideous murders were perpetrated in or around the Temple Mount and elsewhere in Jerusalem. Young women were slain, their corpses drained of blood. Now, Jerusalem may attract the righteous, but it also houses the citizens of hell. At first the city authorities believed that some madcap was waging his own unholy war, because the victims were Muslim, but then Frankish women were also found murdered. Rumours whispered that their deaths were linked to the black arts, magic, sorcery, witchcraft. Allegations were laid. There was a witch, Erictho, possibly English; she'd arrived in the city and steeped herself in the secret knowledge. The patriarch and the governor of Jerusalem offered rewards for her capture, but Erictho seemed to live a charmed life. Rarely glimpsed, a true shape-shifter, she was never arrested. However,' he paused, 'gossip had it that she had been seen either visiting or near the Temple precincts. Other whispers hinted that a Templar might be involved; worse, that a secret coven of sorcerers had infiltrated our order. Henry Walkyn certainly did not help matters. He had gained a sinister reputation for slipping into the city, visiting the strumpet-mangers, whorehouses, brothels, taverns and bathhouses frequented by prostitutes. Nothing substantial, not enough to bring charges, but such rumours turned into accusations of witchcraft against the Temple.' Berrington held up a hand. 'Of course, such allegations have been levelled before against our brethren. Our scribes and scholars study the secret knowledge of both the Jews and the Arabs, and that, in turn, provokes unrest amongst certain prelates of Holy Mother Church, but this time the allegations were serious. Henry Walkyn's name kept being mentioned. Dominus Tremelai consulted with me as a leading English knight here in Jerusalem. Walkyn's chamber was searched. He owned

coffers and chests with secret drawers and compart-
ments. They contained enough proof to hang or burn
him many times over.'

'Such as?' Parmenio asked quietly.

'Bowls, phials stained with blood, items of jewellery
taken from the girls, books of spells, herbs. Walkyn
denied the charges. Tremelai, however, insisted that he
stand trial for his crimes, though not in Jerusalem: the
scandal would have been too great. He wished to keep
matters *sub rosa*. He conferred with me and decided
that I should take Walkyn back to England, where he
would be tried at the Temple manor near Westminster.
At the same time, I believe, he sent a letter to you,
Master Baiocis, asking you to make careful scrutiny of
what you knew about Walkyn in England, as well as
summoning you here.'

'Yes, yes, he did.' Baiocis flustered. 'I was much
perturbed when I received the summons. Dominus
Tremelai asked me to make careful searches about
where Walkyn had come from. How he had joined the
order.'

'And?' de Payens asked.

'Very little.' Baiocis shrugged. 'Henry Walkyn was
born and raised in the manor of Borley in Essex. His
parents died when he was young; the manor was put
in wardship. When Walkyn became of age, he too served
with Mandeville. Later he turned his manor over to our
order, to which he sought entry. I admitted him. He

served a brief novitiate in London, then asked to go to Outremer.'

'What kind of man was he?' Parmenio asked.

'Pious, dedicated, a good knight, secretive.' Baiocis shrugged. 'Certainly not a chatterer or a gossiper.'

'The same was true in Outremer.' Berrington spoke up. 'Walkyn kept to himself. Oh, he dined in our refectory – you must have met him, Mayele.'

'Yes, on a few occasions. A man you would not notice.' Mayele smiled. 'Not unless he brought himself to your attention. Of medium height, blond hair I remember, very blue eyes; he could be gracious and pleasing but I had little conversation with him.' He pulled a face. 'I knew he was from Essex, that he'd fought for a while in the civil war, but that is true of most English knights.'

'And you, de Payens?' Montebard asked. 'Did you know him?'

Edmund shook his head. 'Not at all, my lord. I served a brief apprenticeship in and around Jerusalem before being sent to Chastel Blanc.'

Montebard nodded in agreement. 'Continue.' He gestured at Berrington.

'Walkyn continued to declare his innocence, but the proof against him pressed hard. Dominus Tremelai decided that I and two serjeants would escort him to the port of Tripoli and then take ship to England.'

'And Erictho?' Parmenio spoke up. 'What happened to her?'

Montebard stretched his hands. 'Searches were made through the Holy City. She seemed to have disappeared, though rumour had it that she still hid in Jerusalem.'

De Payens remembered the gruesome figure he had glimpsed on leaving Jerusalem for Hedad, but decided to keep his peace, as he would try to on all matters.

'Anyway, we left the city,' Berrington continued, 'and journeyed through the Jordan valley towards the coast. We reached Jacob's Well, just to the east of Nablus. I intended to travel on into Samaria and camp near the tomb of St John the Baptist. Walkyn had changed. He no longer acted the innocent. He began to hint that the charges were true. I am not too sure whether he was boasting or not. He said he nursed a great grievance against King Stephen and hoped that when he returned to England he would be able to purge that on the king's own body.'

'What?' Parmenio pushed himself away from the table.

'That is what he claimed,' Berrington declared. 'That he had a grievance, a blood feud with King Stephen. He boasted that the Temple would not hold him. He'd be freed, cleared of the charges, then he and others had business to settle.'

'Why?' de Payens asked. 'Why did Walkyn change? You claimed that he first protested his innocence.'

'I don't know,' Berrington chewed the corner of his lip, 'but I have reflected. In Jerusalem, perhaps he believed he could refute the charges. Chained, manacled and destined to take ship to England, he probably

130

realised that such protestations would not help him. He seemed confident, assured, rather arrogant. He made no reference to anyone else, but of course, he must have had his followers in the city. Now, a Templar knight and two serjeants,' Berrington spread his hands, 'no brigand would trouble our passage. Moreover, we passed other outposts and could call for help.'

'You were attacked?' Mayele asked.

'Late at night,' Berrington declared, 'at an oasis just near Jacob's Well. I'd set the guard. I made sure that Walkyn was still manacled and chained. God knows the truth, but just before dawn they attacked, about a score of them. They crept into the camp; I am not too sure if one of the serjeants had been bribed. The hand-to-hand fighting that followed was bloody and vicious. I stood my ground, but our assailants were well armed with bow, lance, spear and mace. The serjeants, whatever their true allegiance, were killed. I tried to reach Walkyn. I knew the attack was meant to free him. I would have executed him there and then, but by the time I reached the place, he was gone. I then hid, and our attackers withdrew. I had suffered cuts and bruises. When the sun rose, I discovered that all our supplies and mounts had been taken. How the mighty had fallen,' he whispered. 'A few hours earlier I had been a Templar knight, armed, mailed, mounted on a good war horse; then I was nothing, dressed only in my shift. I couldn't stay there. I did what I could for the dead, then left them and began to walk. Later that afternoon I was attacked by desert wanderers. They soon realised who they'd captured.' He shrugged. 'I was passed from hand to hand. I begged them to let me write to our Grand Master in Jerusalem, telling them that he would ransom me, but they refused. I was brought to Ascalon and placed in the slave pens. It was then that I decided to escape. I hid in the city, trying to plan what to do next. I was desperate to get back to Jerusalem.' He shrugged. 'And then the rumours became fact. King Baldwin was marching on Ascalon. The city was put under siege.' He nodded at de Payens. 'I had no choice but to do what you did: lurk in the slums, hide away and pray that deliverance would come.'

'So Walkyn escaped?' Parmenio observed. 'Master Richard, before the siege of Ascalon, your Grand Master sent us on an embassy to Nisam, the caliph of the Assassins at Hedad. He told us that Walkyn had visited there.' Parmenio cleared his throat. 'Apparently the Walkyn who visited Hedad was no more than a wandering beggar. Was this the same man who organised such a dramatic escape?'

Berrington breathed out noisily. De Payens kept his own counsel. He had decided that that was best. He would not divulge what Nisam had secretly told him: that Walkyn had been resolute, a man busy on his mischief. Indeed, what the caliph had told him agreed with Berrington's description of Walkyn as a dangerous adversary.

'I do not know,' Berrington retorted. 'Master Parmenio,

I have heard of you. You know the Assassins. Did they tell you the truth? After all, Tremelai suspected them of being involved in Count Raymond's death.'

'I have read the caliph's reply,' Montebard intervened. 'He claimed that he and his kind were not involved in what happened to Count Raymond. He asked that Tremelai put his own house in order before meddling with other people's. Oh, he was diplomatic, tactful, full of praise and gifts, but his message was clear enough.'

De Payens could see that Parmenio was agitated and full of questions. The Genoese, for all his help in Ascalon, still remained an enigma. What had he been searching for at Hedad? Had he known about Walkyn's visit beforehand?

'And why was I sent to Tripoli?' Mayele asked.

'For two reasons!' Montebard snapped. 'First, you're English. You'd met Walkyn; perhaps you might recognise him. Second, you are de Payens' brother knight.'

'I confess,' de Payens spread his hands, 'that I suspected our Grand Master's motives in sending me first to Tripoli then to Hedad.'

'No, no.' Montebard shook his head. 'God rest Tremelai. What he did sometimes was very stupid; he could be arrogant and impetuous, but he had a high opinion of you, Master Edmund. You were sent to Nisam first because you were in Tripoli, and second as a mark of respect: your name is held in great honour not only by Christians but by our foes.'

'But there was a blood feud,' Parmenio declared,

'between Nisam and the de Payens family. Tremelai knew that.'

'Yes, he did, and that is another reason why he sent Edmund. He knew the full story of that blood feud: how Lord Hugh in those forays had spared Nisam's wife and unborn child. He knew that de Payens would be safe in Hedad, that no harm would befall him. It was a token of trust. Edmund, your family, for whatever reason, never discussed the blood feud with you. Tremelai must have sensed that, and he would not reveal it lest you refused to go. In the end, he knew you would be safe.'

The chamber fell silent. They sat half listening to the sounds drifting from outside: the call of a horn, the neigh of a horse, the clatter of hooves, servants shouting, laughter from around the well, where water was being drawn. De Payens stared at Montebard. The Grand Master looked haggard and tired. How much of this was true? de Payens thought. Had Walkyn been a witch, a warlock, a sorcerer? Had he tried to lie his way out of the charges against him but, when arrested, revealed his true self? What Berrington said made sense. Very few people would dare attack a Templar convoy, certainly not a knight with two serjeants. Walkyn must have had followers in the city, men and women dedicated to him as the Fedawi were to Nisam. And Parmenio, what was his true role? Why had Tremelai, and now Montebard, accepted the Genoese into their secret councils? Was he responsible for that crossbow bolt outside Ascalon? Yet, on reflection, that bolt had clearly been aimed high, whilst Parmenio had saved his life in the city. And Berrington, Mayele and Walkyn? They shared so much. All three were English knights who had fought in the civil war against King Stephen, enrolled in the comitatus of this Mandeville, Earl of Essex. De Payens voiced this. Berrington smiled; Mayele just shrugged.

'Edmund,' he almost drawled, 'I have made no secret of my past. I fought for Mandeville, as did Berrington for a while, and Walkyn. Three names amongst thousands. Remember, Mandeville was driven into rebellion by King Stephen's injustice, not that we care about that. We fought as mercenaries. Many did. In the end, only the Temple tried to defend the earl's name and give him honourable burial.'

'But Walkyn seems different. He talks of a blood feud against King Stephen.'

'You know me, Edmund. I watch and smile, but men like Walkyn nursed a deep personal loyalty to Mandeville. They view King Stephen as guilty of the earl's death, a king with the blood of their lord on his hands. Wouldn't you agree, Richard?'

Berrington nodded, tapping the table. 'Many English knights fought for Mandeville,' he agreed. For most, such knight service is a routine task; for a few, well, it is different, unique. Indeed, once Walkyn began to reveal his true self, such allegiance was not just a memory but a burning issue. He even called King Stephen an assassin who should pay for his crimes.'

'Enough of that for the moment.' Montebard spoke up.

'The affairs of England concern me, but for the moment, Edmund, what you have heard here: has it resolved your anxieties and those of your comrades?' The Grand Master drew a deep breath before continuing. 'You and Mayele were sent to Tripoli to guard Count Raymond because that lord had heard rumours that he was under threat. He reported these to our Grand Master, asking for his help. Tremelai, anxious about the whereabouts of Walkyn and the disappearance of Berrington, sent you as a gesture of confidence: the descendant of the great Lord Hugh. You, Mayele, were also sent because you might recognise Walkyn. In the end we do not know who truly organised that assassination, but our Grand Master, God rest his soul, was still perturbed. He decided on dispatching you three to Hedad to extract guarantees that the Assassins were not involved, as well as to receive pledges from the caliph that such interference would never take place.'

'And Ascalon?' de Payens asked, clearing his throat. 'The Grand Master's desire to break into the city: was that connected with you, Berrington?'

'Yes, it was,' Montebard intervened. 'Rumour was its own messenger. Gossips chattered in the bazaars and markets how a Templar had been captured and sold on; such news reached Jerusalem. Tremelai may have suspected that Master Richard, or even Walkyn, was imprisoned in Ascalon. Perhaps that could explain our Grand Master's impetuosity, his desire to break in, the foolish, very foolish risk he took.'

'After Berrington's disappearance,' Parmenio spoke up, 'surely the Grand Master sent out scouts, an expedition, to discover what had truly happened? They must have followed the same route?'

'They did,' Montebard replied. 'Unbeknown to anyone, Tremelai dispatched a convoy of knights and serjeants. At the oasis near Jacob's Well they found a few remnants of the conflict but no corpses. Tremelai was a proud man. A Templar knight and two serjeants had disappeared. An apostate Templar was on the loose. It was not a matter he'd wish to boast about. Little wonder he was determined to break into Ascalon.'

'And Walkyn?' de Payens asked.

'Gone, disappeared like some mirage in a desert,' Montebard replied, 'but we think . . . Well, let me voice my suspicions. I believe that Walkyn, and possibly the witch Erictho, fled from Tripoli by sea. At this moment they are journeying back to England, or may have even reached those shores. There is a risk, a real danger, that they may try and inflict hideous damage against King Stephen or his cause. As you know, the civil war in England between Stephen and his kinsman Henry Fitzempress is like an open sore on the body of that kingdom.' Montebard paused. He glanced quickly at Boso. 'Dominus Tremelai was very, very anxious that the House of Temple increase its power and influence in England. King Stephen has proven to be a good friend, granting us properties in London and elsewhere. You can see the path I am following? I do not want the

Templar name besmirched by some assassin. To put it succinctly,' Montebard pointed down the table, 'Magister Boso here will be travelling back to England. You, Edmund de Payens, Philip Mayele, Richard Berrington, and yes, you, Master Parmenio, will accompany him. Your task will be twofold. First,' he held up a hand, 'to warn King Stephen of the danger. And second, to search out Walkyn, and execute him.'

# PART TWO

ENGLAND
AUTUMN 1153

# Chapter 7

First of all he arrived at Wallingford
with a great army . . .

'Set, lock, loose!'

Edmund de Payens flinched as the catapult cups flew
forward, casting their fiery missiles across the swollen
waters of the Thames. A few fell short. Others smashed
into the hordes of men massing on the far bank or,
better still, engulfed portions of the pontoon bridge
Henry Fitzempress's men were trying to build. If
successful, they could then destroy the fortress of Castle
Gifford, which King Stephen had hastily constructed

where the Thames flowed narrow around the town and dark mass of Wallingford Castle.

'Once more.' The knight banneret, his royal livery of red and gold all dirty, raised his sword and roared at the sweating men-at-arms. 'Once more before sunset. Give the bastards a bloody compline, then first thing tomorrow, wake them for matins!'

The men laughed and cheered. Once again the catapults were primed and released their dreadful song; a scorching arc cut the dark-blue sky already shot red by the setting sun. De Payens leaned against the heavy wooden stockade and stared across the river.

'All the same,' he murmured to himself. 'Killing and death! We love it, it's in our blood, the very core of our being.'

'To whom are you speaking?'

De Payens whirled around and stared down at Isabella Berrington, who stood, her lovely face almost hidden by the ermine-lined dark-green hood.

'My lady, you should not be here.' De Payens hastened down the ladder.

'Nonsense, Edmund!' She stepped closer, those beautiful, laughing eyes bright with mischief. 'Richard says the enemy will never find our range. We are like children, aren't we, standing around a mill pond taunting and teasing each other but doing no great harm.'

As if mocking her words, a massive boulder hurled by a catapult on the far bank crashed into the water, whipping spray up against the towering stockade fence.

Isabella laughed and drew closer, clutching at de Payens as if frightened. He grasped her hand, kissed her fingers, then let her go.

'Four months.' He turned as if embarrassed, staring across the bailey at the long hall of plaster and wood. 'Four months since we left Outremer. I never thought we'd reach safety, yet now here we are . . .'

They walked across the bailey, reminiscing for a while about the journey from Ascalon to Cyprus across the Middle Sea, journeying along road, river and mountain path. The weather had been good, high summer with only a few storms, whilst the letters sealed by Montebard had ensured comfortable lodgings and fresh food at Templar houses or Cistercian monasteries. Their two servants had fallen sick and had been left in a hospital outside Avignon. Parmenio had also contracted a fever, tossing and turning, shouting in Latin, babbling nonsense. Lady Isabella, with the help of a leech in a Benedictine infirmary, had nursed him back to health. In the main they had travelled as strangers to each other, often separating depending on passage aboard ships or delays caused by horses and ponies casting a shoe. When they did meet they concentrated on the daily tasks facing them rather than what was to happen in England. Now that they were here, they seemed at a loss.

Isabella and de Payens paused by the main gate leading out of the castle. Torches were being lit. Scullions, servants and grooms hastened about, preparing the evening meal or settling the horses for the night.

'Edmund?'

He blinked and stared down at that lovely face, as he had done often through their journey. He was fascinated by her strange violet-blue eyes, the constant smile. Isabella was full of sunlight and joy. Indeed, he conceded, she was the true fair lady of the legend: beautiful, enticing, formidable, but locked in her own silver tower, its doors sealed not only by herself but by his vows of obedience and chastity. The tension her presence caused often irked his waking hours and plagued his sleep.

'My lady, I'm sorry.'

'You're always dreaming.' She stood on tiptoe and tapped his cheek with one gloved hand. 'Master Baiocis and my brother sent me. You are not part of this war, Edmund; the house of the Temple is not to become involved.'

'We are involved,' de Payens retorted, 'simply because we are here. I had to see, but in truth, war here is no different from war elsewhere. Anyway,' he tried to brighten his mood, 'why send a lady?'

'Because I wanted to come, and I do have an escort: the ever-watchful Mayele,' she added impishly. 'He now awaits us.'

De Payens collected his horse from the stables and, wrapping the reins around his hands, led his mount under the makeshift gateway across the fetid-smelling moat and down the ramp where Mayele slouched on his horse, Isabella's palfrey busy cropping the grass beside it. There was the usual banter and teasing, before de

Payens helped Isabella into the saddle, then mounted his horse as Mayele listed the news. Master Baiocis, whom Mayele secretly called 'the Toad', needed them in the refectory of Wallingford Priory. Apparently King Stephen, his son Eustace and two of his leading advisers – Henry Murdac, Archbishop of York, and Simon de Senlis, Earl of Northampton – would join them for a splendid feast now being prepared by the priory kitchens.

'The King, His Grace,' Mayele made a mocking flourish with his hand, 'wants to question us and, I suppose, find answers. None of which we will be able to give.'

De Payens half listened to Mayele's biting criticism of the anxious busyness of the Toad. They'd had little time to speculate during their arduous journey. Baiocis had been plagued with fears that Walkyn might already have reached England and be carrying out his malicious mischief. In fact, despite their haste and the bone-jarring crossing on board the cog that had brought them safely into Dover, they had discovered nothing about the malignant they were pursuing. The constable and harbourmasters at Dover held no record of Walkyn entering the kingdom. Baiocis, using his authority, had sent letters to other ports and harbours. They had waited at Dover for a reply whilst they all recovered from crossing the Narrow Seas, a terrifying experience. A summer storm had swept the waves, spinning the cog, making its timbers creak and groan in protest. Once ashore, they rested at a pilgrims' tavern, the Good Samaritan, drying out their possessions, eating, and hiring horses. The lack of news about Walkyn depressed them, but Baiocis proudly announced that as he was now back in his own English bailiwick of the Temple, he had authority over the small preceptories throughout the kingdom, the principal one being the moated fortified manor of the Temple in the parish of St Andrew's, Holborn, just north of the Thames. Accordingly messengers were also dispatched to London and elsewhere demanding information on Walkyn. The replies arrived after they'd left Dover, intent on joining King Stephen as swiftly as possible. No one reported anything about the man they were hunting. This only heightened Baiocis' anxieties as they became immersed in events happening around them.

The civil war between King Stephen and his kinsman Henry Fitzempress was intensifying, as each strove to bring his opponent to battle and utterly destroy him. Stephen had chosen to attack the Fitzempress fortress at Wallingford, a strategic stronghold controlling both the Thames and the main roads through the kingdom. He had laid siege, building Castle Gifford to block all routes, hoping to provoke Henry to march to Wallingford's relief and so decide matters in a set battle. 'Tired swordsmen circling each other' was how Mayele described the conflict. The signs of war were obvious as they rode north: burned villages, deserted fields and sinister bands of armed men who quietly melted away at the sight of the piebald standard and pennants of the Temple. Troops trudged the roads, war carts and siege machines rattling behind them. Black columns of smoke dirtied the blue summer sky. Distant red smudges of flickering fires lighted the darkness of the night. Scaffolds and gibbets were commonplace, well stocked with rotting corpses. Even so, de Payens was much taken with the strange new countryside, a blessed cool relief after the ever-scorching fly-blown heat of Outremer. Berrington and Mayele were delighted to be home, revelling like pilgrims who had reached their chosen shrine. Parmenio, about whom de Payens had remained suspicious, acted the surprised traveller, though now and again the Genoese made mistakes, mere slips of the tongue, which made de Payens wonder if he had not visited this island of mist before. For the rest, de Payens secretly marvelled at the dark coolness, the abrupt change of sun to rain, the clouds that swept the sunshine across open fields of brown and gold, the well-stocked, clear streams, the forests and woods stretching like an ocean of green to the far horizon.

On one occasion after leaving Dover, he tried to count the different shades of green alone and became lost in their beauty. Uncle Hugh had visited these islands some thirty years before, and de Payens realised why the Temple was so eager to stretch its roots deep in such a rich and fertile land. Nevertheless, the kingdom also possessed a haunting eeriness, particularly in its woods and forests, which recalled the stories of

Grandmother Eleanor: mysterious places of sudden noises, of bracken and grass moving as if some silent terror crawled beneath them. Trees, ancient as the world, their branches curling up above him to stretch black against the sky. Flower-filled glades where birds of every colour swooped, and beyond these, marshes, swamps and stagnant pools quiet as the grave, as if some noonday horror had swept over them. Ancient rocks and ruins where priests had once worshipped sinister gods were commonplace. Mayele heightened the mood with stories about the wild woodland being the haunt of goblins, sprites and other phantasms, legends about the grotesque gargoyles who lived deep in these woods, ever ready to prey on the weary traveller. He told these tales winking at Lady Isabella whilst watching de Payens' face. The Templar carefully hid his own fears, but at night the stories darkened his sleep, and nightmares surfaced about being lost in such a place without horse or arms, having to flee through darkening glades pursued by midnight shadows.

'Edmund?'

He startled. Mayele and Isabella had reined in. They were almost through the royal camp pitched outside Castle Gifford, a sprawling collection of bothies and ox-hide tents around glowing fires. It was bat-winged time, and the night air was thick with the smell of cooking, and the rank odours from the latrine pits and horse lines.

'Edmund,' Isabella's mocking tones recalled those of

Nisam, 'you're dreaming again.' She gestured at the camp. 'Mayele believes this turmoil cannot last much longer. Henry Fitzempress must make peace. What do you think?'

They were still discussing the war when they passed under the cavernous fortified gate of Wallingford Priory into the great cobbled bailey housing the stables, forges, kitchens, sculleries and butteries. De Payens dismounted, ensured that an ostler tended his horse and found his way back to the narrow chamber allocated to him in the guesthouse. The bells of the priory tolled for vespers. He stripped off his armour, washed, put on his cloak and joined the brothers in the shadow-filled stalls of the church, a hallowed sanctuary of Caen stone full of pillars and arches, statues and gargoyles, where candlelight flickered eerily on the polished oak lectern and other furnishings. A bell chimed and the prior began the divine office: 'Oh God, come to our aid . . .'

The brothers, cowled and hooded, chanted the reply: 'Will you totally reject us? Will you no longer march with our armies . . . ?'

De Payens' mind drifted back to that council chamber in Ascalon. Since then he had, as if learning a psalm, been through the logic of what he'd been told. The macabre murders in Jerusalem; the sightings of Erictho; the accusations against Walkyn and the evidence that proved them correct; Walkyn's arrest and intended deportation to England; his escape and consequent attempts to ingratiate himself with the Assassins. De

Payens pondered the possibility that Walkyn had been responsible for the murder of Count Raymond. It was logical: he could have stolen that medallion and those daggers from Hedad, all part of his plot to kill a great lord so as to stir up chaos for Tremelai, who, despite providing an escort, had been unable to prevent Count Raymond's murder.

'You have made the earth quake, torn it open . . .' the monks chanted.

Yes, Walkyn had certainly shattered the peace of the Temple. De Payens and Mayele had failed Count Raymond, whilst Tremelai had had no choice but to send them to Hedad to find out the truth about possible Assassin involvement. They were the logical emissaries. They'd both witnessed Count Raymond's murder, whilst de Payens' presence would be a mark of honour to Nisam, who had a special relationship with the founder of the Temple. The same was true of their presence in Tripoli: again a logical gesture of respect to the count, whilst Mayele might have recognised a fellow countryman.

'You have made us drink wine that has confused us . . .'

Payens smiled to himself. Perhaps his own confusion might thin. His presence in Tripoli may have been intended as a deterrent to the conspirators. Surely they would not strike at a Frankish lord protected by Templars, one of whom belonged to the de Payens family? In the end this had been proved wrong.

'Glory be to the Father, to the Son and to the Holy Ghost,' the monks chanted.

And the rest of the plot? de Payens wondered. Berrington had been captured and found himself in Ascalon. He had been responsible for Walkyn; it was logical that he'd be sent back to England with Baiocis to hunt Walkyn down, and that Mayele and de Payens should join him. Mayele was an Englishman, whilst again, the name of de Payens would be a way of conveying to the English crown how seriously the Templars regarded this situation.

'Oh God, visit your holy temple,' the good brothers chorused. The monastic choir was now moving on to the next psalm, but de Payens remained lost in his own thoughts, staring at the face of a woodwose enshrined in foliage, a striking carving on top of a pillar opposite. He resolved to put the past aside and concentrate on what was happening now. Two problems remained. First, where were Walkyn and the witch Erictho? No evidence of their presence in England had yet been found. Second, the secretive Genoese, Thierry Parmenio – who was he really? Why had he been in Tripoli? Why had Tremelai trusted him so much?

'They have poured out blood like water in Jerusalem,' the lector chanted. 'We have no one to bury the dead.' De Payens recalled Jerusalem and quickly struck his breast in sorrow. He felt guilty about Tremelai. The Grand Master had been both foolish and arrogant, but there was no proof of any bad faith. Moreover, if Tremelai had trusted Parmenio, why shouldn't he? Finally that secret cipher: why had he been given it? Why had Nisam striven so hard to tell him something but concealed it in a form he could not translate? De Payens stared around. The hour candle on its great bronze spigot at the entrance to the choir caught his eye. He quickly crossed himself and genuflected. The flame had nearly reached the next hour ring. It was time to be gone.

The priory refectory, a long whitewashed chamber dominated by huge black crucifixes fixed on either end wall, had been specially prepared. Soft rushes powdered with herbs covered the floor. The trestle tables had been draped in thick white cloths and a silver carved statue of the Virgin and Child placed in the centre. The prior had supplied the best plate of his house. Copper herb casks positioned beneath the windows exuded a fragrant warmth. King Stephen, his pale face peaky under a mop of red hair, green eyes constantly blinking, his fingers forever stroking his neatly clipped moustache and beard, had arrived with little ceremony. He'd taken off his half-armour and thrown this at a grinning squire, stretching and yawning before noisily washing his hands and face in the proffered bowl of rosewater. Eustace, his son, similarly dressed, was the very image of his father, though sullen and more reserved. A truly ruthless man, de Payens reflected, betrayed by the set of his mouth, lower lip slightly jutting out, eyes constantly squinting as if Eustace was making a judgement about everything he saw and heard. The King's leading ecclesiastic, Henry Murdac, Archbishop of York, was clean-shaven, grey-faced, his black hair neatly tonsured. He was garbed in the white robes of a Cistercian monk, a silver tasselled cord around his plump stomach, black sandals on his feet. Simon de Senlis, Earl of Northampton, the King's principal adviser, was a white-haired, bearded man, his blunt soldier's face furrowed and lined, eyes red-rimmed with the smoke from the fires at the nearby siege. As soon as he arrived, Northampton roared for wine, and when that was not served swiftly enough, he grabbed a tankard from a tray in the window recess and downed it in one gulp, the yellow drops staining his moustache, beard and the top of his gold-lined cotehardie.

De Payens had glimpsed the royal entourage earlier, near Castle Gifford. The king had personally directed the catapults after studying the movements of the enemy on the far bank. Now he and his companions were hungry, thirsty and impatient for food. The prior delivered a short blessing then withdrew, closing the refectory door behind him, and the banquet was served. One course swiftly followed another: quail soup, venison in spices, suckling pig garnished with fruit and vege-tables, beef cooked in ginger and thyme. Despite his hunger and tiredness, Stephen was courteous, smiling at de Payens and his companions, paying special atten-tion to Isabella. She had dressed magnificently for the occasion in a high-necked blue gown with a brocaded front, her long blonde hair braided with green ribbons, a silver circlet around her forehead. Murdac and Northampton were equally courteous, but Eustace was as foul-tempered as a rutting boar. He had apparently been quarrelling with his father and his councillors and was intent on continuing this during the meal. Henry Fitzempress was marching with great force to the relief of Wallingford. The king, uncertain about his own troops, had decided to break off his attack on the town and seek a peace with his rival, a decision Eustace violently disagreed with. Northampton and Murdac tried to calm Eustace's fiery invective, loudly declaring that the king had no choice, that his barons were tiring of the fight and wished to withdraw. Moreover, Henry Fitzempress might be amenable to peace talks. Eustace would not accept this, threatening to disengage his own forces and harass the enemy in East Anglia.

The king was half minded to agree to this, and opened a debate with de Payens and the assembled company. The Templars were reluctant to be drawn in. Stephen, eyes blinking, pleaded with Berrington, de Payens and Mayele: if Eustace did withdraw, would they at least accompany him into the eastern shires? Murdac and Northampton had already agreed to do this. De Payens was confused. He stared at Baiocis for advice, but the English master sat silently, anxious, as if nursing some secret pain. Berrington tactfully pointed out that the Temple had remained neutral during the civil war. Eustace yelled that there was no such thing, whilst Stephen, eloquently assisted by Murdac, pleaded that

all he wanted the Templars to do was act as inter-
mediaries with his son and give him good advice on
strategic matters.

Eustace was eager to hear the Templars' reply. The
argument with his father had raged all day, and if
the Templars acquiesced, the king would give him his
blessing. Berrington finally agreed, and only when this
matter was settled did the king broach the Templars'
mission to England. He reminded Baiocis of his many
grants to the order in London and the outlying shires,
and asked why a Templar would wish to do him harm.
Baiocis, white-faced, clutched his stomach and gestured
at de Payens and Berrington to explain. De Payens
nodded to his comrade, as he still found the Norman
French at the English court slightly different from that
of Outremer. It was more precise and clipped, not pitted
with the lingua franca of the Middle Seas. Parmenio had
informed them that this reflected the isolation of the
English court, and in doing so had also revealed that he
was conversant with the common Saxon tongue and
amused them with his imitation of it. Now the Genoese
sat stony-faced as Berrington explained what had
happened. The refectory stilled at the story. Even Eustace
stopped his drinking for a while, the wine glistening on
his lower lip. He protested that the Templars enjoyed a
reputation as ferocious as that of the Assassins, and if
an apostate was scouring the kingdom intent on murder,
this was more dangerous than any enemy arrow.
Northampton was quick to support the Prince, pointing

out how assassination was now rife in this mist-strewn kingdom. Parmenio had mentioned that three of the great Conqueror's offspring had died mysteriously in the New Forest, one a crowned king; whilst the present civil war had erupted because Mathilda's only brother, Prince William, had perished in the mysterious wreck of the *White Ship* out in the Narrow Seas. According to the Genoese, many claimed that the Prince's death, and those of others, had been the work of the Angel of Darkness. Eustace's constant interruptions reminded the assembled company of this. Once Berrington had finished, the king sat tapping his fingernails against his goblet.

'My father,' he began quietly, 'joined the First Crusade. You've heard the story? He abandoned the cross-bearers at Antioch and returned home. Perhaps this is part of some curse . . .'

'Nonsense, Your Grace,' Murdac intervened. 'Your father made reparation. He died a true Christian warrior at the Battle of Ramlah. Now, Mandeville, he was cursed.'

De Payens glanced at Mayele, who simply smiled and winked back.

'Mandeville,' Murdac repeated, 'self-styled Earl of Essex, perjurer, blasphemer, warlock . . .'

'Children's tales,' Mayele broke in.

'Black sacrifices,' Murdac insisted. 'You, Mayele, fought for Mandeville.'

'As did I for a short while,' Berrington declared, 'as well as many knights now camped outside Castle Gifford. True, Your Grace?'

Stephen nodded in agreement. 'True, true,' he murmured. 'Mandeville won a fearsome reputation. He plundered monasteries and abbeys.' He pointed at Berrington. 'So you fought for him for a while but left in disgust. Yes?'

Berrington smiled his agreement.

'I remember now,' Stephen continued. 'You won the name of being a most honourable knight. The monks of Ely claimed that you defended them against the earl. But,' the king lifted his goblet, 'some of the others were fiends incarnate.'

'Half of my retinue,' Eustace joked, 'are Satan's men. They fear neither God nor man. Your Grace,' he gestured at the archbishop, 'you know that. Mandeville was a great earl, a warrior. Thousands flocked to his standards.'

'And so did many wizards, sorcerers and witches.'

'Mandeville was once my most fervent and loyal supporter,' the King intervened. 'I made a dreadful mistake. I arrested him for alleged conspiracy against me. Mandeville rose in rebellion.'

'He plundered churches.' Murdac lapsed into Latin. 'He pillaged great monasteries like Ramsey and Ely in the wetlands of the Fens. Your Grace, he died excommunicate, body and soul damned to hell, which is why his coffin still hangs in chains from a tree in that cemetery at Holborn. The Temple should be careful.' Murdac, his grey face hard, froth flecking his lips, was no longer the pious churchman.

157

'Your Grace, Your Grace,' Northampton soothed, eager to dissipate the tension, 'many fought for Mandeville or some other great lord. Walkyn is now the danger. He nourishes bitter grudges against both the crown and his own order. The Templars regard him as a renegade. Our guests are here to hunt him down. Now,' he tapped the table, 'the clerks of the Exchequer and Chancery have made careful search but have discovered little about Walkyn, except that he owned the manor of Borley in Essex . . .'

'Go away!' Eustace shouted at a servant who had opened the door. The prince sprang to his feet, seized a platter strewn with bones and hurled it at the door.

The king's dogs, nestling close to one of the braziers, immediately lurched forward to squabble noisily over the bones. Eustace, snatching up his war belt, went amongst them, lashing out, until Senlis caught him by the arm, spoke quietly and gently guided him back to the chair on his father's right. De Payens watched intently. Eustace was violent; a sickness of the mind? He recalled the stories about how though King Stephen enjoyed great popularity, churchmen, particularly the Archbishop of Canterbury and the Holy Father, had issued strict instructions that Eustace was never to be crowned as his heir apparent. The papacy was obdurate on this, determined to bring the civil war to an end. If Stephen won, then perhaps Eustace might be crowned, but if he was defeated, the spoils of war, the crown of victory would go to Henry Fitzempress.

Studying the prince's face, mottled with anger, white froth staining his lips, the speed with which he downed cups of wine, de Payens could understand the reluctance of the great lords to serve such a master. Eustace might have a fearsome reputation in battle, but . . .

Mayele touched his arm. 'Baiocis?' he whispered.

The English master had half risen, as if troubled by Eustace's violence. He clutched the table, hand moving from belly to chest. He was grey-faced, beads of sweat lacing his brow, eyes popping, mouth gasping for air. He was breathing noisily, half coughing, as if clearing his throat. De Payens watched in horror as Baiocis flailed his hands, gagging and choking.

'In God's name!' Eustace bawled.

The other guests moved even as Baiocis fell to the ground, convulsing violently, arms and legs jerking as his head banged against the floor. The confusion spread. Servants hurried in. The priory apothecary was summoned, but Baiocis was beyond all physical help. The prior arrived even as the master of the English Temple suffered his last convulsion. Cowl pulled up, a stole around his neck, he swiftly anointed the dying man, loudly whispering the words of absolution from the sacrament of extreme unction. Parmenio moved to Baiocis's leather-backed chair. He picked up and sniffed both the wine goblet and the water cup, then wrinkled his nose and pushed the goblet away. He sat watching as Baiocis died, just as the prior finished his ministrations.

'A seizure?' Eustace asked.

'Poison!' Parmenio lifted the goblet. 'Tainted and foul-smelling.'

De Payens walked over and picked up the goblet. It was half empty. He noticed the fine grains of powder amongst the dregs, and sniffed. The rich claret was strong, but there was a more subtle tang, very like a medicine he had once been given when he had a fever. He pushed the goblet away. Royal retainers, alarmed by the news now sweeping the priory, burst into the refectory, only to be screamed at by Eustace, who ordered them out.

'What poison?' Stephen had not moved from his chair.

'What poison?' the prior repeated, wiping his hands on a napkin from the nearby lavarium. He gestured at Parmenio and the apothecary, examining each goblet, flagon and jug on the table. 'Your Grace, our infirmary stocks every herb. Our gardens are rich with crocuses, nightshade, Solomon's seal, foxglove . . .'

'Who could have done this?'

Both the prior and the apothecary shrugged and shook their heads. Eustace angrily gestured at them to leave. Once they'd gone, the prince repeated his question.

'In heaven's name,' Mayele declared, 'if we knew who it was . . .'

'I sat on Baiocis's left,' the Prince continued as if he hadn't heard Mayele. 'You,' he nodded at Isabella, 'to his right.'

'He never left his seat,' the Genoese replied. 'He had

his hand constantly on his goblet. No one approached him.'

'Except servants,' Mayele declared. 'I was sitting opposite him. I swear no one approached so close as to poison his goblet.'

'And that is the only one?' Berrington asked.

'Yes.' Parmenio picked up his own goblet, sniffed and drank from it.

Eustace hastened to the door, shouting for the prior. Parmenio shook his head.

'Whoever was responsible,' he whispered, 'is long gone, I'm sure.'

'We must have the corpse removed,' Berrington declared.

Was Baiocis the intended victim? de Payens thought. Or had there been a mistake? Was it the king or the prince who was supposed to have drunk that poison, or was Baiocis murdered because of who he was?

'Our order.' De Payens voiced his anxiety. 'The bailiwick of England. Who will be its master now?'

'I shall be.' Berrington shrugged. 'I am the most senior knight. It will take time for the chapter of the bailiwick to assemble; even longer to inform the Grand Master in Jerusalem.'

He took a cloak from a peg on the wall. De Payens helped him drape this over Baiocis's corpse. Never handsome in life, Baiocis's face was contorted by the rictus of a gruesome death, eyes half shut, yellow stumps of teeth in a gaping mouth, a lacy froth trickling down his chin.

The prior, summoned by Eustace, re-entered. A frightened man, he could offer little help about which servants served what. The king brought the interrogation to an end and ordered the corpse to be removed. De Payens glanced quickly at Isabella. She sat clutching her goblet, face white and tense, lips moving as if in silent prayer. He went over and placed a hand on her shoulder. She smiled shyly up at him, but he was struck not so much by her fear as her determination. '*Courage here,*' she whispered up at him, '*has to be harder, spirits stouter, hearts sterner. Here lies our lord brought low, our best man lies in the dust. If any warrior thinks of leaving the battle, he can howl for ever.*'

'My lady?'

She blinked and stared up at him as if seeing him for the first time.

'Edmund, my apologies. I quote from an old Essex poem about a famous battle.' She lifted her hands, fingers fluttering. 'What is to be done here, what is to be done?'

De Payens moved to his seat.

'What is to be done,' the king declared loudly, echoing her words, gesturing at Eustace to retake his seat, 'is to decide what was intended here. Berrington?'

'Your Grace?' The Templar shrugged. 'Baiocis lies dead. Was he secretly dosing himself with a physic that proved noxious? Has he been murdered by Walkyn and his coven? Was he the intended victim, or was that someone else? As for the perpetrator? Your Grace, this

162

priory teems with men, violent souls, men of war, steeped in blood . . .'

'As well as witches and warlocks,' Murdac broke in. The prelate quickly crossed himself. 'I listened to your tale about the abominations in the Holy City. You think the name Erictho is not unknown here? My chancery is in York; Theodore, Archbishop of Canterbury, has his own records. Both would recognise the name Erictho.' He waved a hand. 'Oh, not much, just tittle-tattle.'

'So it's true?' de Payens retorted. 'Erictho is of English birth?'

'Undoubtedly one of the many *gregarii*.' Murdac used the term of contempt for those who wandered after armies. 'She would have joined the devil horde who left for Jerusalem to seek out fresh victims.' He crossed himself again. 'What I know is only gossip from the villages and towns. Some say Erictho is a harridan; others that she is a great beauty, horribly disfigured for her sins. They have ascribed powers to her. How she can thicken the powers of the night, summon carrion birds and mix poisons from the froth of a dog or a snake-fattened badger.'

'I would like to meet her.' Eustace roared with laughter at his own joke.

'She is a poisoner?' Parmenio asked, ignoring the prince's outburst.

'One of the many accusations levelled against her.'

'Children's prattling,' Northampton murmured. He sighed as he lurched to his feet, much the worse for drink. 'She collects dragon's eyes and eagle stones.' He laughed sharply. 'The likes of Erictho can be found, legion in number, along the filthy runnels of Southwark or on the devil's land around St Paul's. Your Grace,' he turned to the king, who sat plucking at his lower lip, 'these Templars have delivered a warning. Some madman has concocted a fey-witted scheme to kill you.' He shrugged. 'Henry Fitzempress's army has the same purpose, so why worry?'

The king smiled in agreement and rose, his son and councillors with him. He thanked the Templars courteously, and the royal party swept from the refectory, the king shouting at Eustace that they must have private words before they parted. De Payens listened as the footsteps faded in the corridor.

'We are done.' He sighed and stared around. 'The king does not truly believe us, does he?'

'His Grace is distracted,' Berrington replied. 'He is most concerned about his son, about the great lords withdrawing from the battle, the approach of Henry Fitzempress. He is surrounded by murder and intrigue. He has a son whom no one wants crowned, so why should he worry about one cut amongst many?'

'He should.' Parmenio sat down in the king's chair. 'Baiocis's murder is a warning.'

'Yet we cannot pursue Walkyn,' Berrington declared, 'because we do not know where he is, how he hides or where he goes. During the meal, His Grace assured us that his clerks had scrutinised the records of both

164

Chancery and Exchequer. No trace of Walkyn was found, no sign of him entering or leaving the kingdom. Now,' he rose to his feet, 'we are to accompany the King's son. We cannot refuse. To bring a warning to His Grace then decline his request to accompany the prince would be grave offence. Who knows, perhaps where we go, Walkyn will follow. He certainly made his presence felt here.'

'Was Mandeville a warlock?' de Payens asked abruptly.

Berrington leaned against the table and stared across, eyes hard, face resolute. 'Mandeville was truly the rider on the pale horse mentioned in the Apocalypse; certainly all hell followed him. One of the reasons,' he added brusquely, 'why I left his company and journeyed to Outremer. Now,' he pointed to the black wooden crucifix, 'Baiocis's corpse is to be laid out in the priory church. His body is past all help, but his soul still needs our prayers . . .'

# Chapter 8

And Eustace . . . greatly vexed and
angry, met his end.

They spent three more days at Wallingford Priory.
Eustace gathered his troops, hundreds of ribauds, rifflers
from London, Flemish mercenaries, whoremongers,
looters, hard men who had battened fat on almost twenty
years of civil war. They flaunted the royal livery, but in
truth, de Payens concluded, they were wolves in wolves'
clothing. He realised how a great lord like Mandeville
could attract rapists, murderers, thieves, warlocks and
witches to his standard. No wonder the likes of

Berrington, sickened by what he saw, sought to cleanse his soul by admission to the Temple. For the rest, Baiocis's death remained a mystery. All they could do was supervise his funeral rites. A requiem mass was sung in the gloomy, shadow-filled priory chapel. The death psalms were chanted amidst the glow of candle-light and gusts of smoke. The corpse was sprinkled with holy water, incensed and blessed and taken out in a makeshift coffin, fashioned out of an old arrow chest, then laid to rest in the Potter's Field, the yew-shrouded corner of the priory cemetery reserved for strangers.

An hour later, as the bells chimed nones, Prince Eustace took leave of his father, and with his three-hundred-strong retinue, left Wallingford in a flurry of dust, lowing horns and fluttering banners. De Payens rode at the rear with his companions, Isabella mounted on a palfrey especially loaned from the royal stables. Simon de Senlis, Earl of Northampton, together with Murdac of York were to act as Prince Eustace's advisers. He pointedly ignored them. The prince's cavalcade moved swiftly through the summer countryside along rutted trackways and on to the old Roman roads, dried hard by the summer sun. Beautiful weather. The fields were primed for the harvest. Orchards hung heavy with fruit. Watermills stood freshly repaired and painted for the autumn crop. Eustace transformed all that. The black banners of war were unfurled as he swept through the shires towards Cambridge, burning, pillaging and looting the manors and estates of his father's enemies.

Barns were fired, granges left smoking black ruins, harvest fields ravaged, orchards plundered, stew ponds and streams polluted. Any who resisted were cut down or hanged from the nearest oak, sycamore or elm. Peasants, farmers and merchants heard of this devil storm and fled to churches, monasteries, castles and fortified manor houses.

After six days of such ravaging, Eustace's cavalcade reached Bury St Edmunds, a stately abbey built of light grey stone, set behind its own lofty walls and well stocked with granges, fish ponds, orchards, barns and outhouses. A place of peace and harmony, with its sun-washed cloister garth, a garden filled with luxurious rose bushes in full bloom, their fragrance hanging heavy in the afternoon air. The abbot had the good sense to meet Eustace on the road leading up to the main gate-house. Flanked by cross-bearers, thurifers and acolytes all garbed in white, he delivered a short homily in Latin, welcoming the young prince but tactfully pointing out that his retinue would have to stay in the fields and meadows outside. Eustace, drunk in the saddle, agreed. He and his immediate household, the Templars included, were escorted into the abbey and apportioned chambers in the grey-stone guesthouse. De Payens lodged in a narrow room. He immediately took off his armour, arranged his few possessions and demanded that he and his companions meet in the small rose garden below. He was saddle-sore, weary and furious: he and Parmenio soon clashed with Berrington over what was happening.

'Outlaws!' de Payens shouted, giving way to the anger seething within him. 'We are no more than outlaws, burning farms and watermills, for the love of God!'

Parmenio nodded vigorously in agreement. Since leaving Wallingford, he'd become even more secretive and withdrawn.

'Well?' de Payens demanded.

Mayele simply smiled, as if savouring some secret joke. Isabella sat on a turf seat, examining the bracelets on her wrist.

'Why?' de Payens yelled at Berrington. 'Why are we here? This marauding? We are Templars, not *gregarii*, ribauds!'

Again Parmenio agreed. Mayele turned away. Isabella put her face into her hands.

'We have no choice, Edmund, you know that.' Berrington walked over and grasped de Payens' shoulder. 'As I said before, we brought a hideous warning to the king. We could not ignore his request; to refuse to accompany his brutal son would have damaged our interests.'

De Payens protested, yet in the end he had no choice but to agree. Back in his narrow whitewashed chamber, he sat on the edge of his cot bed and stared at the coloured hanging celebrating the martyrdom of St Edmund.

'Illusions,' he whispered, recalling Nisam's accusation, 'we are just chasing illusions. What is the reality? Is it Walkyn, or something else?' He stripped, lay on

169

the bed and drifted into sleep, still wondering about what should be done. He was wakened later in the day. The light through the lancet window had dimmed. For a brief while he ignored the pounding on the door, Parmenio yelling his name. Then he recalled where he was and hastily donned his long tunic, put on his boots, grasped his sword belt and drew back the bolts. The Genoese, breathing hard, beckoned him out.

'For the love of St Edmund, come. The prince . . .'

De Payens followed Parmenio out of the guesthouse and round into the cloisters, where Eustace, sword drawn, was screaming at the abbot, who stood defiantly before him, shaking his head, now and again crossing himself in protection against the prince's torrent of blasphemy. Berrington and Mayele stood to the right of the abbot. Isabella, sitting on the cloister wall, got up and approached de Payens, finger to her lips.

'The prince,' she whispered, 'wishes to empty the abbey's granaries.'

'God's teeth!' Eustace bellowed, shaking his fist at the abbot. 'I will have my purveyance, my rights in this matter.' He stormed off, mouthing threats, yelling for Murdac and Northampton, standing in the shadows of the cloisters, to follow him. Then he paused and spun around, fingers falling to the hilt of his sword in its brocaded scabbard, and stormed back to the abbot. De Payens half drew his own sword; Parmenio caressed the hilt of his dagger, while Berrington hastened forward as the prince advanced threateningly. The abbot stood his ground, one hand grasping his pectoral cross. Eustace stopped, glared at the abbot, then abruptly burst into laughter. He tapped the abbot on the shoulder, stepped back and sketched a mocking blessing in the air. Northampton and Murdac came hastening over, but Eustace's mood had changed.

'No trouble, my lords,' he shouted. 'We shall take close counsel in my chamber later.' He waved a hand at them to withdraw, then linked his arm with that of the abbot, walking him through the cloisters, talking softly, as if they were the closest of brethren.

De Payens watched them go, hand still on the hilt of his sword. Berrington and the others sauntered across.

'The prince is mad,' de Payens whispered. 'In heaven's name, Berrington, Mayele, what a tangle we have ourselves in. Every bush is a bear. Every word is a possible curse. Black smoke against blue sky. Houses and cottages burning like bonfires on a sea of green.'

'That is why we left England.' Isabella spoke up softly. 'Edmund, what you see is not as malignant as what we witnessed.'

'*Homo diabolus homini* – man is a devil to man,' Berrington murmured. 'It was no better in the other shires: storm-riders, night-prowlers, fire and iron . . .'

'Here we are,' de Payens shook his head, 'supposed to be pursuing a warlock who seems no more real than a marsh wisp. We should leave. Baiocis is dead, murdered. We should return and tell the Grand Master what has happened. This is impossible.'

171

'And Montebard will reply,' Berrington observed, 'that we did not carry out his orders. Indeed, we jeopardised the Templar cause in England. Remember, Edmund, we are only here because he asked us to be.'

De Payens glanced at Parmenio. The Genoese stood, hands on hips, staring at the ground.

'What shall we do?' murmured the Templar.

'What shall we do?' Parmenio echoed. 'Little wonder the Holy Father in Rome and many of the English bishops do not want Eustace crowned as king-in-waiting. We follow a wild man with a violent past and little future.' He glanced up. 'I hear what you say, Berrington, yet Edmund is correct. We cannot ride the trackways of England for ever and a day searching for Walkyn.'

'But he must be close,' Berrington declared. 'Baiocis's death proves that.'

'It proves nothing,' de Payens snapped, 'except that someone poisoned Baiocis.'

Berrington, face drawn, eyes even more narrowed, shook his head.

'How else was Baiocis murdered? Did anyone see any of us lean over and pour that noxious potion into his wine? If we had, someone would have noticed. No, he was killed in a subtle, clever way, by Walkyn or one of his minions.' Berrington paused. 'Walkyn might well be responsible. We are here, however, to prevent mischief to the crown.' He took a deep breath. 'If that happens and we fail, then perhaps we should think of leaving. Even so, Baiocis's death creates fresh problems. I cannot leave the bailiwick of England in such confusion.'

De Payens walked off across the cloister garth. He stopped and stared up at a carving of a lizard, a two-legged serpent crawling up a lily stem towards the petals, each of which represented a human soul. Next to this peered a gargoyle with the face of a pig and the ears of a monkey. On the breeze floated the faint plucking of a lyre and a young, clear voice chanting a hymn to the Virgin.

'We should wait,' Berrington called out, 'we should wait a little longer. The prince must return to London, to Westminster; by then we may have finished our duty.'

De Payens just shrugged in agreement. He left the cloisters and visited the abbey church, admiring its treasures, especially a sombre wall painting describing the fifteen signs of God, which, according to St Jerome, would precede the Last Judgement. Dramatic, soul-searing events painted in vivid colours: mountains tumbling, tidal waves surging, stars dropping from heaven, crashing to an earth engulfed in the fires of hell. He then visited the Lady Chapel and the chantry dedicated to St Anne. He spent some time there before leaving and going down the tree-lined path into the Petit Paradis, a little garden arranged in concentric circles full of flowers in all their glory and colour. He sat on a turf seat before a small fountain carved in the shape of a luxuriously feathered pelican striking its breast, from which water gurgled. He heard a sound. Lady Isabella, dressed in a tawny robe fringed with white bands at cuff and neck, her lovely face hidden under a *coupe de mail*, came sauntering down the path. She sat next to him and grasped his fingers, tightening her grip as he tensed.

'Edmund, Edmund.' Her lips were so close he could smell the mint on her breath. 'In heaven's name,' she teased, 'fair knight, be at ease. I'm no *belle dame sans pitié.*'

He turned.

'We all want this finished,' she murmured. 'Soon it will be. Walkyn will be hunted down and killed.' She turned to face him squarely, her fingers white and delicate, the cuff of her sleeve soft against his neck.

'Never trust a soldier . . .'

De Payens whirled round as Berrington and Mayele came into the paradise.

'Sirs, are you spying on me?' Isabella teased.

'No, sister, but the good brothers of St Benedict are; they told me where you'd be.'

'Where is Parmenio?' asked de Payens, eager to divert attention.

'Gone wandering, as he always does.' Mayele crouched down and squinted up at de Payens. 'You know, Edmund, I don't trust the Genoese. He appeared like some sprite in Tripoli and since then he has never really explained his presence here.' He paused as the abbey bell clanged noisily, booming out the tocsin.

De Payens sprang to his feet. Above the tolling of bells, shouts and cries of alarm drifted across the walls of the paradise. Berrington raced back up the path, de Payens and the rest following. They left by the wicket gate and paused as a lay brother, sweaty-faced and out of breath, clutched Berrington's arm and gasped out the news in a tongue difficult to understand.

'It's the prince, Northampton, Murdac,' Parmenio called, hastening over, jerkin undone, the shirt beneath sweat-soaked. 'All three,' he gasped, 'murdered!'

'All three!' de Payens exclaimed.

'God pardon them,' Parmenio gasped. 'The prince and Northampton have been poisoned. They are already dead.' He waved his hands. 'Murdac is barely alive and has been taken to the infirmary. The abbey leech is examining the wine goblets. You'd best come.'

Eustace's chamber was on the ground floor. The great double shutters over the arched window had been flung open to allow in more light to reveal the grim horror. Both Eustace and Northampton lay sprawled on the floor. The prince was dead, eyes staring, his face contorted, a frothy foam trickling from his open mouth. Northampton sprawled nearby on his side, face all ugly in death. It seemed as if the earl, in his last agonising throes, had tried to creep towards the great crucifix nailed to the wall. Berrington asked for the chamber to be cleared except for the abbot and the leech. The prince's captain of mercenaries, face flushed in anger, did so, beating at the brothers and servitors with the flat of his sword. He fastened the door behind them and went and stood over his dead master. De Payens stared around. The chamber was luxurious, with gleaming walls, well-polished stools and benches, a great chair with padded leather backing and a huge four-poster bed hung with drapes. Dominating it was a long trestle table, most of which was covered with scrolls, rolls of parchment, scraps of sealing wax and ink horns. Next to these stood three goblets and platters of unfinished food. The high-legged stools thrown back on their sides told their own macabre story. De Payens walked across and picked up the wine jug. It was empty. He sniffed but could detect nothing and put it down. The prince was a toper, a lover of wine, and Northampton was no better. Two of the goblets, one of which was Eustace's, at the top of the table, were drained even of their dregs. The third, which stood to the right of the prince's chair, was almost full. De Payens, heeding the warning of the leech, picked this up and smelled the strong tang, like that of an empty skillet left over a fire. He wrinkled his nose in disgust and glanced towards the window. The sunlight was dimming. He went across and looked up at the sky, where clouds massing dark and low threatened a sudden summer storm.

'I think all three goblets contained poison,' the leech declared. 'The jug is drained, so it's difficult to tell.'

'Domine?'

De Payens turned. The captain of the mercenaries

176

had taken off his helmet and pushed back his mailed coif to reveal a narrow scarred face, his red hair shaven on all three sides.

'Yes?' the Templar asked.

'Domine, the jug was brought by a lay brother; he is outside. I tasted the wine before it was taken in.' He spread his hands. 'I feel no ill effects.'

'And the goblets?' Berrington asked.

'They must have been here before,' the captain replied, 'but surely if such noxious potion was in them, His Grace the Archbishop would have noticed. Once I had tasted the wine,' he continued, 'I allowed the lay brother in. His Grace took the flagon and filled all three goblets. The prince and the earl were already seated. They say,' the captain's voice turned ugly as he pointed at the abbot, 'that the prince was cursed by St Edmund for plundering his abbey, in which case . . .'

'In which case,' de Payens intervened quickly, 'we'd best leave St Edmund alone. Bring in the lay brother.'

The old abbey retainer could add little to what they already knew. Trembling with fright, he announced that he worked in the buttery. He had drawn the wine in the presence of the cellarer, who could confirm this. He had then immediately carried the flagon to the prince's chamber. No one had approached him. The captain on guard outside had taken a generous sip, then he had brought the jug in. The prince had immediately demanded a goblet; the archbishop had obeyed, and as he poured the wine, the lay brother had withdrawn. The captain confirmed this, adding that no one else had entered the chamber.

Berrington took the goblets and put them on a tray. He picked this up and bowed to the abbot.

'Reverend Father, I will take these to the infirmary, where His Grace the Archbishop lies. He may be able to tell us more. Captain, I order you on your loyalty, tell your men to remain settled. Further disturbance will not help. Father Abbot, once we have talked to His Grace, I will need the use of your chancery, the abbey messengers and the fastest horses from your stables. The captain here will provide an escort. They are to leave, search out the king and advise him about what has happened here. Now . . .'

Carrying the tray, Berrington led them down to the dark-beamed, white-walled infirmary. The leeches' assistants were busy in the principal chamber, tending the archbishop. Berrington put the tray of goblets down and they all went in, except for a pale-faced Isabella, who simply sank down on a bench outside. Mayele saw this and went back to her. The rest gathered around Murdac's bed. The archbishop had been purged and fed with a concoction of herbs and salted water to make him retch; the room stank of vomit. The archbishop, his ghost-white face sheened with sweat, was conscious, eyelids fluttering. The abbot crouched on a stool by his bed and talked softly; the archbishop, voice weak, murmured his replies, which the abbot translated.

'He filled both goblets and his own. The prince

declared that he was thirsty, as did Northampton. They drained the wine and demanded the goblets be refilled. His Grace obeyed, then sipped his own. A short while later, even as he felt the first symptoms, the prince and the earl became violently ill. Both claimed they were choking.'

The abbot patted the cold, vein-streaked hand; Murdac whispered some more.

'He tells the same story of how the wine was served.' The abbot sighed. 'He smelled nothing remarkable. He now wants to be away from here, to be taken back to his favourite manor in Dorset.'

That day and the succeeding ones were filled with frenetic activity. De Payens, with the help of the abbey coffers, negotiated with the prince's mercenaries to withdraw south and join the king in London, leaving a small retinue to guard the dead. The two corpses were washed, embalmed and blessed, then laid out in state before the abbey high altar. Couriers were dispatched and received. The king, both distraught and angry, was careful not to allocate any blame; his letter explained how he was now involved in complicated negotations with Henry Fitzempress. He gave detailed instructions about how the Templars were to supervise his son's corpse, which was to be taken with all solemnity to the family mausoleum at Faversham Abbey in Kent, where Eustace's mother lay buried.

Common gossip around the abbey and amongst the prince's retainers maintained that Stephen's second son,

William of Boulogne, would succeed as heir apparent. A few days later the proclamation of a lasting peace between Stephen and Henry Fitzempress dispelled such rumours. Both leaders had sworn great oaths. Stephen would remain king, whilst Henry Fitzempress would be solemnly adopted as his heir presumptive. Speculation grew rife. Berrington, lean face all puckered with concern, convened a meeting of his entourage to discuss the news. Mayele remarked ironically how Eustace's death could not have occurred at a more favourable time; nor that of the fervent royalist Northampton, not to mention the grievous sickness of the Archbishop of York, who now lay at death's door. All grudgingly conceded that the secretive, mysterious Walkyn had carried out a most successful revenge against Stephen and his family. Already the swift change of fortune was making itself felt. The abbot had dispatched couriers to congratulate Prince Henry. Berrington said he would do likewise, so as to win the new ruler's approval for the Temple.

'We are finished here,' he proclaimed.

'Finished?' Mayele barked back.

'I have reflected upon what Edmund said earlier,' Berrington declared. 'What more can we do? I could continue the hunt for Walkyn. I propose that Edmund and Parmenio be dispatched back to Outremer, bearing letters to our masters in Jerusalem describing what has happened here. I shall stay to reorganise the Temple holdings, contact the various preceptories and,' he smiled thinly, 'join everyone else in paying my respects to the new star rising in the east.'

'And me, brother?' Isabella asked. 'If you wish, I could join Edmund . . .'

De Payens remained silent, lost in thought. He was tempted to accept what Berrington said, yet he felt irked at being used as a messenger boy.

'I could leave as well,' Isabella repeated.

'If I want to go,' de Payens retorted.

'If he should go,' Parmenio added.

They were sitting in the Petit Paradis; now the Genoese rose swiftly to his feet, clearly agitated.

'Brother?' Berrington demanded.

'I am not your brother,' Parmenio retorted. 'I, we, you, Edmund, we all hold a commission to hunt down Walkyn and whatever malignants have joined his coven and kill them all; those are the orders of our Grand Master.'

'But,' Berrington interrupted, 'I can continue the hunt. Mayele can assist. Earlier, both you and de Payens said you wanted to leave. I thought this would be an honourable compromise.'

'That was before,' Parmenio repeated heatedly. 'We wondered if Walkyn had come to England. Now we know the truth. We have witnessed at first hand his mischief. Moreover, Stephen is still king. We have told him why we are here. Should some of us leave now and give up the task because Walkyn has succeeded? I do not think King Stephen would reconcile himself to that. The situation is now more serious. If we had left before these murders, that would have been tolerable, but now we are committed. The king may not even give us licence to leave. Whatever, I will not return, not yet.' He glanced at de Payens. 'Edmund,' he pleaded, 'at Ascalon I saved your life. On this matter, I beg you: we must stay, at least for a while.'

De Payens, intrigued by the Genoese's passionate appeal and convinced by his logic, nodded in agreement. Deep in his heart he also felt resentment at the way Berrington had decided how matters should be. True, earlier he had wished to return to Outremer, but that had been anger. Now Eustace and Northampton were dead, whilst Murdac was dying. Surely such deaths should be avenged? It was too late to leave now. Berrington looked as if he wanted to argue the case, but then he pulled a face and passed on to other matters, such as supplies, and the need to return to London to collect revenues from the Templar coffers. The meeting ended, each going their different ways. De Payens tried to draw Parmenio into conversation, but the Genoese simply murmured that he had said enough for a while.

The days flew by. In the middle of September, the Templars, with full panoply, escorted the embalmed corpses of the prince and Northampton to Faversham Abbey for their solemn interment. The king was present, as was Henry Fitzempress. The Angevin was red-haired, florid-faced, heavily built, with the long arms of a born swordsman. One hand rested on his dagger, the other on a very tall, pale-faced, dark-haired cleric whom

Berrington whispered was Thomas à Becket, a clerk well known in both London and Kent. King Stephen met them in the Galilee porch of Faversham abbey church. He welcomed them coldly, though he thawed as Lady Isabella expressed her own compassionate condolences. He declared that they'd done enough to protect his son, but added that they must be in London around the Feast of the Confessor, in the middle of October, when they could account for what had truly happened before the Great Council.

The following day they returned to Bury St Edmunds. Berrington became busy over their departure for Westminster. Isabella helped him, Mayele being used as a courier. De Payens, left to his own devices, wandered the abbey. He became accepted by the good brothers as a royal guest, a fellow monk from a different order. De Payens worked hard to make himself at home in that cavernous, sprawling house of prayer. He often strolled through the great cloisters, reciting his beads. He visited the long dark nave of the church, and joined the monks in the library or scriptorium, where their precious manuscripts were chained to polished lecterns. He chattered to the abbey chroniclers, who sat with sharpened quills and freshly brushed vellum, ink horns at the ready, their great writing benches littered with parchment knives, wax, pots of paints and curls of ribbon. He assembled with the good brothers in their stalls for matins, lauds and the rest of the sacred hours. He immersed himself in the daily horarium in the abbey, even helping where he could in the stables and forges, whilst using such occasions to probe events around the death of the prince. In the end he discovered nothing new. The brothers whispered behind their hands how Eustace's death was the work of St Edmund, who had inflicted punishment on the prince for his sins. They also murmured about Parmenio: how the Genoese was prying into the murderous affray that had taken place in their abbey, though keeping himself very much aloof from them.

De Payens had to agree. Parmenio had grown estranged from his companions, often absenting himself from the guesthouse refectory. Berrington and Mayele commented on that, but ignored Parmenio, as if he were no longer a member of their retinue, resentful at his opposition to Berrington's wishes. Isabella grew cooler, whilst her brother concentrated on Templar business, being visited day and night by couriers and messengers. Berrington voiced his suspicion that Walkyn might have hidden himself in London, and announced that they would journey there as soon as possible to resume the hunt. In the meantime, other business demanded his attention.

De Payens considered spying on Parmenio, but dismissed this as dishonourable. The Genoese had his own business, and de Payens decided that little could be done until they moved to London. Instead, struck by the beauty of the countryside, he took to riding out along the trackways, turning off into the nearby forest to admire the gradual change of the riot of greenery to a feast of brown and gold as autumn swept in. He was fascinated by the constant turmoil of life: the bracken snapping and crackling as fox, hare, rabbit, squirrel and other creatures burst their way through, hunting for food or each other; the ever-present canopy above him, always alive with the fluttering and calls of birds; the darkness on either side of the trackway where the great trees clustered so close, only to abruptly open on to sun-washed glades sprinkled with wild flowers; swift, narrow streams that bubbled vigorously into meres, pools and ponds.

On his rides, de Payens became aware of other sights, dark, fleeting figures. The good brothers laughingly assured him that these were only forest people – charcoal-burners, poachers from nearby villages, woodsmen – not the hags, elves and gargoyles of popular legend. De Payens found such outings comforting, as he reflected on what had happened since that *dies irae* in Tripoli almost a year ago. It provided him with an opportunity to probe the dogging sense of unease about the search for a warlock whom he had never known or seen.

On the feast of St Dionysius, he decided to ride out again. He attended the dawn mass for that illustrious martyr, then broke his fast at the ale table in the buttery, where Brother Grimaldus cheerfully provided sustenance for his journey with a linen bag containing bread, cheese, apples, some dried meat and fresh plums. De Payens collected his horse from the stables, and within

185

a short while was deep in the dense copse of trees, broken by glades ringed by ancient stones. He had grown accustomed to the forest sounds, and became deep in thought about the tangle of mysteries. He wondered if the abbey library could help translate the cipher still in the small leather pouch on a cord around his neck. Memories from the past came and went: Parmenio in that Greek church in Tripoli, darting forward with a dagger; Mayele loosing arrows so deadly against his chosen victims; Nisam in his garden pavilion staring at him sadly; Baiocis dying in the refectory. The Templar recalled how the master had looked ill from the beginning of that meal, clutching his goblet as if already anticipating his death. Then Eustace and Northampton struck down so swiftly, but how? The abbey leech had later reported that the archbishop's goblet was definitely laced with some noxious potion, but the other cups, drained even of the dregs, were a mystery as he could detect no real taint.

De Payens broke from his reverie and tightened his reins at sounds behind him different from the rest. He paused, staring around as if studying the trees, then he glimpsed them: three small, dark shapes moving on the other side of the glade. He rode into the trees and slipped from his horse, quietly urging it on as he slid into the tangled undergrowth. He undid his war belt, drew his dagger and waited, motionless. Three small figures came darting down the path. De Payens lunged and caught one, grasping the small body around the waist. Despite the screams and yells, he held his prisoner fast, then grinned at the bright eyes and dirty face glaring at him through a tangle of black hair. He laughed and put the little girl down. She backed away, eyes rounded in fear, then paused at the sight of the silver medal, a likeness of the Virgin, which de Payens always carried in the wallet on his belt.

'Come,' he beckoned, 'take.'

The girl chattered back. De Payens couldn't understand what she said. He beckoned her again, crossed himself and leaned over. She grasped the medal and he let her take it. Then he got to his feet, strapped on his war belt and walked slowly down the snaking path to where his horse was cropping the grass. He undid the pannier, took out the linen parcel of food and turned. Three children now stood on the trackway with the sunlight behind them, little black shadows holding each other's hands. De Payens felt a stab of self-pity tinged with envy. He had never experienced that; no brother or sister, just Theodore and the formidable Eleanor. He quickly murmured a prayer of thanksgiving for that, undid his wallet and took out two more of the shining medals. Then he unclasped his cloak, spread it on the trackway, put the medals in the middle and undid the linen bag. The children, dirty faces almost hidden by tousled black hair, came and knelt opposite him. He pointed to the medals, then quietly drew his dagger, and ignoring their gasps cut the food into four portions. Little arms snaked across, each seizing their portions as well as the medals. De Payens closed his eyes, crossed himself and murmured the Benedicite. When he looked again, all three children were pushing the food, a mixture of apple, bread, cheese and meat, into their mouths, large eyes rounded in pleasure. De Payens laughed. He talked to them but they couldn't understand. Instead they made the sign of the cross and crammed the plums into their mouths. Once finished, they wiped their mouths on the back of their hands and patted their stomachs. De Payens rose. He sketched a blessing, put on his cloak, remounted and rode on. When he turned in the saddle to wave, all three had disappeared.

# Chapter 9

King Stephen returned in great glory to London.

Eventually de Payens reached another glade, and on the breeze came the distant tolling of the heavy abbey bells. He decided to return following the same path back. The sun was in his eyes, sparkling through the interlaced canopy of trees. He reached the place where he'd fed the children, reined in and looked down just as a burst of bird wing alerted him. His hand went to his sword even as the crossbow bolt whirled by his face, its feathered quarrel almost brushing his skin. Another skimmed over his head. He pulled on his reins, and his horse reared. A third bolt, whirring like some deadly bird, plunged into the animal's neck, sending it squealing and kicking before collapsing in agony. De Payens pulled his feet out of the stirrups, crawling away as the horse lashed out in its death throes. He gazed around. His left leg was hurting, his back and arms bruised by the fall. He drew both sword and dagger and glanced pityingly at the horse, a good mount now sprawled in a pool of blood, limbs twitching. He stared ahead and glimpsed shadows moving. These were no common outlaws, who'd be too poorly armed to attack an armed knight. Moreover, the ambush had been carefully prepared. They had waited for him to return, with the sun in his eyes. Professional assassins, hired killers, probably four or five of them, because the bolts had all been loosed in swift succession. As he tried to reach a tree, so that he could at least protect his back, the bracken crackled and snapped. The assassins were drawing close. Abruptly a horn sounded, a long, carrying blast. The undergrowth behind him rustled. Arrows sped over his head in the direction of his hidden attackers. Again the horn blast. Men armed with spears and clubs were threading through the trees on either side of him. One turned and hurried towards him, hand up in the sign of peace.

'*Pax et bonum*, Templar.'

By his dark brown robe, the cross on a cord around his neck and the clean-cut tonsure, de Payens recognised a priest. He came and crouched beside the Templar, his weathered face wrinkled in concern, kindly green eyes searching for any wound.

'You certainly have enemies, Templar.' He spoke the lingua franca of the Middle Seas. 'Oh yes.' He grinned. 'I was a chaplain in the retinue of Lord Balian. I have worshipped in the Holy Sepulchre, but now, for my sins and in reparation for my pride, I am parish priest of St Botulph's-in-the-Wood, a benefice of St Edmund's. Well,' he patted de Payens' leg, 'you're injured?'

'No, just bruised and humbled,' de Payens replied, pulling himself up. 'Otherwise I'm sound. My horse?'

'Poor beast.' The priest extended a hand, and de Payens clasped it. 'I am John Fitzwalter, as I said, priest and former chaplain.' He helped de Payens up, and they went and stood over the dead horse. The forest people emerged, shaking their heads, talking quickly to the priest in their guttural tongue. 'My beloveds,' Priest John translated, 'say that your attackers were assassins skilled in forest-lore.'

'Who could hire such men?' de Payens asked.

The priest pulled a face. 'We've heard the gossip about you and the other Templars at the great abbey. How you were in the retinue of Prince Eustace. As for your question, this is England; the shires are full of such men. They only believe in one verse from scripture: They fear neither God nor man. Thank the Lord you were kind to the children. They glimpsed your assailants and hurried back to the village with the news. Now, your poor horse.' He patted de Payens on the arm. 'You've read the great

Anselm? He said that cruelty to animals comes directly from the Evil One. Ah well.' He crouched and helped de Payens loosen the saddle and bridle. 'Leave the animal here, Templar. The poor will eat it. Some good will come from this evil. Small recompense for your saviours.'

De Payens stood up. One of the villagers gently took the saddle from him, another the harness. The Templar opened his wallet, shook out the remaining coins and medals and pressed them into the priest's hands. He then stared closely at his rescuers, forest people dressed in shabby green and brown tunics bound around the waist with rope; rough sandals and leggings protected their ankles and feet. A few were young; others looked indistinguishable, with their mass of dark hair, bushy beards and moustaches. They smiled at him and spoke quickly to the priest.

'They thank you. They always follow you when you come here.'

'Why?'

'I'll explain.' The priest added grimly, 'Those children were a lure, but you were very kind. Come.' He grasped de Payens' arm. 'We will escort you back to the abbey gatehouse.'

They went back along the path. The priest described his village church, how he'd repaired it, the vivid wall painting he was preparing to illustrate themes from the bible, especially the Final Judgement.

'God knows what will happen on that day. Now listen.' He spoke slowly, enunciating every word. 'As I said, we knew about the prince. We heard about his death and those of the others. We are also concerned, Templar. Men have appeared in our woods, strangers, dangerous nighthawks, dark wanderers, well armed, visored and hooded. They camp here and watch the abbey.'

'Does anyone come out to meet them?'

'I cannot say. We only see their fires at night, smell their woodsmoke. Indeed, one of my parishioners has met them.'

'What?'

The priest paused, shouting at the forest people, who drifted back.

'Thurston,' he called. A young man stepped forward, spear in one hand, club in the other. The priest spoke to him; Thurston replied, his gaze never leaving that of the Templar.

'What did he say?' de Payens asked. 'I recognise the name Walkyn.'

'Thurston is a skilled poacher,' the priest murmured. 'There is not a rabbit alive he cannot catch. Now there's a warren deep in the forest, a source of fresh meat. Thurston was there; he trapped three or four, enough food for my parish. He was returning when two strangers slipped out from the trees. They were courteous enough, but asked him to hand over the meat. Thurston of course could not refuse, but in the forest fashion, he asked their names. One of the men replied that his name was Walkyn, that all he wanted was the meat, then Thurston could go on his way.'

'Walkyn?' De Payens stared at the villager. 'You are sure of that?'

The priest translated, but Thurston was stubborn and kept repeating the name, nodding vigorously.

'The strange thing is,' the priest smiled at de Payens, 'Thurston asked what his companion's name was, and the same name was given. And that is not all.' The priest indicated that they should walk on, calling to his parishioners to do likewise. 'All kinds of men flee here, outlaws from the towns and villages. A few join us. Many do not survive, but these strangers certainly have. In the main they leave us alone, as we do them. Very rarely do we clash, but recently, in the last month, things have changed.'

'How?'

'Young girls,' he murmured, 'well, young women; at least three in the last weeks have just disappeared. Now that is not so surprising. Some of our young men and women get tired of forest life and flee to the towns and villages, but these were different. They had families, lovers; one was betrothed to be married. They just disappeared like frost under the sun.'

De Payens repressed a shiver as he recalled the stories about similar macabre disappearances in Jerusalem.

'And no corpses have been found?'

'Templar, look around. You could bury the cadavers of an entire city in this forest and never find a grave. But to answer your question bluntly, we do not think these young women ran away. Something hideous has happened to them.'

'And you think these strangers could be responsible?'

'Perhaps.' The priest shook his head. 'We even wondered about you. We watched you ride out, hence those three children. My parishioners,' he added drily, 'were watching you all the time. *Deo Gratias*, they also saved you.'

'How long have you been here, Father?'

'Oh, at least fourteen summers in all. Why?'

'You know about the great rebel, Mandeville, Earl of Essex?'

'Oh yes, that demon.'

'Why do you call him that?'

The priest paused, looking up at the sky. 'I've heard the stories about him being a warlock, a sorcerer, but that is not true. Mandeville was like the rest of the great lords, greedy for wealth and lands. He committed hideous blasphemies, occupying monasteries and abbeys, despoiling holy places. By doing so he attracted a host of dark spirits, men who dabbled in all sorts of wickedness. I am a pastor, Templar. I deal with the care of souls. Do you know what I think?' He glanced sideways at de Payens. 'We human beings, our souls are like manor houses, haunted by angels and demons. We all make a choice about which should dominate. Whatever,' he sighed, 'we heard the stories about Mandeville's followers. Some of them were steeped in wickedness; they carried out bloodthirsty rites, revelling in what they did. Look at Prince Eustace. We heard about his wild ride through the shires. What chance do my parishioners have against mailed men on horse, armed with swords and crossbows? They ride into a village and can do what they want; no sheriff, no bailiff can object. The king's peace is shattered. It's so good to hear that King Stephen and Henry Fitzempress have been reconciled.'

They reached the forest edge, and approached the abbey gatehouse. The priest took the saddle and harness from his parishioners; only he went forward with de Payens. He paused at the small drawbridge across the narrow ditch.

'Templar,' he handed over the harness, 'God be with you.' Then he was gone.

De Payens' dramatic return to the abbey provoked consternation amongst the good brothers. Parmenio, Mayele and Isabella came hurrying down. Once de Payens had assured the brethren that he'd suffered no real hurt, they all gathered in the guesthouse refectory, and he gave his companions a cursory description of the attack, even as he studied their faces, particularly that of Parmenio, who looked troubled. On his return, de Payens had immediately asked the porters and door-keepers if any of his companions, or indeed anyone else, had left the abbey, only to be assured that they had not. On reflection, he concluded, it wasn't possible for a malignant to leave St Edmund's, thread through the woods, then lurk to kill him within such a brief space of time. Nevertheless, he did not wish to remain beetle-blind. He could have died in the forest. And had not a similar attack occurred outside Ascalon, when Parmenio had been with him? He deliberately did not tell them about the forest children or the details of his meeting with the priest, but he did mention the strangers in the forest, hooded and visored, all calling themselves Walkyn.

'Perhaps it's the name they have taken for themselves,' Parmenio observed. 'It's quite common to assume the title or designation of the leader of a group. The retainers of great lords do likewise.'

Berrington and Mayele agreed.

'Edmund,' Berrington declared, 'while you were gone, we received information, a messenger from Essex: rumour has it that Walkyn landed on the Colvasse peninsula near Orwell, a lonely estuary not far from his manor at Borley. He would want to avoid port reeves and harbourmasters, and it would be easy in some foreign port to hire passage on a cog, a pirate ship, which could land him and any others on a lonely strip along the Essex coast.'

'But how could he do that?' de Payens countered.

'What do you mean?' Parmenio demanded.

'Well,' de Payens stretched out his hand, 'look at me, a poor Templar knight. You, Berrington, and the rest have come to England paid by monies drawn from the exchequer in Jerusalem. We are dependent on what we receive from our order, the hospitality of the good brothers, the kindness of the king in loaning horses. Where did Walkyn get such wealth? He was a poor Templar knight.'

'He was also leader of a coven.'

'Yes, but he was captured,' de Payens insisted. 'He was seized, held captive by you, Berrington, bound as a prisoner, manacled, seated on a poor horse, I presume. He had nothing on him, did he?'

'Of course not,' Berrington agreed. 'But remember, his coven attacked us. They stripped us of our armour and whatever wealth we carried, and stole our horses. They would also have brought whatever wealth they had from Jerusalem.'

'And Tripoli?' Mayele observed. He gestured at Berrington not to interrupt. 'Remember, brothers, Count Raymond was killed, then the rioting and massacre began. Part of the city was plundered; wealthy merchants had their houses stripped of all possessions. If Walkyn was responsible for that, he may have amassed a small fortune, true?'

'Yes,' Parmenio leaned his elbows on the table, 'yes, that would make sense.' He talked as if speaking to himself. 'It's been mentioned before. Perhaps that was the reason for the attack in Tripoli: to kill the count and cause chaos and mayhem as a guise, a cloak. Walkyn's real intention was to plunder the houses of the rich to acquire the wealth he needed.'

'Which he would use,' Mayele declared, 'once he began his travels. Silver and gold in foreign ports would soon buy passage on a private cog, whilst in Essex he would use the same to recruit and summon up members of his coven and hire assassins.'

The discussion about Walkyn's intentions grew heated. Isabella slipped on to the bench beside de Payens, face all worried. She rested a hand on his arm, shaking her head.

'Edmund, Edmund,' she whispered in a return to her old flirting. 'I could have accompanied you on your rides.' She grinned impishly. 'A fair maid on the green sward . . .'

'Sister!' Berrington got to his feet. 'Edmund, you cannot go out alone again.' He walked up and down. 'It's possible that armed men, cowled and masked, are gathering in the woods, a natural place for Walkyn to hide. He may even have followers here in the abbey. We've outstayed our welcome here. Tomorrow we leave for London. Walkyn might follow us, and there we can trap him.'

Edmund de Payens stood in God's Acre, a plot of land stretching between the wall of St Andrew's, Holborn, and the Templar enclosure with its rounded church, half-timbered hall, barracks, guesthouses, forges, store-rooms and other outbuildings. He stared in astonishment at the great oaken casket hanging by stout chains from the branches of an ancient, gnarled yew tree. All around him rose the memorials of dead Templars and those who had served them, but this was unique: the coffin of a great earl who had died excommunicate, a body refused burial in consecrated ground until the Pope in Rome lifted the sentence of eternal damnation.

The ox-hide covering, blood red in colour, was fading and weathered, the huge chain links rusting. The coffin swayed slightly, creaking as if the corpse inside housed a blackened soul still struggling to begin its journey towards the light.

De Payens whittled at the stick he'd picked up as he studied the ground beneath the coffin. Someone had taken great care over this plot; no nettles or weeds, their roots matted like basketwork, thrived here. The ground had been torn with a tooth-rake, reaping out the crawling, snake-like roots and breaking up the clods of earth, and a meadow plot planted of green grass jewelled with lilies of the wood, daffodils, daisies, forget-me-nots and speedwells. De Payens crouched down, relishing the flower scent. Even though it was October, autumn had arrived late here and the full glory of summer was not yet spent. He thanked God for the clement weather and crossed himself. He and his companions had left St Edmund's following, where possible, the old Roman road south. They had bought horses, palfreys and sumpters as well as whatever harness they needed. Each day they'd travelled immediately after the dawn mass until the hour of vespers, when they'd sought shelter in some monastery, church, hostelry or pilgrim tavern. They'd ridden into London from the east, close to the soaring white donjon built by William the Norman, making their way along the north bank of the Thames, past the castles of Montfichet and Baynard, through Newgate, into the Temple enclosure.

They'd arrived nine days ago. Berrington, acting very much the master, had summoned the seneschals, clerks and bailiffs. He'd inspected the Templar buildings and allocated them chambers, except for Isabella, who took lodgings in the nearby Bishop of Lincoln's Inn, a fortified manor house within walking distance of the Templar manse.

Two days later they had been summoned to the king's house at Westminster. They'd heard mass at St Paul's, leaving even as the masons, stone-cutters and carpenters swung themselves up on to the scaffolding around the still unfinished cathedral. They'd ridden through the strengthening morning light and entered the north gate of the palace. The great bailey beyond was already busy with falconers, hooded hawks on their wrists. Hunters were fussing with wolfhounds and wiry vulperets. Grooms and ostlers grouped around horses, destriers and palfreys. They'd left their mounts and pushed their way through a throng of clerks, men-at-arms and serjeants, and along vaulted passageways into the royal chamber, hung with canvas newly dyed a deep crimson, the gaps between emblazoned with the king's arms. A grand table under a gold-fringed canopy stood on a dais at the far end of the chamber; this was ringed with high-backed chairs and stools. On each side stood small trestle desks holding parchment rolls, tubs of sealing wax, vellum, bound books and steel-ringed coffers. Sconce torches flickered, candles glowed and brazier baskets crackled and smoked; the chamber was very warm and full of fragrances.

They had to wait for a while until a blare of trumpets and the shouts of chamberlains announced the arrival of the king. Stephen entered garbed in a short mantle of russet fastened at the right shoulder by a large jewel brooch over a long red tunic flowered with gold and fastened at the throat by a silver clasp. His tight-fitting scarlet hose and boots of black leather, still spurred, were splattered with the blood and mud of the hunt. He was accompanied by a whey-faced clerk dressed in black, which only emphasised the cleric's pinched features beneath a mop of neatly tonsured hair. Other courtiers and officials followed, but they stayed near the door. Stephen swept to the chair in the centre of the table, the chancery clerk to his right. Berrington and the rest were told to approach and take their seats. The king was pale, thinner. The death of his son had clearly shaken him, but he did not indulge in recriminations.

'My son was murdered,' he whispered once Berrington had finished speaking. His face lightened when he caught Isabella's smile of compassion. 'Yes, yes,' he waved a hand, 'my lady, you and your brother must dine with me in the hall, but for now . . .' He beckoned at de Payens, who felt a stab of jealousy and frustration at not being invited as well. 'Please,' the king insisted, 'tell me again. Tell me what happened.'

De Payens described the deaths of Senlis and Eustace,

and then added a short description of the murderous assault on him in the forest outside the abbey. Once he'd finished, Stephen nodded and whispered to the chancery clerk, then raised a hand for silence.

'We have done fresh searches.' The king rubbed his face. 'The harbourmasters and port reeves have not reported Walkyn's entry into the kingdom, though,' he added wistfully, 'there are a legion of deserted coves such as Orwell. Our recent troubles have certainly not helped matters. Nevertheless,' he continued, 'without specifying his crimes, Henry Walkyn, former Templar, is to be put to the horn as *utlegatum*, beyond the law. By order of king and council, he can be killed on sight. A reward of a hundred pounds sterling is posted on his head; two hundred if brought in alive. This proclamation will be issued to every sheriff and port reeve, and pinned to the cross outside St Paul's and that in Cheapside. Dead or alive,' he mumbled, 'dead or alive – wolf's-head.'

Afterwards, de Payens, Mayele and Parmenio had returned to the Temple, where they had to wait until early evening before Berrington and Isabella returned, full of chatter about the king and the favour he'd shown them. That evening held a further shift in events. Once again Berrington raised the possibility of leaving Walkyn to the bounty-hunters and reward-seekers. De Payens, however, recalling the murderous attack on him, stood his ground. So it was decided that Berrington would continue as master of the Temple in England.

He would be assisted by Mayele, who'd act as his envoy to the other preceptories. Parmenio and de Payens meanwhile would continue their hunt for Walkyn.

De Payens threw away the stick he was whittling and walked carefully around the yew tree and its grisly burden. Berrington and Mayele often came here, either to view this gruesome sight or to pay their respects to the great lord, he did not know which. The two men still believed that Mandeville had been a formidable war leader. As they stoutly maintained, the dead earl could not be held responsible for some of the people who served him. Parmenio also visited here, though de Payens noticed how he kept his distance, never drawing too close. On the other hand the Genoese had become friendlier, actually seeking de Payens out. He heard a sound and turned. Parmenio stood there, hand on the hilt of his dagger.

'What is the matter?' De Payens walked towards him. 'Do you fear attack even here? Why do you caress your dagger hilt?'

The Genoese lifted both hands and grinned.

'In the presence of the devil,' he tapped the cross hilt of his dagger, 'I ask God and his angels to protect me.'

'From what?' de Payens demanded. 'Why, Parmenio?' He leaned in, his face close to that of the Genoese. 'Why are you so stubborn, so faithful in all of this? Here you are in a strange country, a foreign place. You are like a lurcher who won't be thrown from the scent.'

'You're the same.'

'I'm a Templar. This is Temple business. You are Genoese, far from home. Why bother? Why not go back?'

'He was the devil.' Parmenio ignored the questions and pointed at the hanging casket. 'He used to send his searchers out at night to discover where rich men dwelt, so that he could seize them, throw them into dungeons and demand heavy ransoms. He took his coven by barge through the slimy fens at night and seized the monastery at Ramsey, surprising the brothers in their beds just after they'd sung matins. He turned them out and filled their monastery with soldiers. He seized sacred treasures, relics and vestments. He turned such places into a fort.'

'Others have done the same.'

'Old Mandeville did worse,' Parmenio retorted. 'He turned Christ's church into a robber's den, the sanctuary of the Lord into the devil's abode. He attracted the worst amongst the warlocks and witches, blood-drinkers and demon-worshippers. Hideous abominations were carried out, so intense that even the walls of the church sweated blood.'

'These children of Satan?' de Payens asked. 'They murdered?'

'Oh yes, they took prisoners, innocents who were never seen again: those who hid in the fens nearby heard the cruellest screams.'

'You seem well versed in their practices,' de Payens retorted. 'But to return to my question, which you never answered, why are you really here, Parmenio? You appeared like the Angel of Vengeance in that church in Tripoli. Since then you have dogged our footsteps like a hungry mastiff. You face battle, hunger, thirst, a perilous journey – why?'

'Like you, Edmund,' Parmenio's reply was swift, 'a task has been entrusted to me. I will complete it.'

De Payens was tempted to confront him with a litany of questions, then he recalled the Genoese protecting him in Ascalon.

'Anyway,' Parmenio beckoned him forward, 'someone is here to see you. He says he will only speak to a Templar.'

'Where is Mayele?'

'On errands for Berrington.' Parmenio's reply was sarcastic. 'And before you ask, our noble master and the beautiful Isabella are at Westminster again. Our king is much taken with them.' He grinned. 'Especially the charms of *la belle dame*. Ah,' he smiled ironically, 'the sorrows and pain of widowhood, eh, Edmund?' He turned on his heel and led de Payens back into the Templar manse. They went down the flagstoned corridor that cut past the chambers on either side. Just before they reached the entrance hall, Parmenio paused. 'Oh, by the way,' he whispered over his shoulder, 'she's back, your secret admirer.'

De Payens closed his eyes in exasperation. Over the last few days a young woman – the porters claimed she was a courtesan, a high-priced one – had been glimpsed near the main gate. On one occasion she had approached Parmenio and asked to see de Payens.

'Well?' the Genoese asked.

De Payens opened his eyes.

'You see,' Parmenio smiled, 'she won't see any other Templar, just you!'

'She will have to wait. Now who's this?'

The man waiting for him in the hall rose as they entered. De Payens gestured at the two serjeants to withdraw.

'Well?' he asked.

The stranger was a young man, clean-shaven, with an honest face. He was neatly attired in a bottle-green tunic down to his knees over brown hose pushed into soft clean boots. The mantle on his shoulders had a hood; this was pushed back over sandy hair.

'I speak Norman French.' The stranger's voice was low and cultured. 'I'm a clerk in the Guildhall, Martin Fitzosbert.' He licked his lips, and lifted ink-stained fingers.'

'And what do you want, clerk?'

'The reward for Henry Walkyn alive, or at least part of it.'

'What?'

'Listen,' Fitzosbert gabbled, 'the entire city knows about the proclamation. I work at the Guildhall. I help transcribe the documents putting men to the horn. It's common enough.' He spread his hands. 'We clerks have a sharp eye to a quick profit. Around the sheriff's chamber cluster the bounty-hunters and professional thief-catchers. They swim in the same dirty pools as their prey: vagabonds,

sturdy beggars, counterfeit men of every ilk, outlaws, sanc-
tuary-seekers, night hawks and dark wanderers.' He
paused. 'Morteval the Welshman is the best in London.
He came into the Chancery after the Jesus mass this
morning. He claims to have knowledge about the Radix
Malorum.'

'The what?' De Payens half laughed. 'The Root of all
Evil?'

'A notorious sorcerer, a seller of philtres and potions,'
Fitzosbert declared. 'A self-confessed member of many
covens, who consorts with witches and their like.
Morteval believes the Radix will know the true whereabouts of Walkyn and his coven.'

'How, why?' Parmenio asked sharply.

'Because the Radix knows all about such matters.'

'So why not abduct him and bring him here?'

'Ah, he will do that, Domine,' Fitzosbert smiled thinly,
'but first he keeps the Radix under close scrutiny. He
lurks at a tavern, the Light in the Darkness, in the
slums near Queenshithe, a place haunted by ribauds
and other malefactors. Morteval believes that today,
after the Angelus bell, the Radix is to meet someone
important. He has hired an upper chamber and the
tavern cooks are very busy. Morteval believes that if we
enter, we may find Walkyn and his ilk. All he wants is
a substantial portion of the reward, as do I.' Fitzosbert
paused as de Payens lifted a hand. 'I will not go there
by myself.'

'Oh no.' Parmenio voiced his agreement.

'Your two serjeants.' Fitzosbert pointed at them.

De Payens glanced at Parmenio, who nodded in agreement. The Templar hurried up to his own chamber. He put on his mailed hauberk, covered by a dark cloak; beneath this he strapped on his war belt with its sword and dagger sheaths.

A short while later, accompanied by the two serjeants, Parmenio's farewells ringing in his ears, he followed Fitzosbert out through the great double gate of the Temple into the streets and alleyways leading down to the river. De Payens had not wandered London. Berrington had warned him that after the attack in the forest, he must be more prudent and cautious. Certainly the narrow lanes and runnels they now entered were as dangerous as any lonely forest trackway. The ground was pitted and holed. An arrow-slit sewer, crammed with steaming dirt, ran down the middle. Signs bearing all kinds of garishly painted symbols swung dangerously close above their heads, whilst the doors and shutters of the tenements on either side kept opening and shutting in a never-ending clatter. The constant stench from the midden heaps was as rich as any in Jerusalem, the noise and babble just as strident as the bazaars of the Holy City. The lack of colour, though, was strikingly different. The breeze was turning cold, and passers-by were swathed in dark cloaks and hoods. The roofs were drenched by recent rain; their thatch of reeds, straw and shingles poured down a wetness that soaked the timbers of the upper storeys, thickening the wooden shutters and rusting the hinged lattices of iron. Under this drizzle hens, geese, goats and pigs roamed aimlessly. Scavenger dogs plundered the grease-coated heaps of rubbish, fighting off the yellow-ribbed, amber-eyed cats whilst blocking the passage of carts, horses and pack ponies.

Fitzosbert led them past stalls set up in front of houses supervised by traders and their legion of apprentices, who darted about like imps from hell. Cookshops, pie stalls, wine taverns and alehouses did a thriving business with those eager to escape from the thronging, filthy streets. Now and again the line of houses would break to reveal an open space, where skinny cows grazed on meagre grass, or some little church, with dirty steps and narrow windows, desperate to catch the attention of passers-by with the clanging of its bells or the preaching of its parson from an outside pulpit.

They eventually skirted the grim fastness of Newgate. Before the massive iron-studded gates stood the pillory and thews, busy with its daily line of victims: men and women caught by the beadles and bailiffs, waiting to be fastened in the clamps to stand and be mocked in their own filth until justice was done. Fitzosbert described the list of offences as he came alongside de Payens, with the two serjeants trudging behind him. Life in London was certainly cruel, the Templar reflected. They passed Ludgate, down between the castles of Montfichet and Baynard, where the gallows stood, each scaffold bar decorated with its gruesome victim. Most of the cadavers were rotting, turning slightly on dirty ropes; beneath them, ragged children played their games. A barber, his bowl slopping a bloody froth, offered to cut hair, trim a beard or draw a diseased tooth. His shouting for business cut across the white-garbed Cistercian chanting the general absolution as three malefactors, death warrants pinned to their shabby tunics, were turned off the execution cart to swing and struggle against the ropes suspended from the stout branches of an elm tree. Great lords and ladies on their richly caparisoned horses trotted by, grooms and retainers hurrying alongside. They rode untouched and undisturbed by their surroundings, as if their ermine-lined cloaks, dark robes and thick furred hoods created an impenetrable barrier between themselves and the rest of humanity. Here and there guildsmen in the blue and mustard colours of the city kept a sharp eye on the various stalls. Aldermen, resplendent in their scarlet robes and glinting chains of office, also patrolled, faces full of their own importance. Around these clus-tered liverymen, eager to act on their every whim.

'London means trade,' Fitzosbert whispered, and de Payens nodded in agreement. Everything was for sale, from woollen hangings to Spanish boots, fine steel pins to brocaded cloths, eel pies to sugared manchet loaves, wine from Gascony or furs from the frozen north. Woe betide anyone who fell foul of the regulations proclaimed by criers and enforced by the market walkers. All trans-gressions were met with summary justice. Bakers who

211

sold short were fastened to hurdles with a bundle of hay lashed to their backside and dragged through the city. Ale masters who conned their customers sat in a horse trough with a whetstone around their necks. Fishwives who freshened stale catches had to crouch chained to a post with the rotting produce slung under their noses. Whores caught touting for business were paraded to the noise of bagpipes to barber stools, where their heads would be roughly shaved and their faces smeared with dung. A priest caught with his leman was forced to ride a horse bareback facing the animal's tail, much to the amusement of passers-by, as he kept falling off and had to be hoisted back on.

De Payens sensed the bustle, the violence of the streets, where landless men, beggars, mercenaries and the denizens of the alleyways moved in a swirling crowd. He and Fitzosbert entered a broad thoroughfare and went down past the stately, pink-plastered mansions of the wealthy into a tangle of alleyways and tunnels full of darting shadows. They twisted and turned, the houses leaning over them, until they reached a small square. In the middle a madcap performed a frenzied dance before the statue of some patron saint. In one hand the lunatic held a firebrand, in the other a wooden mallet, which he used to strike the flames to create a shower of sparks. Across the square stood the Light in the Darkness, a gloomy tavern of wood and plaster on a stone base. The door was guarded by ruffians holding cudgels, who stood aside and let them into the tavern room, which stank of onions and rancid cheese. The light was poor, the windows shuttered. Fat tallow candles smoked on the top of the overturned barrels and casks that served as tables. A dwarf, almost swathed in a grey apron, scurried across, his gargoyle face making him even more grotesque in the flickering light. He peered up at de Payens, then at Fitzosbert, who leaned down and whispered. The dwarf tittered behind his hand. De Payens curbed his own spurt of fear; the two serjeants were also uneasy, loosening their swords and daggers, peering through the murk. De Payens could not express his fear; it was like bile in the stomach, stench in the nostrils. He was making to turn away when another figure strolled softly as a cat across the rush-strewn floor.

'Friends, greetings, my name is Morteval.' He stepped into the pool of light, his pockmarked face redeemed by small, clever eyes. He ran a mittened finger through the long tendrils of his oily black hair, which framed bearded features.

'Templar.' He extended a hand. De Payens kept his own on the hilt of his sword. Morteval shrugged and pointed to the ceiling. 'Our guests have arrived. Master Martin will lead the way.'

# Chapter 10

A numerous horde of foes had gathered
to threaten them with unbridled savagery.

They climbed the steep steps built into the corner near
the door. Fitzosbert went first, de Payens and the two
serjeants behind, Morteval at the rear. They reached a
shabby stairwell, its needle-thin window covered by a
strip of dry horn. Morteval pushed himself to the front
and, finger to his lips, pointed at the door. De Payens
leaned his head against it; he heard the clink of cups
and the murmur of voices. Morteval whispered to be
careful, but de Payens was now very wary. Morteval and

Fitzosbert had slipped behind him, so to go back down the stairs might be dangerous. Without warning, de Payens raised his boot and kicked at the leather-covered door. It opened with a crash. The room beyond was in darkness, except for a fiery lantern blazing angrily in its centre. Suddenly de Payens was back in that forest outside the abbey, the sunshine dazzling his eyes through the trees. He shouted a warning and fell to his knees as the cross-bolts whirled through the air. One of the serjeants screamed as a feathered quarrel shattered his face; the other, struck in his chest, staggered forward into the darkened room. De Payens drew his dagger and lunged swiftly at a shape moving towards him, plunging the blade deep into the man's belly. He then threw himself back into the stairwell. Morteval, surprised by the sheer swiftness of the Templar, was too slow. De Payens slicked his throat with his knife, and the thief-taker died in a frenzied whirl of arms and legs. De Payens crashed down the stairs, hurling himself on to the fleeing Fitzosbert. He grasped the hair on the back of the man's head, threw him to the floor and pounded his face until Fitzosbert stopped screaming and lay still. De Payens staggered to his feet, drawing his sword. The dwarf came rushing at him. The Templar smashed him aside with a sweep of his mailed arm. Figures appeared through the tavern doorway; dark shapes crept down the steps behind him.

De Payens made a decision. Keeping to the shadows, he ran at the door, crashing into the men gathering there, his dagger gashing hooded, visored faces. He felt the full fury of battle engulfing him, the sheer joy of lashing out with his sword. Kicking and swearing, he was out into the square, his assailants following. He did not give them time to gather, but closed with them, and when he broke off, gasping for breath, three more corpses lay sprawled jerking in their own life blood. Other assassins massed in the doorway, but its very narrowness constricted their movement. De Payens charged, screaming his war cry, confusing them even more as they tried to fend off the whirling, jabbing steel of his long war sword. For the Templar, this was joy and elation, his blade cutting and slicing the flesh of his enemy. No more reflection. No brooding. Nothing but the sheer fury of battle, of crushing his foes.

His assailants now realised their mistake: they were confronting a Templar knight, a master swordsman, who was using the narrow tavern entrance to trap them as a farmer would a horde of rats in a barn. They edged the Templar out across the dirt-strewn cobbles, trying to outflank him then attack him from behind. Two of them succeeded. The madcap, still whirling his firebrand and mallet, danced across to meet them, shaking the flames in their faces, then screamed as one of the assassins drove his sword deep into the poor fool's throat. De Payens, alerted, darted sideways, jabbing swiftly with the tip of his sword, skewering the assailant in his right eye, then backed away, moving across the cobbles until he felt the statue behind him. His opponents, now spread out in an arc, followed cautiously. The cobbles ran with blood, as if the very ground was wounded. Yells and groans rang out. Wounded men fought to staunch deep slashes in their limbs, chests and bellies. One man, his eyes and face smashed by de Payens' sword, crawled like a blind dog on all fours, pleading for assistance. Doors and shutters were being flung open. A horn sounded, followed by shouts of 'Harrow! Harrow!' as the hue and cry was raised.

'*Non nobis, Domine*,' de Payens shouted. '*Non nobis. Deus Vult! Deus Vult!*'

The attackers closed again, desperate to bring him down. One slid to his knees and slashed at de Payens' leg. The Templar cleaved his skull, splitting it like a log, then brought his blade up so that it scythed to the right and left, slashing the arm of another attacker, who moved back too late. De Payens felt his breath choke. He was sweat-drenched, his eyes were blurred, his strength was failing, arms growing heavy, wrists aching, whilst the cut in his leg was bubbling blood. Four assassins were still edging forward. De Payens glanced past them; more were emerging from the tavern, one of them carrying a crossbow. The Templar mustered his strength as the four charged in a whirl of clashing steel, darting swords and snaking daggers. He used every trick, swaying slightly, blade moving constantly, twisting like a sheet of glancing light. Nevertheless, he was weakening. He fought for breath and began to chant a psalm, even as the first cross-bolt whirled past his head to strike an attacker, hurling him back. Suddenly a horn brayed, and the Templar war cry rang out. Parmenio was beside him. Templar serjeants were pursuing the remaining attackers, who fled like shadows into the darkness of the alleyways. De Payens fell to his knees, then tumbled in a faint against the statue.

'Now God be thanked. Michael the Archangel, standard-bearer of the heavenly host, must have protected you.'

De Payens held the bleary, watery eyes of John Hastang, coroner of the City of London, who had swept into the Temple buildings three days after what he called the Great Battle of Queenshithe to finish his inquiries. De Payens leaned back against the bulky bolster of the narrow cot bed pushed into a corner of the infirmary.

'How is the warrior now?'

'Tired but better.' De Payens glanced to where Mayele, Berrington, Isabella and Parmenio clustered just near the doorway.

'Nothing but a slicing cut,' Mayele grinned. 'Another victory for the champion knight, not pinned this time beneath his horse on a forest trackway to be rescued by wood elves. No, no, Edmund, you confronted your enemies like a master swordsman.'

'And no chantry priest,' Isabella teased, 'no forest people who arrived just in time. All down to your own mighty sword arm.'

Mayele and Isabella continued with their teasing until Hastang held a hand up for silence.

'This is the domain of the Temple,' he intoned formally, fingering the ave beads around his neck before taking a generous slurp from the wine goblet Isabella had pushed into his hands.

'Dominus de Payens, you are the toast of all the taverns from Queenshithe to Galley Gate, to the Tower and beyond.' He leaned forward in a gasp of rich claret. 'Do you realise you killed eleven men?'

'Who were they?'

'Oh, my ruling as coroner,' Hastang smiled, 'is that their deaths were other than natural, but,' he sniffed 'they were richly deserved, richly deserved. You have, Master Templar, the grateful thanks of the City council. You were tricked, baited and trapped, or so they thought. The man who came here as Martin Fitzosbert? Nonsense! He was no clerk, but Peter the Pious, a natural counterfeit who could pose as a holy chantry priest or a devout monk. He was well known to me, the sheriffs and the beadles. He had a gift for lying beyond all others.' Hastang stretched out a hand and touched de Payens gently on the side of his face. 'Do not be ashamed. He has tricked and deceived many. He was the lure. He'll pretend no more. You smashed his face and crushed his cunning brain. Morteval the murderer has been sought by my office for many a year. A professional assassin, Master Edmund, a knifeman, a *sicarius*, a creature of the night, responsible for more deaths than I have had hot suppers. Ah well, he'll kill no more. Your blade emptied his throat.' Hastang was clearly enjoying

219

himself. 'As for the dwarf, mine host in the Light in the Darkness? He was the purveyor of much unadulterated wickedness in this city; now he is gone to his eternal reward with a broken neck. Oh yes,' the coroner smiled bleakly, 'we have much to thank you for. Yet at the same time you are most fortunate.'

'I was tricked, deceived.'

'Undoubtedly. The proclamation against Walkyn has stirred the hearts of many.'

'So why kill me?'

'Now that I don't know.' Hastang, with his back to the others, suddenly narrowed his eyes, and de Payens realised the coroner was not the fool he pretended to be. 'Whatever, Master Templar, somebody with a great deal of wealth wanted you dead. Any other swordsman would not have fared as well.'

'But why?' de Payens repeated.

'Because we are hunting them,' Berrington called out. 'You and Parmenio are responsible. Our enemy now knows that.' He came and crouched beside the bed, his narrow, high-cheekboned face all serious. 'An elaborate strategy, Edmund. Walkyn hired counterfeit men and assassins to kill you because you are hunting him.' He paused. 'Mayele was also attacked outside London. Ribauds, hooded and masked, tried to unhorse him on the road through Woodford. I have been followed in the city. Walkyn must be furious. The king's proclamations have turned every man against him. I'm sure he decided to strike first.'

Berrington patted de Payens on the shoulder and got to his feet. De Payens glanced at Isabella, radiantly beautiful, her fair hair hidden by a wimple and a gauze veil. She smiled through her tears of joy.

'They failed.' Parmenio, standing apart from the rest, walked forward and stared down at de Payens. 'Nevertheless, Master Coroner is correct. Someone with great cunning and considerable wealth plotted that attack at Queenshithe.'

The coroner, slurping from his goblet, nodded vigorously.

'Oh yes, oh yes.' He smacked his lips. 'Men were bought and bribed, promises made, threats issued.'

'But we took no prisoners.'

'None,' the coroner agreed. 'Your two serjeants, God rest them, were killed. The malefactors were butchered; those who survived died shortly afterwards, gabbling in their pain. Now it would take years, if ever, to discover who planned such a cunning trap. Peter the Pious was London's most skilled counterfeit man. He would not have come cheaply. Anyway,' the coroner pointed at Parmenio, 'how did you know? If you had not arrived when you did . . .'

'Observation.' Parmenio chewed the corner of his lip. 'Peter the Pious was advised that we were strangers, foreigners who would be deceived by his clerkly ways and innocent prattle, and we almost were. After you left,' he fiddled with the gold ring on the little finger of his right hand, then pulled at the wooden cross around his own neck, 'I recalled how English clerks always wore a cross or a set of ave beads around their necks. Above all, they wear a chancery ring emblazoned with the royal or city arms. After you had gone, I reflected. Peter the Pious had none of these; he'd dismissed us as ignorant foreigners. Now we'd all been very cautious, rarely leaving the Temple precincts, so it was logical that our enemy would have to lure us out. It was skilfully done. The charlatan had been carefully apprised about who we were searching for.' He shrugged. 'I concluded that if I'd made a mistake then nothing was lost, but if my suspicions were correct . . .' He smiled. 'I summoned the serjeants; thank God I arrived in time.'

Hastang got to his feet. Isabella pushed past him and sat on the stool the coroner had just vacated.

'Leave Edmund alone.' She spoke over her shoulder. 'Let me have a few words with him.' She grasped his hands, rubbing his fingers gently, smiling at him, waiting for the others to leave. Once they had gone, she began to chatter about her days spent at court, the beauty of St Peter's Abbey and the elegance of the nearby royal hall. De Payens realised she was trying to distract him, and teased back about how he'd heard the king was much taken with her beauty and grace. He hid his own spasm of jealousy and listened carefully to her descriptions, studying her hair and her beautiful face.

'Why?' he asked abruptly.

'Why what?' she mocked back.

'You're not married,' he declared. 'You wander the face of God's earth like a pilgrim.'

'What am I, Edmund?' She leaned forward. 'Well, when you left Jerusalem for Hedad, going down the Streets of Chains, I saw you dressed in your white mantle, felt cap on your head, Parmenio going before you, Mayele riding behind. You sat on your horse like a man, determined, dedicated and purposeful. The same is true of my brother and others in the Temple.' She leaned closer. 'I am no different. My brother and I were raised in the manor of Bruer in Lincolnshire. As with you, our parents died when we were young. We were brought up together. Richard always wanted to be a knight, a paladin. Above all, he and I wanted to escape the flat green landscape of Lincolnshire, the boring meetings of the manor, shire and guildhall. You've seen this country, Edmund. Sometimes beautiful, sometimes cold and wet, riven by civil war. Richard and I were restless, and once we began to wander, we could not stop.' She smiled mischievously. 'Now, listen to this. It's a minstrel song I learned at court.' And without further ado, she began to sing in a sweet, melodious voice.

De Payens looked forward to such visits, though they became rare as the weeks passed. Winter in all its bleakness set in. Advent came. The Temple prepared for the great feast of Christmas. Green boughs, sprigs of holly and mistletoe, alongside Christmas roses, decorated the walls and doorways. A chantry priest from the nearby church of St Andrew came every morning to lead them in the haunting O antiphons, whilst a wandering troupe of players was hired to re-enact the story of the Annunciation and the birth of Christ. De Payens' leg healed quickly enough, and he busied himself with walking about, going down to the smithies and carpenters with his sword, dagger and hauberk, all damaged after the ferocious fight in Queenshithe. The scabbard had to be replaced, his sword given a new grip, its pointed edge sharpened, links in the chain-mail hauberk repaired. The hunt, now led by Parmenio and Mayele, continued, but Walkyn proved elusive. Hastang, the coroner, was also zealous in his pursuit of the malefactors. He'd taken a great liking to de Payens and was a constant visitor to the Temple precincts. On one occasion, Hastang and Parmenio visited the Sanctuary of St Mary at Bow, near Cheapside. A wolfshead who'd taken sanctuary was suspected of being involved in the attack on de Payens at Queenshithe, but the outlaw who gripped the edge of the altar was a common malefactor who could tell them nothing.

A sharp-tongued, keen-eyed hawk of a man, Hastang hid his busy wits beneath a mask of diffidence. He and de Payens became firm friends. The coroner was openly delighted at what he referred to as 'the extirpation of a deadly nest of hell's residents'. He openly rejoiced that the Light in the Darkness had now been seized by the city for its own profits.

'A Light in the Darkness!' he scoffed. 'More like a darkness deeper than the rest. Believe me, Edmund,' he wagged a finger, 'that tavern was the root of a great deal of evil. More murder and mayhem were plotted there than in the very heart of hell.' He shook his head. 'Whoever organised that attack on you had a great deal of gold.' He rubbed his face, then winked at the Templar. 'They hired the best. Morteval was killed, as were assassins wanted in at least fifteen shires, men with rewards on their head, professional killers.' He laughed quietly to himself. 'I tell you this, Edmund, if you were to walk back into Queenshithe, no one would dare approach you.'

De Payens grew to trust Hastang, and was flattered when the coroner invited him to supper in his narrow townhouse, which stood squeezed between two splendid mansions fronting Cheapside, the main trading thoroughfare of the city. Domina Beatrice, the coroner's wife, was comely, much younger than her husband, the proud mother of two little girls. She became fascinated by the Templar. At their regular suppers she would question him constantly about Outremer, Jerusalem, the sacred sites, the customs and dress of various people. In turn, Hastang would regale de Payens with stories about the twilight world of the city, the strumpet-mongers, pimps, night-roamers, ruffians and ribauds who swarmed like rats along the alleyways of London. He described in detail the evening chepes, the illegal markets that flourished after curfew had been sounded. A time of bartering and selling in the garrets and tenements of the night-dwellers, who offered stolen goods for sale, then gambled and whored from compline to the bell for the first mass at dawn.

'I have raided such places,' the coroner confided to de Payens. He held up a warning hand. 'I have shaved the heads of harlots, forced them to wear striped hoods and carry white wands to Cock Lane. I have pilloried their pimps, locked them in a cage at the Tun or at the Compter near Newgate. Even more telling, I offered to pardon all their crimes if they could tell me about Walkyn. Yet,' he shook his head, 'nothing! Oh, that malignant and his coven may well lurk here in the city, but no one knows anything about them.' He pulled a face. 'Your Genoese friend? The one who saved you? That's a different matter.' He leaned across the table and filled de Payens' goblet, his sharp face illuminated by one of the glowing candles. He paused, as if listening to Dame Beatrice laughing with their daughters in the small solar above them. De Payens quickly glanced around the room, with its neatly stacked chests and coffers, a small fire under a mantled ledge, its coloured wall cloths, the shelves and pewter pots fastened against the pink-plastered walls, the thick turkey rugs on the floor. A most comfortable chamber, its narrow, horn-filled windows firmly shuttered against the cold; chafing dishes and copper braziers proving resolute defenders against the bitter night air.

'Oh yes.' The coroner tapped the side of his nose. 'The Genoese is a foreigner who has been noticed, his appearance carefully scrutinised. London is not so large as to forget the likes of him, and the whispers float from ward to ward.'

'What are you saying?' De Payens was aware that the coroner was preparing an accusation. 'Master Hastang,' he lifted his cup in toast, 'I travel with my companions; that doesn't mean I trust them.'

'I may have it wrong, Edmund, but your Genoese friend slips in and out of the Temple like a ghost. He is sometimes seen along the wharves, particularly when a cog or carrack, usually Venetian, has completed its long, arduous voyage from Outremer. On occasion he has been glimpsed deep in conversation with a monk, a Cistercian.'

'A Cistercian?' De Payens scratched his chin with his thumb. 'Someone from Outremer?'

'More likely from Normandy. The information I received was that the monk may have slipped into Dover then travelled north. Now, why should the Genoese be meeting such people? Somebody is sending him messages. I thought you should know.'

On that particular evening, Hastang made the Templar reflect not just on the mysterious Parmenio but about the whole sinister world he had entered. He could not break the oath he'd sworn to the Grand Master in the council chamber at Ascalon and divulge the full truth behind his mission to England, yet he could describe the heinous slayings at Wallingford and Bury St Edmunds. The coroner proved to be a shrewd observer. Now and again he interrupted with the odd question, which made it clear that he had always suspected the Templars were involved in secret machinations, though he kept his own counsel on that. He listened fascinated as de Payens described the poisonings of Baiocis, Eustace, Northampton and Murdac. Once the Templar had finished, the coroner pointed to a slender beeswax candle burning brightly on its copper spigot.

'When I was a boy, a lad no taller than a flower, my father used to set me a puzzle in our church during Lent. Twelve candles were placed before the rood screen – they represented the Apostles. Eleven of them were pure beeswax; the twelfth, depicting Judas the traitor, was false. To the naked eye, each was a fresh column of wax, but one of them was counterfeit. My father used to instruct me on how to discover the Judas candle.'

'And did you?'

'Eventually, yes. Simply by close scrutiny and examination, a slight flaw in the whiteness, the curl of the wick . . .'

Hastang lifted his cup.

'So it is with the Sons of Cain, Edmund. In this city, wives poison husbands, husbands kill rivals, if not in hot blood then through a great deal of craft and guile. They hide behind an illusion, a pretence; they bring about a mishap that really masks hideous murder. It is the same with these deaths. Ask yourself what truly happened. Did Baiocis drink the poison at that meal? Ah,' he grinned, 'I see you already have suspicions about that. And the prince? If the jug of wine wasn't tainted,

228

was it something else? The cups? And those attacks on you in the forest and at Queenshithe? Use your wits, Edmund! Reflect. Who knew you were going there? God did not intend you to be a dumb ox.'

On his return to the Temple, de Payens carefully recalled everything that had happened, listing events whilst trying to curb his own growing disquiet. He dared not confide in anyone. Indeed, Berrington and his sister were often absent at Westminster, whilst Mayele had been dispatched on business here and there. Berrington was keen to collect all monies and rents due to the Temple exchequer, and Mayele's task was to journey to the various holdings to remind the bailiffs of their obligations and demand immediate payment. On one matter de Payens agreed with Berrington and Mayele. Two serjeants had been killed at Queenshithe, and the remainder were needed elsewhere, so Berrington hired a comitatus of mercenaries, hard-bitten veterans, to serve as Mayele's escort.

The days passed. Candlemas came and went, and on the morrow of the great feast, Hastang and his retinue of burly city bailiffs swept into the Temple. Berrington and Isabella had gone to join the court at Baynard's Castle, whilst Parmenio had yet again disappeared on one of his mysterious errands. The coroner, cowled and muffled against the biting cold, whispered how that was just as well, and would de Payens accompany him? The Templar immediately agreed, even though the coroner remained tight-lipped about their destination. He asked de Payens not to wear any Templar insignia, offering the heavy brown cloak worn by the rest of his retinue. De Payens put this on, pulling the hood over his head, and they left the Temple precincts, hurrying along the murky lanes down to the riverside. The sharp breeze made de Payens flinch; though his leg wound had healed, he limped slightly. He glanced up: the rib of sky between the overhanging buildings was a dull grey. For a brief while he pined for the sun and heat of Outremer, his home for the last twenty-six years, yet at the same time he was elated at the feeling of being close to a friend, a comrade he truly trusted. He felt as if he had come home, no longer the obedient servant sent here and there with little or no explanation offered. Yet he must remember that this place too was dangerous. London was a trap, and in the shadows lurked his enemies.

The light was fading. Lamps glowed from hooks on doorposts as well as huge poles erected at the entrance to certain streets. Chains were being stretched across to prevent horsemen and carts clattering through. Church bells chimed the hour of evening prayer. Beacon flames flickered in the huge lantern horns set up in steeples. Stalls had been taken down, goods packed and stored away. Dung carts collected the rubbish, the rakers and street scavengers attacking the sprawling heaps of refuse. Shutters clattered closed. Doors slammed. Here and there a voice called. Incense from a church floated across to mingle with the fading odours from the cook-shops, pie stalls and makeshift grills of itinerant traders.

Bailiffs and beadles poured buckets of freezing water over those in the stocks to clean their filth before releasing them with a spate of curses. Half-opened tavern doors provided shafts of light and warmth. Around these, desperate beggars clustered for a crust or a piece of meat. Nobody accosted the coroner and his group as they swept along the alleyways. Hastang was very well known, while his retinue, armed with mace, club and sword, was protection enough.

They passed under the dark mass of Baynard's Castle, turning into an alleyway leading down to the quayside, the cold breeze heavy with the smell of salt, fish and tar. Hastang abruptly stopped and knocked at a shop door, above which hung the gaudy sign of a ship's chandler. The door opened, and the owner, displaying the guild insignia, ushered them across the sweet-smelling shop and up some stairs into the solar, where his wife and children clustered around a table. The merchant ignored his family, leading the coroner's group across to the shuttered window. He opened this slightly, and Hastang gently pushed de Payens forward so that he could peer through the gap down into the street below. He whispered at the Templar to watch the doorway of the tavern opposite, a spacious three-storey building that rejoiced in the name of the Prospect of Heaven.

'The Genoese has been there for some time,' the chandler murmured. 'I know he hasn't left. Gilbert, my apprentice, is still within. He's been there for at least an hour.'

De Payens secretly marvelled at the coroner's cunning. He needed no legion of spies; just tradesmen, craft and guild members who knew the streets and who could recognise a stranger, especially one whose description had been given them. Hastang was determined to discover who Parmenio truly was and what he was about. They waited. The chandler's wife took her children up to the bedchamber. In the street below, shadows slunk in and out of the light. Cats squealed. A large sow, broken loose from its lead, charged down the street, pursued by a butcher and his dogs. A horse-drawn hurdle, some malefactor lashed to it, trundled by. The tavern door became busy, then Parmenio stepped into the light. He paused, glanced furtively around and slipped into the darkness. A short while later, Gilbert the apprentice darted across the street and into his master's house. He ran breathless up the stairs and slumped on a stool, gabbling about what he had seen. De Payens could not understand his tongue, but he passed the boy a coin. Hastang heard him out, then led the Templar away.

'Apparently Parmenio was with a Venetian. Gilbert later made enquiries. A carrack from that city lies at Queenshithe and will leave on the morning tide. Parmenio and his guest sat in a corner; chancery pouches were exchanged. The Genoese seemed disappointed, worried, but what they were talking about,' Hastang pulled a face, 'we do not know.'

'Venetian?'

'They own the swiftest ships, Edmund; they do business with the ports of Tripoli and elsewhere. It's not the first time Parmenio has met such strangers. Someone from Outremer is definitely sending him messages and he is replying, but why?' The coroner turned away. He thanked the chandler and led de Payens downstairs and out into the darkness. Instead of taking him back up into the City, he led his retinue through a tangle of stinking alleyways and runnels, nothing more than murky tunnels, bereft of any light except the solitary chink or glimmer from a shutter, or someone armed with a hooded candle or lantern horn darting across the street in front of them. De Payens, one hand on his sword hilt, the other pinching his nostrils at the stench, glimpsed the occasional figure lurking in the mouth of an alleyway, only to disappear deeper into the murk. A door opened. Women carrying a funeral bier, the corpse on top covered by a shabby shroud, came out and hastened past them into the night. Abruptly a voice called through the darkness.

'Hastang and his bailiffs! They come, they come!'

'On your guard!'

'On your watch.' Other voices echoed eerily through the blackness.

'Night-watchers,' Hastang whispered.

Abruptly a door crashed open as a slattern came out to empty a pot. De Payens glimpsed inside and startled with surprise. Only a glance before the door was slammed shut, but it revealed a great feast being held:

tables arranged in a square and laden with platters of steaming meats, bowls of fruit, jugs, flagons and goblets. The scene was lit by a host of flaring candles. Men and women, all garbed in garish clothes, sat around eating and drinking, their goblets raised in toast to a white-clad man in the centre, his black hair wreathed with a holly crown.

'A beggars' banquet,' Hastang whispered. 'Our city holds stranger sights.'

They cleared the alleyways and reached a stretch of wasteland, silverish in the light of the moon. Far across it a lantern winked high in the air like a beacon light.

'More of my men,' Hastang declared. 'They are guarding what's been found. You must see it, Edmund. I am sure it's Walkyn's work.'

They walked across the wasteland. Here and there de Payens glimpsed the ruins of houses. Hastang explained how a fire, followed by an attack on London during the recent troubles, had laid waste this quarter north of Watling. It was a truly ghostly place: gaunt trees, branches stark and stripped of all leaves, wiry gorse and unseen dips and potholes. When the breeze shifted the mist, de Payens glimpsed the derelict church they were approaching. Owls hooted, the brooding silence broken as a ghost-winged bird came floating over the gorse, hunting for vermin, which scurried in panic through the bracken. A church bell deep in the city began to clang, as if tolling a warning.

'St Blaise on the Heathland,' Hastang murmured.

They crossed the tumbled cemetery wall, as the lych-gate had collapsed, blocking the entrance to God's Acre. A torch flared in its makeshift sconce on the door jamb leading into the nave. The baptismal font had been removed, as had the tiles on the floor, together with the wooden furnishings such as the rood screen, aumbries and even the pulpit. Some of Hastang's men waited in the chancel. They'd fashioned rough torches and pushed these into cracks and crevices, and the juddering light made the shadows dance even more, as if lighting entry to a hall of ghosts. At the coroner's approach, the men clambered to their feet from around the makeshift fire where the altar had once stood.

'No one has moved it?' barked Hastang as he strode down the nave.

'No, sir,' one of the men called back.

Hastang nodded and led de Payens off into the little sacristy to the left. A corpse lay under a makeshift shroud. At the head and feet glowed a lantern horn. De Payens caught his breath. Hastang knelt and peeled back the cloth to reveal a young woman perhaps no more than fourteen or fifteen summers old, her naked corpse a dirty white, coated and smeared with dried blood. Mercifully her long black hair hid her ravaged face, but the rest of the horror was plain to see: her throat had been slit, her chest ripped open and her heart plucked out. De Payens had seen enough and turned away, retching. He tried to murmur a prayer against such horror, the work of lost, damned souls.

'Taken, she was.' Hastang stood beside him. 'Taken from the streets. Some poor wench; not the first, Edmund, to be seized and butchered. A pedlar found her corpse and hurried to tell me. She is not some harlot attacked for pleasure, and as I've said, she's not the first. This is the work of witches and warlocks: a mutilated corpse stretched out in a deserted church.'

'You are sure she was part of some black rite, the work of Walkyn?'

'I suspect so.' The coroner tapped his foot. 'Such bloody business must be brought to an end, Edmund. We need firm rule here. The king must impose his peace. The chaos, the evil mayhem that is a violent cover for such nightmare souls must be brought to an end.' He peered at de Payens. 'Templar, you keep strange company. What is all this about, eh? Think, reflect and trust me.'

De Payens' hand went to his throat, and he touched the small leather pouch containing the cipher of the Assassins. He stared at Hastang, at that lined face with its honest, clever eyes. He wanted to trust this man fully. He must. He took the cord off, undid the pouch, shook out the parchment and handed it to Hastang. 'It's a cipher,' he explained.

The coroner inspected it as he walked out of the sacristy and back into the sanctuary, while de Payens stood staring down the nave: a hellish, macabre place of flickering light. Did this represent his church, his ideals, his order? He thought back to that day in Tripoli, turning his horse to confront those assassins; at that particular moment he had entered a bizarre twisting maze of intrigue and brutal murder. All was an illusion. He had suspected Tremelai of every kind of wickedness. Yet the Grand Master had simply been an arrogant fool who intrigued and dabbled in matters beyond him. Memories returned in a myriad of images: Mayele loosing those arrows; Parmenio stealing upon him with a knife; Isabella's kindness; Berrington, the hard-faced administrator who seemed to revel in power; Nisam staring at him sadly; Montebard, brow all furrowed; Baiocis clutching his stomach at the beginning of the feast; the prince's chamber with the windows wide open; Parmenio's duplicity; the coroner's questions . . .

'Letters and numbers.' Hastang came up beside him. 'Letters and numbers.' He squeezed de Payens' shoulder. 'I can make no sense of it, and neither would you, Edmund.' He winked. 'But I know some clerks – aged, yes, but still sharp-witted – scribes of the Chancery, who spend their days concocting mysteries like this. If you trust me?'

De Payens nodded.

'Good,' Hastang breathed. 'Then let's leave this. I'll make sure the poor wench is churched and buried properly. As for you, Edmund, look to your companions, Parmenio in particular.' He held up the parchment. 'I'll see to this. Now, I have one last person for you to meet. Bring him out,' he shouted.

# Chapter 11

De Mandeville plunged the entire realm into
turmoil, spreading cruelty everywhere and
respecting neither sex nor rank.

From the darkness to the right of the chapel door shuffled a figure. Two of the coroner's retainers, keeping
their distance, flanked him with swords and daggers
drawn. The figure was garbed in black like a Benedictine
monk; a white cloth covered his face, with holes for eyes,
nose and mouth. He walked in an ungainly manner,
using a staff to support himself but de Payens caught
his strength, power and presence. He walked towards

them, staff tapping the ground, an ominous, almost threatening sound.

'So, a Templar here in London!' The voice was surprisingly light and courteous in tone. 'I see you are surprised, Templar. Once I was a knight of the order of St Lazarus? You know it?'

'Fierce fighters,' de Payens retorted. 'Knights who contracted leprosy. Some were infected, others almost cured. In battle they had nothing to lose and everything to gain.'

'Which is my case,' the stranger replied. 'Once, Templar, I was fair, a passionate lover of women. I have fought out in the hot desert where the sun splits the rocks. I have ridden through Jerusalem like a prince. In my pride I broke my vows and slept with a woman who carried a curse, but my story is my own, the song of my soul. Suffice to say I returned here cured.' He laughed, 'But too late. My face frightens all. I am still excluded from the company of men.'

'Who are you?'

'So Master Hastang hasn't told you?' The stranger chuckled. 'I am the Hunter of the Dead, the Keeper of the Corpses, the Leper Knight. In the hours of darkness, when the city sleeps, I float my barge out on to the river. I seek corpses in the shallows, among the reed beds and along the mud flats. I know the river, a fickle, cruel mistress. I discover where she leaves her dead, all pale, cold and green-slimed. I collect them for the City council and take them to my tabernacle, the little

239

chapel of St Lazarus down near the great bridge. I wash, purify and anoint them. I post my bills. Two pence for a suicide. Three pence for a victim of an accident. Five pence for a killing or an unlawful slaying.'

'Are you trying to frighten my guest?' Hastang teased.

'Frighten?' The Keeper of the Corpses sighed so deeply the white cloth on his face moved. For just a heartbeat de Payens glimpsed the bottom of a cruelly ravaged face. 'Frighten? How could I frighten a Templar, the great champion and victor of Queenshithe?' The Keeper tapped his staff on the ground. 'No, I do not frighten him. I don't think I could. Anyway, he will come to worse things by and by.'

'Tell him,' Hastang insisted, 'tell him what you know.'

The Keeper moved closer, resting on his staff. De Payens caught a sweet odour from the man's cloak, some fresh herbs pleasing to the senses.

'As I said, I haunt the river on my barge,' the Keeper began, 'a lantern in the prow, another in the stern. Many know me and just pass me by. I see sights that do not concern me. Royal barges going from Westminster to the Tower and back. Smugglers edging out of the wharfs and quays. Young noblemen, hot and lecherous as sparrows, darting across to the stews, bath-houses and brothels of Southwark. Even spies slipping down the side of foreign ships to boats waiting below.' He paused as Hastang gestured at his two bailiffs to join the rest, still grouped by the fire in the chancel.

'I know the river,' the Keeper continued. 'I drag out

a corpse and can tell you how the unfortunate died: a blow to the head, a blade to the belly, throat or back. Recently, some fresh horror. The corpses of young women, drained of blood, their rib cages smashed, their hearts plucked out, throats slit, white and cold like some hunk of pork hung above a flesher's barrow until all the blood has emptied.'

'How many times?'

'Twice; I believe you've seen the same here tonight.' The Keeper pointed with his staff further up the church. 'But I've also seen more. One night just before Candlemas, the river was smooth, the breeze had dropped. I was off Queenshithe and moved into midstream. A powerful wherry with at least six oars appeared out of the mist. Sometimes evil is like curling smoke: it can offend your soul and chill your heart. I immediately became fearful. The wherry was moving fast, all six rowers, capuchined and masked, bending over the oars. A figure stood in the prow, face hidden. I turned my barge swiftly, and as I did, the light from the powerful lantern horn on the prow revealed two young women, bound and gagged, lying in the stern of that wherry. It was like when lightning flashes, cutting through the darkness, revealing something as if in a burst of sunlight. I glimpsed the sheer terror in those women's eyes. I saw the gags, the cords around their wrists and ankles. God forgive me, Templar, I could do nothing. The wherry went by me, disappearing into the darkness.'

241

'But such kidnappings are common, surely?'

'No, they are not!' Hastang came forward. 'Edmund, you can buy a plump girl for a penny in this city, a full household of them for half a mark. London has more whores than citizens. Why move two young women in the dead of night? I could fill a royal barge with young strumpets all jubilant at earning a crust. Why the silence, the terror, the gags? And where were they going?' He turned to the Keeper.

'Not to Southwark; the wherry was in midstream, as if heading out to the lonely mud flats of the estuary.' The Keeper tapped his staff on the floor. 'I believe I met murder, mayhem, sacrilege and every form of abomination that night. I called it the devil's barge. I have not seen its like on the river!' He stepped back. 'I told my dear comrade Hastang, and he brought me here to view the horror found in the chancel. It's the same as before.'

'And there's something else, isn't there?' Hastang insisted. 'You told me about Berrington.'

'Ah, Berrington!'

'You know him?' de Payens asked sharply.

'I know a great deal about what happens in the City. I have my spies, and the coroner here often shares a cup of claret with me. I've heard of Berrington.' The Keeper grasped his staff with both hands, leaning on it as if favouring some wound in his leg. 'I too fought with Mandeville, the great Earl of Essex, out in the wetlands. Many men flocked to his standard, devils in human flesh. Berrington was not one of those. I never met him, but I heard of his name, someone whom Mandeville did not like: a knight who objected to the plundering of churches and the occupation of monasteries. His name is familiar because of that, nothing more. You must remember that hundreds, aye even thousands, flocked to Mandeville's banner!'

'And Mayele?' de Payens asked.

The Keeper just shook his head.

'Another name amongst many.'

'And Parmenio?' Hastang said. 'I mentioned his name and you recalled something.'

'Ah yes, Thierry Parmenio, the Genoese.' The Keeper coughed, clearing his throat. 'Templar, I have travelled the face of God's earth. When I returned from Outremer, I did not come by sea. Such voyages are not for the likes of me. I travelled overland, and came to Lyons, a noble city. I lodged outside its walls and heard rumours, strange stories about a trial involving witches and sorcerers, local priests who should have had more sense than to be involved in the black rites. On the day I arrived, the executions of such miscreants were being carried out in the city. I am sure that that name, Thierry Parmenio, was mentioned as being somehow involved.' He tapped the side of his head. 'I was schooled well, Templar. I have a good memory, particularly for names. I have certainly heard of Parmenio before, but more than that I cannot say.' He sighed. 'Well, I have to be gone, but first your blessing.'

'My blessing?'

'Why not? You've knelt in the Lord's Sepulchre, yes? You've kept your vows. Your blessing, Templar; few priests will approach me.'

De Payens, slightly embarrassed, recalled the verses often used by Grandmother Eleanor. He lifted his hand. 'May the Lord bless you and protect you,' he murmured. 'May He show you His countenance and have mercy on you. May He turn His face to you and give you peace. May the Lord bless you for ever.'

The Keeper bowed. 'And now I will give you my blessing, Templar. Act justly. Love tenderly, and walk humbly with your God.' Then he was gone, disappearing into the blackness through the doorway.

Hastang and de Payens left the church, two of their escort going before them with torches. They slipped along the deserted alleyways and narrow trackways, the night hawks and dark wanderers fleeing at their approach. Only the occasional beggar whined for alms from some shabby doorway. They'd almost reached the Bishop of Lincoln's Inn when they heard the sound of the tocsin ringing from the Templar compound. De Payens hastened on to find the main gates thrown open, torches burning, serjeants, their swords drawn, patrolling the entrance. He hurried in, followed by the coroner, and glimpsed a splash of blood on the steps to the guesthouse. Inside the refectory, Mayele was nursing a cut hand, while Berrington had a bruise on his face. The infirmarian was tending to both of them. The smell of vinegar, aloes and balm hung heavy. Hastang sent three of his bailiffs up the stairs to check the guest chambers for intruders. De Payens bent down to inspect the splash of blood on the paved floor.

'Assassins.' Mayele came across. He crouched down and stirred the blood with his finger. 'Six of them.' He pointed further down the refectory, where a trestle table lay tipped, food and wine scattered about.

'Berrington and I were having our supper here. A knock at the door; I went and opened it.' He smiled in that cynical way. 'Sheer good fortune. I should have stepped on their swords, but one of them was slow. He hesitated. I did not. I slammed the door shut and shouted for Berrington. I tried to bolt the top, but they were pushing hard. Berrington arrived and tried to help. We decided to spring the same trap. We stepped back abruptly, swords drawn, and met them blade to blade.'

'Six in all.' Berrington spoke up, but paused as Isabella came into the room, face all fearful. She hurried across to her brother, who simply embraced her and whispered. She turned and thanked the servant who had accompanied her from the Bishop of Lincoln's Inn, then slumped down on a stool, blonde hair falling about her face.

'All cowled,' Berrington declared. 'City ribauds, roaring boys hired for a few pence. Two were wounded; the rest collected them, threatened us with their swords and withdrew . . .' He paused as Parmenio came up into the refectory. The Genoese, still swathed in his cloak, soon became disconcerted by Mayele's blunt questions as to where he'd been, mumbling that he'd been unwell and needed to buy medicines. The coroner, who'd been walking around noting the chaos, the sword cuts to the tables and pews, tapped the heel of his boot hard against the floor.

'This is an affair in the bailiwick of the Temple. It does not fall under my jurisdiction. Masters, my lady, I must be gone. Edmund?'

De Payens followed him out into the darkness. Hastang stopped and glanced over the Templar's shoulder.

'Be alert, Edmund! Tomorrow, try to discover how those assassins gained entry and left. In the meantime . . .' And the coroner sauntered off, humming the tune of his favourite hymn: '*O puella vera et pulchra*'.

De Payens returned to the refectory, where Parmenio had righted the table stools. Berrington dismissed the serjeants and bolted the door behind them. He leaned against it and gestured at the table.

'Let's eat, drink, reflect and decide. We cannot stay here where Walkyn, God curse him, can lurk in the runnels and alleyways to plot his attacks.'

'So what do you propose?' de Payens asked.

'Draw him out!' Mayele banged his goblet on the table. 'Leave London. Let's go where the malignant came from, the manor of Borley in Essex. Edmund, you've recovered; the worst of the winter is over. Where we go, I am sure Walkyn will follow.'

De Payens glanced at Parmenio, who nodded his head. Berrington also seemed in agreement.

'It's logical, feasible,' he murmured. 'The king is leaving London for Dover. As regards Walkyn, we are making no progress here. We have finished our outstanding Templar business in London. Isabella and I must settle certain family matters. So, we'll move to Borley, and then,' he smiled, 'we must return to our family manor at Bruer in Lincolnshire.'

Agreement was reached. De Payens made his good nights and returned to his own chamber. He felt a biting anxiety. Hastang's words about studying everything carefully created deeper suspicions, especially about Parmenio's mysterious errands. Moreover, once again they were going to tramp along muddy trackways to some bleak manor house. He stared at the crucifix on the wall and, not for the first time, reflected on his vows and his life as a Templar. Agitated by such thoughts, he undressed, took his small, battered psalter, a legacy from Lord Hugh, from his saddle bag and knelt on the hard floor. He stroked the calfskin cover, tracing the silver-embossed cross, which was gradually fading. The pages inside were yellowing, black and greasy, well thumbed. He moved closer into the glow of candlelight and opened the book to the compline of the day. He chanted aloud the first line of the psalm: 'The Lord turns his face against the wicked, to destroy their remembrance from the earth . . .'

'Does he?' whispered de Payens, recalling the gruesome corpse of that young woman, the revelations of the Hunter of the Dead. He stifled his doubts and tried to read, even as his mind drifted back to that sombre sacristy and the dreadful corpse it held.

The next morning de Payens woke early. He attended the Jesus mass, meditated for a while, then broke his fast in the buttery, where the cooks were serving bowls of oatmeal laced with milk and nutmeg, followed by white loaves smeared with butter and honey. He drank a stoup of watered ale, then wandered out to stand in the cobbled yard. A servitor, armed with a bucket and cloth, was washing the bloodstains from the steps of the guesthouse. De Payens walked over, nodded at the man, then followed the trace of blood out across the yard. He stopped abruptly. He could find no further bloodstains between the inner courtyard and the curtain wall. Mystified, he searched about until he heard his name called. A serjeant hurried over, his breath clear in the ice-cold air.

'Domine, there's a woman at the gate asking to meet you and you alone.'

De Payens followed him out under the gatehouse. The woman the serjeant pointed out was standing close to the stall of an enterprising pedlar, who'd set up shop near the curtain wall selling spools, thimbles, needles, pins and thread. She was bartering over a silver-chased thimble. She paid and turned as de Payens approached, a pale, lovely face, jet-black hair tightly braided with red-gold cord. Earrings glittered from her lobes, a silver torque circled her slim throat, bracelets clinked as she moved her hands. The hood and cloak she wore was of dark-blue wool lined with vair. She spoke swiftly in English, then smiled in apology.

'*Mon seigneur*,' she lapsed into Norman French, 'if you follow me, I will talk about Walkyn.' She glimpsed the alarm in his eyes. 'I am not taking you to Queenshithe,' she whispered. 'Yes, I've heard about that. No, only a short distance, a tavern in Paternoster Alleyway, the Lady of the Sun.' She shrugged. 'I shall be there until the Angelus bell. Well, sir?' She gently tapped him on the chest. 'Perhaps you wish to collect your sword belt. However, I will speak only to you.

'Why?'

'You are the one hunting Walkyn? Yes? The Genoese? The others?' She shrugged prettily. 'I listen to the gossip. The Genoese is elusive. Your companions, well, they are English knights; they may have fought with Walkyn. Moreover,' she gestured back at the Temple, 'your servants watch. They say you are an honest man, though lonely. Can you not spare me a little time? I shall be at the tavern. My name is Alienora.' She walked away, her elegant high-soled shoes tapping the cobbles.

De Payens closed his eyes, whispered a prayer for protection, then hastened back up to his chamber. He strapped on his sword belt, swung a heavy cloak about himself and hurried out of the Temple. He knew Paternoster Alleyway; it was only a short distance, a place reputed to house the better sort. He pushed his way through the throng, knocking away beggars, drunks, the importunate apprentices with their mantles lined with dormouse fur. Fishwives offered mullet, lampreys, mackerel, herring and lobster. Traders bawled how they had sauce dishes, salt cellars, candlesticks, baskets, basins and cups for sale. A beadle stood on a cart, loudly proclaiming that charcoal was not to be bought to be stored or produce sold that had not paid the market toll. A busy, bell-filled morning, with the cookshops and bakeries offering pies and eel, chopped ham, cheese and garlic; a swirl of colour and a tangle of smells from the foul to the sweetest of beeswax.

The Templar reached Paternoster. He walked warily, as the alleyway was paved at an angle either side of a narrow sewer, which cut through the middle. Even at that early hour the runnel was crammed with stinking filth, which the scavengers were covering with shovel- fuls of acrid saltpetre. He reached the double doors leading into the Lady of the Sun, and entered the broad dining hall, its floor coated with rushes, its narrow windows and white-plastered walls draped with red and green cloths.

'A cup of raisin wine?' The tavern master waddled across wiping podgy fingers on an apron. He spoke Norman French fluently, his small sharp eyes taking in de Payens' cloak and sword. 'Raisin wine has the clarity of the tears of a penitent,' he proclaimed. 'It strikes like lightning, and is tastier than almonds; it makes you quick as a squirrel, frisky as a kid at milk.'

'Alienora?' de Payens demanded.

Mine host bowed, hands sweeping towards the stairs.

'Follow me, sir.'

The chamber de Payens entered was spacious, its beams painted a smart black and decorated with coloured signs of the zodiac; the cream-plastered walls were clean and hung with cloths. One small casement window stood open; the other was shielded by a thick yellow cloth. The chamber held some elegant furniture; thick woollen rugs covered the floor, whilst it was well lit by candelabra. Alienora was sitting on the bed, draped in a coverlet of marten's fur embroidered with birds, beasts and flowers. On a stool next to her stood a gilded birdcage with a linnet on a perch. She was feeding the bird morsels from a dish; she finished this and rose as mine host closed the door behind de Payens after loudly announcing: 'A grand and noble visitor.'

'Are you noble, Dominus de Payens?' She smiled.

A funeral horn brayed from the alleyway below. Alienora crossed to the open window, beckoning him to stand next to her. Her mittened hands clasped a bowl of smouldering charcoal as she stared down at the funeral procession below.

'A knight.' She pointed to the riderless horse, all saddled and harnessed, the dead man's helmet, shield and war belt hanging from the saddle horn. Behind the destrier walked a priest carrying a stoup of holy water, accompanied by thurifers with their smoky censers and acolytes carrying candles and crosses. The mourners processed next, all swathed in black, each holding a green bough, softly chanting the psalms for the dead.

251

'*In media vitae sumus in morte,*' Alienora whispered.

'I do not know if I am noble,' de Payens retorted, 'but life is certainly two-edged, and death is part of it. My lady, you asked to see me about the outlaw Walkyn?'

'The outlaw Walkyn?' She laughed. 'Domine, I'm a courtesan, the daughter of a good family. In my green days I was closeted in a convent as a novice until, well . . .' She shrugged. 'Each soul has its own story. Now I live here, Templar. I know the world of men. I recognise the souls of my visitors. I entertain priests, clerics, yes, even Templars, including Henry Walkyn, lord of the manor of Borley in the king's shire of Essex. Walkyn was a tortured man, a Templar who fought the lusts of the flesh. He often failed, which is why he visited me in the weeks before he took ship to foreign parts.'

'And?'

'A warlock?' she mocked, passing the bowl for de Payens to warm his fingers. 'A sorcerer, a wizard? Is this the same man?' Her voice rose. 'Nonsense! Walkyn was nothing but a man torn by fleshly appetites.'

She smiled at de Payens as he handed back the bowl. He looked out of the window; a shadow across the street darted back into the mouth of a runnel. Alienora went to sit on the edge of the bed, gesturing at de Payens to do likewise. He sat down, blushing with embarrassment as his sword became entangled with the folds of the coverlet. He stood up to unbuckle his belt. A knock on the door startled him.

'Mistress,' boomed the voice of mine host. 'Some wine?'

'Wait . . .' She walked across.

De Payens recalled that shadow across the street, the empty taproom below. He'd not asked for wine!

'No, stop!' He flung himself down.

The door crashed back. Two figures, hooded and masked, hurtled in. They knelt and released the catches on their crossbows. Both bolts struck Alienora, one in the chest, the other shattering her face. De Payens scrambled for his sword belt and glanced up. Both felons had fled. He jumped to his feet and followed. Alienora was unrecognisable, killed instantly, her face a mass of pumping blood, shattered bone and ripped skin. One eye socket hung empty. He turned away, reached the door and raced down the blood-soaked stairs. The killers had shown no mercy. Throat slashed, the taverner lay jerking, eyes popping, halfway down. The taproom was still deserted. De Payens glimpsed frightened faces, like those of a host of ghosts, peering through the half-open door to the kitchen. He ran out into the street. Already passers-by were pausing to stare at the tavern entrance. He whirled to the left and right. He could see no assailant, no black-garbed assassin.

'Did you . . .' he shouted at a tinker, then paused. The man could not understand his tongue. He resheathed his sword and returned to the tavern, entering the sweet-smelling kitchen with its fleshing table, its pots bubbling merrily over the fire; beside this the half-open doors of the oven, from which a batch of freshly baked loaves peeked. Cooks, scullions, spit boys and maids crouched terrified. Eventually de Payens found one who understood him, and dispatched her to the Guildhall with an urgent summons for Coroner Hastang. Then he waited in the taproom, guarding the door, until the coroner and his posse of bailiffs arrived. They inspected the corpses. De Payens explained what had happened. He felt weary, sick at heart; he made no attempt to hide his mood. The coroner grasped him by the shoulder.

'Edmund,' he whispered, 'Edmund, either attack or retreat.'

'What do you mean?'

'Well, you could leave for Outremer tomorrow or the day after.'

'Or?'

'Who in your company acts suspiciously? Someone followed you here.'

De Payens reflected on his own disquiet. A nightmare possibility he'd glimpsed but rejected: that Parmenio might be his mortal enemy, a true wolf deep in the sheep fold.

'Retreat,' Hastang repeated, 'or attack. You must choose! As for your cipher.' He pushed his face even closer. 'You tried to translate it. The numbers stand for letters, undoubtedly.' He smiled.

'Norman French?'

'Oh no.' The coroner shook his head. 'I showed it to a cipher clerk in the Chancery who now spends his days as a pensioner at the hospital of St Bartholomew in

Smithfield. He says it is composed of at least three languages, one of them definitely Latin.' He stepped back and looked down at the two mangled corpses being laid out on biers and covered with cloths. 'There's nothing you can do here. I shall rule that these two unfortunates met their deaths other than naturally at the hands of unknown assassins.'

De Payens thanked Hastang, then informed him about his imminent departure to Borley. The coroner pursed his lips.

'The devil's country,' he murmured, waving his hand. 'The prowling place and constant haunt of that old demon Sir Geoffrey de Mandeville. Oh yes, I've heard the stories.' He extended a hand. 'Be prudent. Take care. I shall see you before you leave.'

De Payens returned to the Templar enclosure. Berrington and Mayele had journeyed to Westminster to take their official leave of both king and court. De Payens went around to the Templar church and knelt before an ancient wooden statue of the Virgin and Child, allegedly carved out of wood from one of the trees in the garden of Gethsemane. He placed a winter rose at the base of the statue and knelt back staring at the candles as his mind drifted back to his meeting with Alienora: her memories of Walkyn, those assassins bursting in. Why hadn't they attacked her before? He answered his own question: because they hadn't realised what she wanted, that meeting with him? He felt a stab of fear. Was it Alienora who was meant to die, or him, or both? Had the assassins been waiting for them to meet? Their deaths could have been explained away as a Templar and a courtesan being caught by a jealous rival. He stared around the church. The smell of incense was faint; the glow of candles provided a little heat. He had sworn his oath as a Templar in a holy place like this; he had vowed to take the cross forward. So what should he do – attack or retreat?

He murmured an ave, got to his feet and inspected the hour candle on its stand near a vivid wall painting depicting Christ's visit to Hades. Yes, he had time. He hurried out to the barbican, the weapons store, and asked the serjeant for a crossbow and a quiver of bolts. He checked these, returned to the church and placed them on the floor close to a wall painting of St Christopher. He then brought down his war belt, looped it over a bench just near the entrance and waited. Parmenio, to whom he'd sent a message, arrived almost immediately, pushing open the door and stepping cautiously into the darkened church. De Payens smiled. Parmenio was wary, one hand resting on the hilt of his dagger; he deliberately kept in the shadows. De Payens quietly picked up the primed arbalest.

'Edmund? Edmund?'

'Here.'

Parmenio whirled around. De Payens moved swiftly to the door, pulling across the bolts at top and bottom.

'Edmund, for the love of God.'

'Undo your sword belt.' De Payens walked forward,

the arbalest lowered. 'We first met in a church. We may well part in a church!'

'What do you mean?'

'Your death, perhaps.'

'Why, Edmund? What is this?'

'You are a creature of the night.' De Payens strove to curb his temper. 'Do you see yourself as a hawk, Parmenio, gliding over the meadow, whilst I, like some wary rabbit, scuttle from one bush to the next, fearful of your shadow, the plunging talons?'

'Edmund?' Parmenio took a step forward.

'Stay!' De Payens didn't flinch. He was surprised at his own anger and frustration. 'Alienora – you know she is dead?'

'Yes, I saw you meet, but there again, so might others have done. Rumour flits like a bird along the alleyways. I went to investigate myself. I saw you and Hastang.' Parmenio's voice faltered. 'Edmund, please, put down the arbalest. I am not your enemy.'

'You tried to kill me in Tripoli. I am sure it was you who loosed a crossbow bolt at me outside Ascalon; it must have been. Mayele was alongside me. Who else could it have been?'

'In Tripoli I was mistaken. Outside Ascalon I was trying to alert you.'

'You almost killed me.'

'No. If I'd wanted it to, that bolt would have crushed your skull. I wanted to alarm you, alert you and awake you.'

'To what?'

'To the danger all around you, be it Tremelai or anyone else: Walkyn, his coven.' Parmenio smiled thinly. 'I succeeded. You are a most dangerous man, Edmund de Payens. You are an idealist, a visionary. You thought the world was the stuff of your dreams when in truth it's the work of the bleakest nightmare. I think you now realise that. Your order is changing. It is no longer a legion of pure, simple knights, but men doing business with the lord of this world. There's nothing more dangerous than an idealist who's wakened to the harsh reality of life.'

'And that includes you, meeting visitors from Venice and elsewhere. Strangers who slink into London to consort with you in the shadowy corners of taverns?'

'Ah well.' Parmenio stretched out his hands. 'Lower the arbalest, Edmund, and let me show you something.' He sighed as de Payens just gazed bleakly back at him. The Genoese undid his doublet, fished beneath and drew out a folded piece of parchment from a secret pocket in the padded lining.

'Put it on the floor,' de Payens ordered, 'along with your war belt. Then take three paces back and kneel with your arms crossed.'

# Chapter 12

The realm of England was in this miserable
state of lawlessness.

Parmenio obeyed. De Payens hastened forward, snatched
up the parchment and withdrew. The vellum was of the
highest quality. The purple wax seal boasted the crossed
keys of the papacy, the Bishop of Rome, whilst the
elegant, cursive script proclaimed: 'Eugenius III, by
God's favour and the grace of the Holy Spirit, Servant
of the Servants of God, Bishop of Rome, Pontifex
Maximus'. The letter declared that Thierry Parmenio,
citizen of Genoa, was *legatus a latere*, the Pope's personal

envoy; *malleus Maleficorum*, the hammer of sorcerers, 'God's chosen instrument for the extirpation and destruction of warlocks, witches, sorcerers, necromancers and all who dealt in the black arts, contrary to the teaching of Holy Mother Church'.

De Payens glanced up in astonishment. Parmenio stared sadly back. De Payens re-read the papal writ; it gave Parmenio *totam potestatem in omnibus casibus* – total power in all circumstances.

'Why?' De Payens put down the arbalest. 'Why didn't you tell me?'

'Let me do so now.' The Genoese made himself comfortable. 'Edmund, I'm a clerk in the Secret Papal Chancery. I answer to the Pope alone. The Church,' he chose his words carefully, 'faces many problems; witchcraft is one of them.' He swallowed hard. 'I believe, and I shall repeat it here in the Lord's House, that what we call the black arts, the devil's Sabbath, witchcraft, is in most cases nothing more than chicanery, counterfeit, stupid mummery. Trust me, Edmund, it's nothing. Men and women hinting that they have dark powers to threaten others, or,' he laughed sharply, 'just an excuse to strip naked, drink like topers and revel in every form of filth.' He took a deep breath. 'If they want to dance naked in a moonlit glade or worship some ancient rock,' he smiled, 'what is that? Nothing really, silliness, children's games. Then, of course, there are a few who are masters of illusion or the potion. Believe me, Templar, I can give you a drink that in your mind's eye would have you flying on eagle's wings just beneath the sun.' He paused, choosing his words carefully. 'Finally there are the few, the real masters of eternal darkness. These make no boast; show no sign of who they really are. They are not clod-breakers or mummers but men and women who don masks as clever and as subtle as any. They are to be found not in the dirty hovel, the dingy garret or out on the wild heathland, but in the chancery, the priory, the abbey, the monastery, the moated manor house, the castle, the palace. They are educated and erudite, openly devoted sons and daughters of the Church. In truth they are devil-worshippers, very dangerous.'

'Why?'

'Because they really call on the dark, and use all their power and will to achieve their nefarious ends, and, to do that, they will kill. This is not a matter of dancing in the moonlight, but blasphemy, sacrilege and murder. They truly believe that if they kill a human being, slit their victim's throat as you would a pig's, pluck out the heart, offering it to the powers of darkness, there will be a response.'

'And is there?'

'As the old proverb says: "When you call into the darkness, something, someone always replies."'

'And you hunt them down and arrest them?'

'No, Edmund, I hunt them down and I kill them. They are finished. There is no turning, no repentance. The only thing I can do is send them to God for judgement.'

'And here?'

Parmenio pursed his lips. 'I have been to England before, you probably realise that. This island is a haunt of sorcery. They say that William the Red, King of England, was caught up in such witchcraft and was murdered whilst hunting in the New Forest. Or William, son of the great Henry I: he was drowned when the royal cog, the *White Ship*, was wrecked; his death caused the present war and the rise of men like Mandeville. Rumour has it that the shipwreck was caused by witchcraft.'

'Was Mandeville a sorcerer?'

'No, I don't think so, but he was their protector. He plundered monasteries and abbeys for their wealth and used them as his strongholds. The real practitioners of the black arts were given their opportunity to use and abuse the sacred. Mandeville attracted these souls of deepest darkness to his company. They could hide behind his shield and carry out their abominations. You've seen what they can do in all its horror. Who cares if a young peasant woman goes missing? Who would dare investigate deserted, desecrated churches flaming with light at the dead of night?'

'Yet you went first to Outremer, not England?'

'I was sent there, Edmund, for the same reasons. Over fifty years ago, your great-uncle and others stormed Jerusalem and took it. After centuries of loss they regained all the Holy Places of Christendom. The devout and the pious flocked to worship there.'

'And so did others?'

'Oh yes, they did. Jerusalem, the Holy Land, with its sacred sites and Holy Places, attracts both angels and demons. Rumours began to gather. The Pope received letters from the patriarch and others about witchcraft and sorcery being rife in Jerusalem. I was sent to investigate. I arrived too late. Tremelai, for God knows what reason, had moved swiftly. Erictho the witch, about whom I'd heard, had escaped. Then Walkyn was arrested and committed to Berrington to be brought to England. In the meantime, Boso Baiocis had been summoned from London.'

'For what reason?'

'Tremelai was deeply concerned about the Templars protecting Mandeville's unconsecrated corpse, as well as the reception of characters like Walkyn into the order.' Parmenio pulled a face. 'I have spoken in confidence with Berrington: the records about recruits to the English bailiwick are very sparse.'

'And Baiocis was responsible for that?'

'Yes, he either pruned the records to cover his own stupidity or he brought them to Outremer, where,' Parmenio shrugged, 'they were lost or stolen.'

'And in Outremer?'

'I protected you in Ascalon, Edmund. I thought you'd come to trust me, but there again, why should you? To be honest, I never trusted you. Members of the coven are clever, they hide. They act one way in the light and become another creature after dark. I suppose I'm no different. I'm a master of tongues. I act in disguise, I

263

pretend. I can mingle with the worst and gossip with the best. Anyway, my spies in Tripoli talked of assassins being gathered by a mysterious Frankish knight, perhaps a Templar. I heard about Walkyn's escape.' He stared down the church. 'The shadows are leaving their corners, Edmund, we must be careful.'

De Payens glanced at the arbalest, still primed, lying beside him. Parmenio followed his gaze.

'Edmund, I'm no killer, no assassin. I went to Tripoli. I searched and I failed. Count Raymond was murdered. As for the massacre and looting that followed, I did wonder if there was a reason for that. Perhaps I ignored the obvious. Count Raymond was killed to create confusion and chaos, an excuse to loot and plunder.' He shook his head. 'I don't know. Anyway, I fled to that Greek church. I saw you, a Templar, astride your horse, gazing bleakly out. I'd just come from a house where a young woman had her throat cut and her baby's head dashed against the wall. My anger welled over. I thought you were involved in similar butchery; of course you were not. Such confusion was deliberately plotted. As for the rest,' he spread his hands, 'Tremelai had to trust me. I showed him my commission; he had no choice. He believed that Walkyn had a hand in Count Raymond's murder and that the plunder the renegade Templar had looted in Tripoli would be used for his return to England. The Grand Master had one hope . . .'

'About a Templar possibly sheltering in Ascalon?'

'Of course; one of the reasons why he was so ardent in his support for the assault on that city. He wondered if Walkyn, or even Berrington, who had disappeared, was still in Ascalon. Tremelai really believed the Temple had to put its own house in order. If he had survived Ascalon, undoubtedly we would still have been dispatched to England.'

'Why?' De Payens moved to ease the cramp in his leg. 'Why would Walkyn want to return to England?'

'It's his country, his coven lurks here. Above all, he and his kind have a deep blood feud against King Stephen, whom they hold responsible for the death of Mandeville; their protector. Really it was just a matter of coming home and settling scores.'

'And at Hedad?'

'I'd heard of a Templar visiting the Assassins. Remember, Edmund, the isolated communities of Outremer: Catholic, Orthodox, Jewish, Muslim and the rest. If a stranger appears in their midst, he is noticed. We were fortunate to survive in Ascalon. Think of Nisam and Tremelai busy collecting all the chatter and gossip of Outremer. Walkyn must have done his share of spreading the whispers in order to cause confusion, to bring the Templar order into disrepute. I listened to the chatter at Hedad. I was intrigued, but in the end, I discovered nothing.'

'And so where is Walkyn?'

'Only God knows.'

'And you will travel to Borley?'

'Of course. What choice do we have?'

De Payens rose to his feet. He leaned down and picked up the arbalest but kept it lowered. Parmenio heaved a sigh of relief, swiftly cut off as de Payens raised the crossbow.

'And the strangers you meet in taverns? Messengers from Outremer?'

Parmenio glanced behind de Payens as if studying the wall painting. The Templar watched and waited. He was sure the Genoese was telling the truth, but not all of it. Something vital was missing.

'What if,' Parmenio pursed his lips, 'what if,' he repeated, 'we are chasing shadows, Edmund? Is Walkyn really here?'

'Berrington believes he is.'

'But truly here? What if he has not left Outremer but sends messages to his coven in England whilst he lurks elsewhere.'

'And?'

'Before I left Ascalon, I asked the Grand Master and the patriarch to make careful search for Walkyn; hence the messengers.' Parmenio's voice, slightly raised, betrayed his nervousness. He stepped forward, hands outstretched. 'Edmund, I am not your enemy.'

De Payens did not respond. He studied this secretive Genoese.

'You listen to the chatter,' he murmured at last. 'You've admitted as much. So tell me, the old English Templar Trussell? He confided in me. He was growing frail but he trusted me. He died suddenly while we were at Hedad. Was his death a natural one? What do the gossips say?'

'Trussell died.' Parmenio shrugged. 'He did not like Tremelai, whilst the Grand Master hated him. Trussell was a thorn in his side. I heard a little gossip. How Trussell sickened and died within the day. Tremelai, of course, hurried him to his grave. He must have been relieved to be free of such a venerable critic.' Parmenio paused. 'But yes, Edmund, such a death, at such a time, in such circumstances, might be suspicious. You are now suspicious. Good!' He smiled thinly. 'That's why I loosed that crossbow bolt at you outside Ascalon. I wanted to rouse you. I did.' He stretched out his hand. 'Edmund, I repeat, I am not your enemy.'

'Parmenio,' de Payens clasped his hand, 'the real question is, are you my friend?'

The Genoese just smiled, bowed and walked past the Templar. He loosened the bolts on the chapel door and went outside. De Payens sat down and reflected on what he'd been told, sifting through the various strands before returning to Parmenio's question: was Walkyn truly in England, or were they hunting someone else?

De Payens became engrossed with the problem as Berrington and the others prepared to leave for Borley. They discussed Alienora's murder, but no one could offer any solution, whilst Berrington was adamant that they must continue with their own business. He was confident that Walkyn and his coven would follow them out into the countryside, where it might be easier to trap and kill them.

Four days after Alienora's murder, Coroner Hastang slipped into the Temple accompanied by a watery-eyed, winter-faced old man dressed in the blue and green garb of an inmate of St Bartholomew in Smithfield. They met in de Payens' chamber. Hastang introduced the old man, whom he virtually carried up the stairs, as Fulbert of Hythe, former Chief Clerk to the Crown in the Secret Chancery. For all his venerable ways, Fulbert was sharp as pepper, appreciative of the Rhenish wine and the platter of sweetmeats de Payens brought up from the buttery. The old man chomped toothlessly, then slurped the wine, his eyes, bright as a sparrow's, never leaving de Payens' face. While Fulbert feasted himself, Hastang gave his news.

'In civil strife, precious metal becomes rare. Well . . .' The coroner dug into his purse and took out a pure gold coin, which de Payens recognised as one minted in Jerusalem. He studied the inscription and handed it back to Hastang. 'Coins like this, silver and gold, are in the London marketplace.'

'Walkyn?' de Payens asked.

'Perhaps, and there is something else.' Hastang tapped the old man on the shoulder. 'We searched the records of the Chancery. Mayele certainly fought for Mandeville, but there's hardly any mention of Berrington.'

'So Mayele may have been one of Mandeville's henchmen, whilst Berrington . . . ?'

268

'Perhaps just a knight who fought for a while under Mandeville's banner, tired of it and left.'

'I know of you,' Fulbert interrupted, spluttering out a mouthful of sweetmeat. 'I met your uncle, Lord Hugh. Oh yes,' he chirped merrily, 'oh yes, I met them all, Godfrey of Bouillon, Bohemond . . .'

De Payens glanced at Hastang, who smiled.

'Master Fulbert was at the storming of Jerusalem some fifty years ago.'

'Nearly became a priest, I did,' Fulbert continued in a rush. 'I worked in the Chancery. I wanted to be a black monk, fat and cheery.' He paused. 'But I couldn't.' He tapped the goblet. 'Wine and a lust for women, especially plump ones, round and juicy, ripe for the squeezing.'

Hastang winked at de Payens.

'Ah well,' Fulbert sighed. 'So now we come to your cipher. Tell me more about it. When you're old, stories fill your days, one of the great riches of being alive.'

He listened, eyes closed, as de Payens described what had happened at Hedad. The old man sat rocking backwards and forwards, giving the odd grunt of agreement. When the Templar had finished, Fulbert opened his eyes and whispered to Hastang, who handed over the battered chancery pouch. Fulbert shook out its contents and handed de Payens the Assassins' script.

'Every cipher . . . my apologies, most ciphers are based on the alphabet, with a number for each letter. There are many variations. The number one can stand for A, two for B and so on. Of course these can be jumbled but still easy to translate. This cipher was both very difficult and different, because Nisam used not one but four languages: Greek, Latin, Norman French and the lingua franca. Very clever; then he jumbled the numbers!'

'Why?'

'Because he was following his own code of hospitality and fidelity, yet, Domine, I think, based on what you've told me, he had a great softness for you. He wanted to warn you whilst not betraying the confidence of others. In the end he voiced his own suspicions through that cipher but made it as difficult as possible for you to translate.'

'And so,' de Payens replied, 'if I translated it, then that would be the will of Allah?'

'Precisely. A riddle not resolved by you but through God's own favour.' Fulbert picked up a piece of parchment from his lap. 'The first sentence is in the Greek Koine, a quotation from the Acts of the Apostles. I discovered it through the word *ketra*, which means "goad". The verse is from the description of the conversion of St Paul. It reads: "Is it so hard to kick against the goad?"' He peered up. 'That, I suppose, is a reference to your own doubts and uncertainties. The second sentence, in Latin, from the poet Juvenal, was used by the great Augustine in his Sermon on the Resurrection. The guards at Christ's tomb were told to report that his body had been stolen and that he had not risen from the dead. Augustine ridiculed such a story with a question. The text goes: "*Quis custodiet ipsos custodes?* Who shall guard the guards?" The third part is a mixture of both Norman French and the lingua franca. This time it's a quotation from the Book of the Apocalypse: "Rise up and measure the Temple of God."' Fulbert stretched out and stroked de Payens' cheek gently with the icy tips of his fingers. 'Only you, Domine, will know what that means . . .'

'You are sure?'

Richard Berrington, cloaked and cowled, moved his powerful destrier a little to the left and leaned down so that de Payens could grasp his gauntleted hand.

'I'm sure, Richard.' De Payens smiled back, then nodded at Isabella, seated on a grey palfrey.

'We will miss you, Edmund.' Mayele, his face almost hidden by the broad nose-guard of his war helmet, handed the piebald standard to the captain of mercenaries and moved his horse closer. 'We'll miss you,' he repeated.

'No you won't.' De Payens grasped his brother knight's hand. 'You'll just miss mocking me.' He peered up at Berrington. 'You'll go straight to Borley – yes? Then on to your home manor at Bruer in Lincolnshire?'

Berrington nodded.

'I'll stay here with Parmenio.' De Payens gestured to where the Genoese stood in the doorway, muffled against the cold. 'I'll use Hastang to search the tenements along the river. I am sure Walkyn still lurks here. If he doesn't,

I will call off the hunt. This island, its weather! It's time I returned to Jerusalem.' He grinned. 'Our Grand Master cannot expect miracles.' He nodded at Berrington. 'But we shall meet again.'

The cavalcade left, hooves sparking the cobbles to the jingling and creak of harness and mail. Isabella lifted one gloved hand in farewell, then they were gone towards the gate, the thick morning mist boiling up around them, dark figures in the shifting grey light. De Payens listened to the fading sounds, then walked over to Parmenio.

'You'll break your fast, Edmund?'

'No. I shall retire to my own chamber. Say that I am sickly. I want no visitors, no interruptions.'

'Why have you stayed, the true reason?'

'I want to remain here and continue my hunt for Walkyn. I think I can trap him.'

'Do you trust me, Edmund?'

'As you do me.'

Parmenio bit his lip. 'For how long will we stay?'

'A few days. If you wish, you can always accompany Berrington . . .' De Payens did not finish his sentence. He glanced across the mist-strewn bailey. 'A little more time,' he murmured. 'In the meantime, I do not want to be disturbed. I have done this before, in preparation for my knighthood. I want to be alone, to fast for three days, pray, reflect and meditate.' He caught the look on Parmenio's face. 'Yes, the three-day fast. It's necessary.'

De Payens stayed in his chamber, never leaving except

272

to use the nearby garderobe or attend the dawn mass. He refused all food and visitors, including Hastang. He knelt on his prie-dieu in his narrow closet and recited the psalms. He sipped water and chewed hard bread. He murmured the words of the *Veni Creator Spiritus*, begging for help in reaching the truth, the evidence to turn the suspicions milling in his mind into facts. He asked for pen, ink horn and vellum. He listed the main events, from the attack at Tripoli to that murderous assault on himself and Alienora and the translation of the cryptic message from the Assassins. Every sign pointed to the one path he must follow, with all its consequences. Again he prayed, emptied himself of all illusions, concentrating on the problem. He lay on his bed, staring at the ceiling, now and again drifting into a fitful sleep. He'd wake, splash his face with water and study the crucifix nailed to the wall. One conclusion he could not escape.

'I acted like a child,' he whispered. 'No more than a child, suckled and left in the dark.'

On the morning of the fourth day, de Payens shaved his head, moustache and beard, then stared at his reflection in the shining disc of steel.

'A new man.' He smiled to himself. 'When I was a child,' he continued to quote St Paul, 'I did the things of a child, but now that I'm a man . . .'

He attended the Jesus mass. Afterwards he sat on the ale bench in the buttery and slowly ate a delicious bowl of oatmeal, followed by soft loaves of white bread

273

smeared with butter and honey. Then he sent a courier into the city and met with Parmenio, who, surprised by the Templar's appearance, quickly agreed that he would accompany him. He went to ask questions, but de Payens turned away.

'You still don't trust me, Edmund,' the Genoese accused.

'And you, Parmenio, have you told me everything?' De Payens turned and stood over him. 'We'll see, we'll see.'

The Templar returned to his chamber. He checked his weapons and armour. He undid the secret pocket on his war belt and took out the pure gold coins of Outremer. He put these in his wallet and sauntered down to the main gate. The usual traders thronged there, but so did strangers, dark-faced creatures from the alleyways, their pointed hoods thrown back, hanging down like loose flaps of lizard skin. De Payens deliberately walked past as if interested in the shabby stalls of the tinkers, then quickly turned and caught the glances of these men with hollow eyes and the stare of ghosts. Once his curiosity was satisfied, he returned to the Temple, where he waited for the coroner to arrive just before the Angelus bell. Hastang teased him about his monkish appearance, then listened intently as de Payens described what he wanted. The coroner heard him out and whispered his disbelief. Nevertheless, he took the gold coins de Payens pushed towards him and promised to hire a comitatus of trusted men. Once he had left, de Payens made his own preparations. He remained tight-lipped as regarded Parmenio, and kept his distance from the Genoese; it was the best way, the only way. He must rein in his anger, which was as intense against his own stupid foolishness as anyone else's.

They left the Temple four days later. Hastang led the way out of the cobbled bailey, followed by de Payens, Parmenio, six city serjeants in their blue and mustard livery and about twenty mercenaries whom Hastang had hired with the Templar's gold. These were veterans, well horsed and harnessed, with steel helmets over their chain-mail coifs, leather hauberks, sword belts draped over their saddle horns, the rest of their baggage heaped on sumpter ponies. They made their way north through the busy city, a babble of voices and a sea of shifting colour. De Payens realised that such an imposing cavalcade would be closely observed, but this did not worry him. He was about to enter the tournament. He now knew his enemy and, God willing, would ride him down. Before they left, he had attended the dawn mass; afterwards he had lit tapers before the lady altar and prayed earnestly for those unfortunates who had died, as well as others who would do so before this horror-inspired nightmare was brought to an end.

De Payens was glad to be busy, alert to everything around him. They passed the grim prison of Newgate, where a madman chattered to a corpse dangling from a scaffold. Next to him an old man and woman danced to a tune a boy piped, all anxious to earn a coin or crust.

275

They passed the haunt of prostitutes and whores, who clustered at the mouths of alleyways aptly named Love Tunnel or the Runnel of Secret Moles. Pimps in rat-skin hoods stood, thumbs in belts, keeping an eye on their charges or any potential customers. An iron cage next to the Death Man tavern housed a lunatic, who, when poked by the warder, would dance for the amusement of passers-by. A water-carrier found selling dirty produce stood clapped in the nearby stocks with a cowbell around his neck. De Payens noted all these keenly, as he'd observed the face he'd glimpsed three streets away, or the figure lurking in the shadows as they left the Temple. He glanced up and saw a man with hooded eyes like those of an owl peering down at him from an open casement of the Death Man. He was sure he'd seen that face before, but there again, what was the danger? Matters were moving to a conclusion, whilst he was closely guarded and protected by Hastang and his comitatus.

They journeyed on, only pausing when a line of mummers' carts cut across their path as the travelling troupe made its way down to one of the parish churches to stage a Passion play. The actors were all garbed ready for their performance. Herod in his bright orange wig, moustache and beard. The soldiers in their leather tunics followed a cart full of angels all clothed in dirty white with gold cords around their heads and Salome holding the dripping severed head of John the Baptist. Once the mummers had passed, the cavalcade continued through Aldgate on to the old Roman road stretching north into Essex. A cold, hard, fast ride. The fields on either side were covered in dazzling ice. A swirling silver-grey mist curled through black-branched trees heavy with glossy-feathered crows. They cantered through villages damp and dark showing the ravages of war as well as the inclement weather. Grey-skinned villagers emerged hollow-eyed, begging for food. They passed churches with their doors rent off and glimpsed plumes of dark, threatening smoke against the sky. Yet there was also a change. De Payens sensed this not just in the weather, with its first clusters of sturdy spring flowers, but in a growing peacefulness. The roads were empty of marching troops. Merchants, traders, tinkers and pilgrims were on the move. Fields were being swiftly ploughed. Carts of produce trundled along trackways. Royal messengers thundered by on sturdy horses. Taverns and inns were open and welcoming. Henry Fitzempress's peace was being proclaimed at crossroads, markets, on the steps of churches and at ancient shrines. Hastang whispered how King Stephen was sickening, even dying, whilst his surviving son William of Boulogne lay grievously ill with a leg injury, the result of a mysterious riding accident outside Canterbury. Henry Fitzempress was apparently growing stronger by the day.

They stopped the last night at a priory, the good brothers only too eager to sell food and lodgings in their guesthouse, and approached Borley late the following morning. The manor was built on a slight rise ringed by a palisade and a dry moat, the soil heaped on the inner edge. The main gate hung askew, whilst the bailey was littered with dirt and broken pots, shattered coffers and chests. Scrawny chickens pecked at the ground. Doves swooped and glided from their muck-encrusted cote. Geese strutted noisily around the slime-covered stew pond. The house itself had apparently been built on an old dwelling of stone, the foundation of which had been used as the base for a house of strong beams and thick plaster. It was now in decay. The door hung from its leather hinges, the window shutters were gone and the sloping thatched roof was rent and torn.

De Payens dismounted and went into the murky entrance hall. The rank smell and dirt-slimed walls were offensive. He suppressed a shudder. There was something about this place, a cloying horror, as if some malignancy lurked deep in its rotting darkness. Hastang and Parmenio also felt it. They didn't want to stay here, so they walked back into the fresh cold air.

'Strange,' de Payens observed, 'a deserted manor during a time of war. Surely people would flock here, peasants, outlaws?' He asked his escort to search the outlying buildings.

'What are we looking for?' Hastang asked.

'Anything strange,' de Payens replied, 'out of the ordinary.'

The retinue did as they were told, joking and laughing, glad to be off the ice-covered trackways, yet as they searched, the mood of these hard-bitten veterans changed. They became uneasy, eager to be gone, asking loudly where they would camp for the night. They searched the lonely yards and outbuildings, and eventually one came hurrying across to where de Payens waited in the door porch of the barbican.

'Someone has stayed here recently.' The man pointed back across the yard. 'Fresh horse dung in the stables. They also ate in the small outhouse buttery.'

'Berrington and Mayele,' de Payens murmured. 'They must have stayed the night.'

Parmenio hastened across and plucked at de Payens' cloak.

'Come! I want to show you something.' He led him across the manor yard to the little chapel: no more than a stone barn with a bell tower built alongside. An ancient, dark place with high narrow windows and a heavy-beamed roof, its stone-flagged floor eaten by time. An abode of ghosts, sombre and echoing. Parmenio had lit candles and lanterns taken from their baggage. The light did little to soften the mood of the place, bathing in a meagre glow the peeling wall frescoes and paintings. The Genoese led them into the sanctuary, a semicircle of rough-hewn brick, though the floor was tiled. A wooden altar dominated the centre. Parmenio had pushed this away and set down two candles; the ring of light revealed how the floor was stained and blackened.

'A fire,' Parmenio whispered, 'quite recent. Wood and

charcoal were used, and look . . .' He picked up a candle, moved to the side of the sanctuary and pointed a gloved finger at the dark splash on the paving stone. 'Blood, I'm sure of it.'

De Payens squatted down.

'Mayele and Berrington have been here,' said Parmenio.

'And so,' de Payens smiled grimly 'has Walkyn.'

# Chapter 13

In the meantime, as Fortune proved herself
fickle and changeable to both sides . . .

De Payens inspected the dark, sticky stain, murmured
a quiet prayer and walked down the nave, the heels of
his boots echoing like the tap of a drum. In the poor
light the babewyns carved on the top of the stout
rounded pillars seemed to be leering and squinting at
him. He stood in the shadow of the battered porch and
stared across the cemetery, a wild, overgrown spot, the
bracken and weeds almost smothering the tattered head-
stones and decaying wooden crosses. He was about to

turn away when he caught a glimpse of movement in the cemetery. He stared again. Yes, he was sure: someone garbed in brown and green to blend in with the sombre colours of the ancient yews, hardy shrubs and creeping foliage. He glanced up at the sky, greying with the first touches of the night. Soon it would be owl time, and this place . . . He recalled a ghost story told by Theodore, how each cemetery was guarded by an earth-bound spirit, the soul of the last person to be buried there. Was he seeing visions? He smiled at the faint crackle amongst the undergrowth. A heavy-footed ghost? Parmenio came hurrying down the nave.

'What is it?' he murmured. 'I sensed . . .'

'A malignant place,' de Payens replied. 'Evil lurks here like some beast hungry at the door, famished for souls. I'm not too sure who it is,' he turned to face the Genoese, 'but someone hides in the undergrowth. I doubt if they're hostile. No one would dare attack a company like ours. Ah well,' he sighed, 'perhaps a little honesty might dispel the gloom.' And without waiting for a reply, the Templar walked into the cemetery. He came across an ancient table tomb, crumbling, gnawed by the years and the passing seasons, once a magnificent resting place, now nothing more than a derelict slab. He climbed on to it and unsheathed his sword.

'Parmenio,' he said, 'if you could translate . . .'

The Genoese, fingering his face, reluctantly came alongside. De Payens held up his sword by the cross hilt.

'Whoever you are,' he called, 'whatever you may fear, I am not your enemy. I wish you peace. I swear by the Holy Rood, by all that is sacred, that you are safe. Yes, even in this demon-infested place you are safe.' Parmenio repeated his words in the harsh island tongue, then de Payens took one of the precious gold coins from his wallet and held it up to catch the light. 'I swear by the Holy Face that this is yours if you come forward.' He lowered his hands and stepped down.

The undergrowth stirred. Three men came out dressed in dark green jerkins and brown hose, hoods pulled well over their heads. They were armed with crossbows, daggers pushed through their belts. Two stayed where they were, while the man in the centre walked slowly forward, folding back his hood to reveal a narrow bearded face, eyes glistening from the cold, cheekbones chapped and weather-worn. He approached de Payens, one hand extended. The Templar clasped it.

'Churchyard,' the man declared in stumbling Norman French, 'my name is Churchyard.' He jabbed his thumb at his two companions. 'If I, we, could have some food, wine, meat?'

De Payens called over to Hastang standing in the porch. The stranger would only talk to the Templar, so he took him to the buttery, where Churchyard warmed himself over the makeshift brazier, then wolfed down the food Hastang brought. As he ate, de Payens studied him. Churchyard's fingers were blackened, his garb stained and sweat-soaked, but he was sharp, intelligent and, by his own admission, educated in the horn book and psalter. He might have been a clerk, Churchyard confided; instead he had become Walkyn's franklin or steward. He grinned at de Payens' look of surprise.

'I tried to tell the same to the others who came here, but they drove me off.'

'Who?'

'Lord and Lady Berrington.' Churchyard grimaced. 'Well, it wasn't them; more the cold-faced Templar. We needed no second warning. I recognised Philip Mayele, an expert swordsman. I knew him when he fought for Mandeville.'

'You fought with Mandeville?'

'Of course. Walkyn had no choice. You've seen this manor, a lonely outpost in the wilds of Essex. Armies roamed like fleas on a carcass. What was the use of tilling and sowing if you never lived to harvest, or if you did, someone else took the produce? Lord Walkyn, myself and others drifted into war. Borley was left deserted.' He got up and walked to the door, speaking over his shoulder. 'You're here to learn about Walkyn, aren't you? You must be: there is nothing else here except, of course, the demons.'

'Demons?'

'This was once good land.' Churchyard came back and sat down. 'Hard work but good. I'll tell you my story: Walkyn's parents died. He was alone, raised by an old kinsman who later went the way of all flesh. Walkyn became the manor lord at a time of war. He decided to join that war, so we all followed.'

'What kind of man was he?'

'Why, of mankind,' Churchyard joked back. 'No greater sinner than you or I. He liked his wine and the soft flesh of any peasant girl he could seduce; a good fighter but a weak man. We joined Mandeville's standard. We were no better or worse than any others . . .' He paused as de Payens raised a hand.

'You talk of demons. They say sorcerers, warlocks followed Mandeville.'

'True, I heard the rumours, but they never bothered me. All kinds of wickedness crept out to bask in the sun. Why should I worry about that, Domine? I've seen enough in my life to believe in demons: corpses thrown into wells, swinging from gibbets, trees, roof beams. Men, women and children burned alive. Stew ponds coated with blood, flames licking the black night.'

'And what about Walkyn?'

'He grew tired of it all. We left the war and came here. Only then did we learn what had happened. This place had become an abomination: desolate, empty, soulless, reeking of evil. No one dared approach this manor, not even the most desperate for food and shelter. The stench of wickedness was as strong as woodsmoke. We discovered how Borley had become the haunt of storm-riders, night-dwellers, witches and warlocks. How fires had been seen glowing in the dead of night. How chilling screams pierced the darkness. We made careful search out there in the cemetery.' He paused. 'We unearthed hideous remains. We never discovered their names; now they are only bones and dust, the victims of terrible sacrilege and blasphemy. Borley had become an abode of evil; that's how Walkyn described it, his family home a nest of vipers.' Churchyard supped noisily from his pewter beaker. 'That's what happened during the war. Certain castles, churches and manors were seized by one group or another. Walkyn could not bear it. He blamed himself. He felt guilty; that his own sins would eventually catch him up. He left for London. He talked of taking the cross in Outremer to atone for his violence and lust. We heard rumours that he'd entered the Temple, that he'd gone overseas, but . . .'

'But what?'

'Well, after Walkyn left, we joined another company, which went deep into the countryside, pillaging and plundering. Whispers came, rumours that Walkyn had returned. You talk of demons? Walkyn's name was one of those. I found it difficult to believe; I listened and I sifted. Hideous stories about him being a leader of a coven. By then, Domine, I could believe in anything. Mandeville was in a hot furious rage against both king and Church. This shire had become a place of war. Barges full of armed men floated along the waterways, horsemen thundered along its trackways. No place was safe. One of my company called it "the shire of Hell".'

'But you never met Walkyn again?'

'Never.'

'You recognised Mayele, though?'

'Yes, he was one of those scurrier knights bringing messages to various camps. Mandeville's henchman, a good swordsman, nothing more.'

'And the witch Erictho?'

'Oh, I've heard the name, stories, fables; a name to be frightened of, but nothing else.'

'And Richard Berrington, of Bruer manor in Lincolnshire?'

'Domine, I know nothing of him. I glimpsed him and his sister when they came here. My companions and I hid in the greenwood and watched them leave. I swear, I've never seen or heard of Berrington before.' Churchyard took a gulp. 'Anyway, the war continued. Mandeville was killed. Royal troops entered Essex and the other eastern shires. I and my companions drifted into the forest. We became outlaws. It was a hard life, so we came back here.' He laughed abruptly. 'We found ourselves the guardians of this place. Henry Fitzempress has now proclaimed his peace. Perhaps the manor will be taken from the Temple and granted to someone else. The new lord might cleanse, purify and reconsecrate it.' He glanced greedily at the gold coin de Payens kept twirling between his fingers. The Templar handed it across and decided to trust this man. Churchyard had little to gain by lying. He told him exactly what Walkyn had been accused of, his escape and possible return to England. Churchyard listened in open astonishment.

When de Payens had finished, he just shook his head in disbelief.

'Impossible!' he breathed. 'Either Walkyn was two souls in one flesh, or someone else has assumed his name. I could ask for a description of the Walkyn you knew.'

De Payens shrugged. 'I know nothing. More importantly, a man can change his appearance. Never mind.' He rose. 'If you wish, you can join our company.

Churchyard shook his head. 'Guardians, we call ourselves. I'll remain here.' He got up, clasped the Templar's hand and shuffled out of the room.

Hastang and Parmenio came in to discuss what Churchyard had said. Both seemed surprised. Hastang too wondered if Walkyn was perhaps two souls. They were debating what part of the manor to lodge in for the night when one of Hastang's serjeants burst into the room, saying that they must come. They left, hurrying across the yard. The ancient church looked even more sinister in the fading light, the derelict cemetery sombre, ghostly, alive with eerie sounds.

'Your visitor,' the serjeant gasped as he led them, brushing aside brambles, 'he rejoined his companions and lit a fire . . .' They rounded a soaring, tangled clump of gorse and went through the broken cemetery wall. A glow of light flared through the trees opposite. 'I was simply being friendly,' the serjeant muttered. 'I could see they were hungry, and one of them had been accepted by you, sir . . .' He let his voice trail away. They entered the trees and reached a small glade a little way in. The fire now burned weakly, and two corpses lay there: Churchyard and one of his companions, sprawled face down. Ugly, squat feathered bolts were embedded deep between their shoulder blades, mouths all bloody and sticky with that final rush of breath that had taken their souls.

'There were three,' Parmenio declared, staring around.

De Payens stood up. 'The third was probably Walkyn's man, a spy, ordered to watch. He killed Churchyard for talking to us, then took the gold. He is on foot, so we'll be swifter.' He walked through the darkness of the trees, aware of all the chilling sounds around him. The day was drawing on. Darkness was approaching, as was the climax to all this horror. De Payens recalled an ancient prayer, closed his eyes and whispered it fervently:

'Lord support me all the day long, until the shade lengthens and the evening comes, the busy world is hushed, the fever of life is over and our work is done. Then, Lord, in your great mercy, grant me safe lodgings, holy rest and peace at last . . .'

They reached Bruer after five days' hard riding. De Payens was determined to arrive unannounced. The manor stood on a slight rise at the end of a narrow valley that cut through sullen, wild heathland. The sides of the valley were heavily wooded, the trees densely clustered along the trackway that wound up to the moated, high-walled grange. A hazy, sombre day. The swirling mist shifted and curled. The air was icy cold, the silence broken only by crows wheeling above the frost-laced trees and bracken. Pinpricks of light from the manor provided a welcome beacon, drawing them in across the lowered drawbridge, under the fortified gateway and into a cobbled bailey, where Berrington, Mayele and Isabella waited to greet them. They'd been alerted by a guard just before de Payens had reached the gatehouse. All three were surprised but acted cordial enough. Berrington, despite his effusive welcome, appeared ill at ease. Isabella looked tired, with dark rings around her eyes. Mayele, muffled against the cold, was his usual sardonic self, his lined, bearded face twisted into a grin, though his eyes were as watchful as a hunting wolf's. They offered refreshments, which were politely refused. All exclaimed in surprise at de Payens' appearance and the presence of Hastang and his comitatus. Nevertheless, all three continued the pretence of being the busy, welcoming hosts.

De Payens and his companions were shown around the precinct. Bruer was a large manor, with its own chapel, outhouses, even a small farm. They were eventually ushered into the solar above the great hall, a long, timbered chamber, its walls covered with painted cloths, the rafters draped with pennants and banners, soft rugs warming the tiled floor. A fire burned merrily in the hearth. Cresset torches and candles provided ample light. The grand table on the dais had been hurriedly set, gleaming with dishes and candelabra. The kitchen behind the screen, housing the ovens and spits, provided fragrant, sweet smells. De Payens had a quiet word with Hastang and, through the usual exchange of courtesies with his reluctant hosts, learned how Berrington had brought six of his mercenaries here. Apparently he had dismissed the servants who'd looked after the manor and hired cooks, scullions and servants, five in number. Berrington ushered de Payens, Parmenio and the coroner to their seats, clapping his hands to attract the attention of the servants. He was highly nervous, de Payens concluded, as was his sister; even the cynical Mayele was growing uneasy. They'd been given little time to prepare or plot. This evil fellowship had dismissed him as naïve, a fool, even witless, the madcap knight who blundered wherever they pushed him. Well, that would change.

De Payens placed his war belt on the floor beside him, even as he caught Berrington's worried glance at Isabella. He heard a sound from outside. Hastang's mercenaries and bailiffs had pushed their way into the solar. Isabella, flustered, tried to serve wine. De Payens glanced a warning at Parmenio and Hastang. All was ready! It would end, here, in this warm, sweet-smelling solar, with the fire flickering and the candles glowing, a far cry from the hot, dangerous desert or that sun-drenched gate of Tripoli where he had turned his horse with the assassins slipping towards him.

'Edmund!' Isabella was openly alarmed. Hastang's comitatus was now filing around the chamber. Shouts and cries echoed from the buttery and the entrance hall outside.

'Edmund.' Mayele half rose to his feet, glancing long-ingly at his war belt hung on a peg near the door.

'Sit down!' De Payens' gauntleted hand beat the table so hard the platters, ewers and goblets shifted and clattered. 'Sit down,' he repeated. He felt a sense of relief. Hastang quickly whispered that they'd been told the truth: his serjeants had reported how the strength of the manor was only the six mercenaries Berrington had brought from London and the five servants recently hired. 'Please.' De Payens held up a hand. 'Berrington, Isabella, my one-time brother Mayele, remain seated.' He could hardly bear to look at Isabella, her face now tense and watchful. All three were grouped at the far end; Berrington in the middle, Isabella and Mayele on either side. Parmenio and Hastang sat halfway down, either side of the table. The Genoese was acting perplexed, gnawing his lips, fingers never far from the hilt of his dagger. De Payens glanced around. Hastang's men-at-arms, crossbows primed, guarded the door and all entrances.

'I have found Walkyn,' de Payens announced. 'When I arrived here, I briefly mentioned that I thought he was in York. That was a lie. He is here!'

'What?' Mayele exclaimed.

'You!' de Payens retorted. 'You!' He pointed at Berrington. 'And you!' He jabbed a finger in the direction of Isabella. 'All three of you are Walkyn.'

'Nonsense!' Isabella hissed.

'Truth!' de Payens replied. 'Henry Walkyn, lord of

Borley manor in Essex, was undoubtedly a sinner, a man much given to hot lust, but his flesh, his bones, God knows where they lie. Rotting under the hot sun of Outremer, perhaps, or buried deep beneath some rocky outcrop, picked clean by the vultures and buzzards. The same is true of those two hapless Templar serjeants sent to guard him.'

'Lies!' Berrington snarled.

'Listen.' De Payens rose and walked the length of the table. 'I do not know when this began. I do not know if Isabella Berrington is truly your sister or whether she is your leman, your strumpet!'

Berrington pushed back his chair, but the click of the crossbow catch Hastang now lifted on to the table kept him still.

'She is certainly the witch Erictho.' He leaned down and held the hard eyes of the woman he'd once thought he loved, certainly glorified as the lady of legend. 'You and Berrington are steeped in the black arts, the bloody rites, the demonic psalms and all the other heinous practices. You came together when the civil war raged, a time ripe for your malignancy, when God and his saints slept. You moved from here and joined Mandeville in Essex, forming your own coven, drawing in the likes of Philip Mayele, whose face was already turned against God. Little if any record exists of you, Berrington, in Mandeville's retinue, but you were there, though I suspect under a different name. I wonder if the Berrington the king and others mentioned so favourably

293

was your elder brother? You claim to be the second son. You are certainly Cain's offspring! Others flocked to sit at your table, a time of utter freedom for your abominable rites. No sheriffs, no king's justices, only war, murder, plunder and rape. Who would notice? Who would care about peasant maids being snatched up as your offerings? Who would busy themselves about disgusting ceremonies being carried out in the black hours of the night in sanctuaries once sacred to God? No peace, no law, nothing but anarchy.' De Payens paused. 'But King Stephen, God bless his name, resolutely opposed Mandeville, and the earl was killed. The Church refused consecrated burial to an excommunicate, so the Temple received his coffin and hung it from a tree in a cemetery close to their house in London.' He paused as he heard a cry from outside, then dismissed it. Parmenio was fiddling with his wine goblet but never raised it. De Payens had given strict instructions not to eat or drink anything offered at Bruer.

'Your coven,' he smiled at Berrington, who still sat surprised at the turn of events, 'became notorious. It attracted the attention of abbots, bishops even the Pope in Rome. Accordingly Thierry Parmenio, *malleus maleficorum*, the Pope's hammer of witches, was also alerted.'

'So that's what you really are, Genoese,' Mayele drawled, 'a pimping spy. I wondered as much.'

'Your notoriety was growing,' de Payens continued, returning to his seat, 'but Essex became dangerous. You could not continue your secret life as royal armies swept through the shire. You decided to leave. You, Berrington, approached Boso Baiocis, the master of the English Temple. Mayele also, acting the penitent sinner, the knight who'd killed a cleric and been ordered to take the cross in reparation. You were veteran knights with no impediment, eager to serve the cross in Outremer. Baiocis would be only too keen to recruit you. Isabella, as your devoted, pious sister, would also accompany you. Your wish was granted. You reached Jerusalem, a haven for so many of your kind. Tremelai accepted you with open arms. He was eager for recruits, desperate to strengthen the order, zealous to expand its influence in this island. You were admitted into the brotherhood, whilst your so-called sister took lodgings in a convent, but of course, in time, like any dog, you returned to your vomit. Erictho the witch emerged, a grotesque figure with her straggling wig, masked face and bizarre clothes, glimpsed but never really seen.' Isabella laughed sharply, then glared at Berrington and Mayele as if urging them to do something. 'You returned to your heinous rites, choosing victims for your bloody sacrifices . . .'

'An easy task.' Parmenio, realising the drift of de Payens' allegation, was eager to intervene. 'An easy task in Jerusalem, with its sacred places, its beggar children, hordes of young girls and women, vagrant and vulnerable, but,' the Genoese spread his hands, 'Jerusalem is not the wilds of Essex. No Mandeville emerged to protect you, no horde of mercenaries to shield you, just a legion of spies and informers who swarm around what in truth is a very small city. Rumours began to drift. Tremelai told me about Erictho being glimpsed with a Templar, as well as entering the Temple precincts.' Parmenio ignored de Payens' glare of accusation. 'Peace, brother. Until now, I dared not trust any Templar. I did not really know who was in the coven and who was not. During our journey to Hedad I tried to draw Mayele, to discover more about his past; hence my closeness with him.' He smiled. 'But as we now know, that was his best defence! The cynical mercenary, with little faith or none. The rebel who would find slight cause with either God or the devil. He simply acted according to character, though he hid his blasphemous, murderous ways.' He turned back to the accused. 'Rumour certainly whispered that Templars were involved in satanic rites, not for the first time in your order's history. Tremelai grew highly anxious, as did the Patriarch of Jerusalem. I was summoned from Rome, but . . .' Parmenio gestured at de Payens to continue.

'You, Berrington, decided to act. The rumours were thickening. You decided that Henry Walkyn would be your sacrificial lamb, a man intoxicated with fleshly pleasure, who had often been seen around the brothels and houses of disrepute in Jerusalem. He was English, lord of the deserted manor at Borley. You and your coven had undoubtedly used both that place and his name to perpetrate your abominable practices. A toper given to loose living, Walkyn was vulnerable. You placed those artefacts in his room, helped spread the malicious whispers. The conclusion was inevitable. Walkyn was arrested.'

'But why should Tremelai turn to me?' Berrington asked.

'First, because you are English. Second, I suggest you played a prominent part in detecting Walkyn. Third, you must have exploited Tremelai's fears that a coven existed within the order, perhaps comprised of English knights. You would argue how it might be best to get Walkyn out of Jerusalem, stifle a scandal, send the miscreant back to the bailiwick of England for judgement. How Tremelai could trust you and your fellow countryman Philip Mayele. Who else could the Grand Master turn to, other than English knights? How many of them are there? How many of those could be trusted? Tremelai would rise like any fish to the bait. He'd get Walkyn out of Jerusalem, kill the rumours and prevent a scandal. At the same time, however, he must have been secretly furious about what had happened. Perhaps at your instigation he decided to hold Boso Baiocis to account. Little wonder Tremelai summoned the English master back to Jerusalem, to be questioned about how the likes of Walkyn were admitted to the order in the first place.'

'And why should my brother be so keen to take Walkyn?' Isabella asked, regaining her composure.

De Payens secretly marvelled how easily she could replace one mask with another, so skilled in deceit! 'You know that already,' he retorted. 'You and Berrington must have discussed it often enough. You'd been out of England for some time. You were tired of Jerusalem, wary of how close and narrow a place it was. How dangerous it was for you, vulnerable to capture. You wanted to return to your old haunts. You were now in a position of power. Berrington and Mayele were Templars. Once you returned to England, you could remove Baiocis, which you did, and exploit his death for your own secret purposes: chief amongst these was your deep, fervent desire for revenge against King Stephen, who'd brought about the downfall of Mandeville, your protector.'

'Brother!' Mayele scoffed.

'Don't call me that!' De Payens gestured at Berrington. 'Tremelai was only too pleased to commit Walkyn to you, to see him disappear back to England. You left Jerusalem. Walkyn, manacled and chained, was guarded by two serjeants.' He glared at Berrington. 'Was that your idea? To ask for two guards, a fairly paltry escort? Easier to kill? Your sister was left behind in Jerusalem. She would follow you to Tripoli and join you there, or so you publicly proclaimed. Everything was planned, safe enough. Who would dare to attack the Temple?' He waved at Isabella. 'You would! Once out in the lonely wasteland, you, Berrington, turned on those serjeants. You murdered both of them, as well as Walkyn. Afterwards, Isabella hurried back to Jerusalem to act the lonely sister, whilst her brother remained free to continue his plotting.'

'So I followed my brother?' Isabella exclaimed. 'I wandered the desert?'

'I didn't say that,' de Payens retorted. 'I can imagine that camp: Walkyn by himself, the two serjeants busy. Were all three given some opiate, a poison? You're skilled in physic, my lady, you proved that on our journey to England. Were they drugged before their throats were slit and the lady Isabella, accompanied by Mayele, entered the camp to check all was well? To remove weapons, clothes and horses? Ensure that Berrington was ready to move on to the next part of your plan?'

'I was in Chastel Blanc!' Mayele shouted.

'No you weren't – you would have been on one of your many journeys as a messenger. Who would suspect if you took a day or two longer?'

'But why kill Walkyn?' Berrington jeered. 'He was supposed to be my reason for returning to England.'

'Oh, for a number of reasons. Walkyn was innocent. I wonder if Tremelai had his doubts. The old Englishman William Trussell definitely did. What would Walkyn say if he was put on trial? He'd certainly had enough time to reflect on what had happened. Perhaps he too nourished his own suspicions about being used as a catspaw. He had to die. Second,' de Payens spread his hands, 'that's why we are here, isn't it? Henry Walkyn was the warlock, the sorcerer, the assassin who'd fled his captors and had a hand in the murder of Count Raymond before fleeing back to England to exact vengeance against the

299

crown. Oh yes, Walkyn dead was much more valuable than Walkyn alive. He became the devil incarnate, the sinister will-o'-the-wisp who had to be hunted down. Tremelai, once he'd heard the news of Walkyn's alleged escape, realised the terrible danger confronting him. A rogue Templar loose in this misty island, summoning up his coven to assist in the destruction of the king. Think of the damage that would do to the order's reputation!'

'And Tripoli?' Parmenio asked.

'Edmund, Edmund!' Mayele still believed he could bluff his way out. 'You were with me in Tripoli.'

'So was Berrington,' de Payens countered. 'Here, your plot became more intricate. Walkyn and the two serjeants were dead. Berrington, you and your coven are against all authority. You had no love for the Temple. Tremelai had brought your refuge in Jerusalem to an abrupt end. You wanted to cause chaos, you would like that, but there were other more pressing reasons.'

Berrington's sneer could not hide his fear.

'Some people are so evil,' Parmenio interrupted, 'that all they want to see is the world on fire. Everything turned upside-down! The flames of destruction all-consuming.'

'Certainly you wanted revenge against the Temple,' De Payens declared. 'More importantly, you needed gold and silver.'

Berrington opened his mouth for some jeering remark. Isabella made to rise. Hastang, fascinated by these revelations, shifted the primed arbalest. She and Berrington sat back in their chairs.

'Yes, wealth!' de Payens snapped. 'You are a poor knight, a wanderer who wanted to return to England. Out in Outremer there are no abbeys to plunder or monasteries to attack. To do anything openly, such as ambush a caravan or a wealthy merchant, would be too dangerous; it would expose you. Tripoli, however, is wealthy; it is also a city bubbling with factions. Any disturbance might provide opportunities. How else could you acquire the wealth you'd need once you returned to England, to assemble your coven, pay assassins, buy potions, dress Isabella to be so appealing to the king? The hiring of barges, boats, horses and messengers, not to mention the purchase of weapons and food, all these cost money. You were determined to cause an uprising in Tripoli and create chaos, which you would exploit. You also wanted to continue the pretence that Walkyn was the villain, deepen Tremelai's fears, make our Grand Master more amenable to pursuit, which would bring you into England.' De Payens paused. Mayele had moved slightly, eyes hungry for his sword belt. De Payens sensed this would end in violence. Mayele would never surrender.

'The murder of Count Raymond would be the cause of this chaos,' de Payens continued. 'Then, Berrington, you did something very audacious. You needed assassins, so, head and face shaved, you went to Hedad to speak to Nisam. You pretended to be Walkyn. The caliph

301

would not know the difference, while you could sustain the pretence of being the rogue Templar on the prowl.'

'Very dangerous,' Mayele intervened. 'I visited Hedad, remember?'

'Not dangerous at all,' de Payens retorted. 'The Assassins, for all their reputation, are honourable. Berrington would be accepted as a guest, a petitioner. He offered them no threat. He was protected by the strict rules of hospitality. More importantly . . .'

Parmenio held his hand up and glanced at de Payens, no longer distrustful but rueful, as if conceding to his own admiration. 'You are a Templar.' He pointed at Berrington. 'Nisam would be very interested in your chatter, though he was also determined not to offend the Grand Master.'

'Nisam refused you.' De Payens took up the charge. 'Nevertheless, once again you had blackened Walkyn's name. You had linked Count Raymond's murder with the rogue Templar. You started that rumour as part of your plot. After you were refused, you travelled on to Tripoli and decided on a more dangerous task: to hire your own assassins, lure them in with promises of plunder. You would use whatever wealth you had, the monies given to you by the Temple. You could hide behind a disguise; nevertheless, it was a perilous undertaking. Rumours began to drift about a knight, possibly a Templar, being involved in a hideous conspiracy, Parmenio heard these whispers and hastened into the city. Tremelai also learned of them and became more anxious, desperate about the escaped Walkyn, sick with worry about you, Berrington, and where you might be. More importantly, Count Raymond also suspected mischief.' De Payens collected his thoughts. 'I have no proof of this, but the count probably demanded the Temple's protection against any threat. Who better to send than Philip Mayele, an English knight, and Edmund de Payens, scion of the noble founder of the Templar order, a mark of respect, an assurance of the Temple's good wishes?'

'Yet Count Raymond still died?' Hastang spoke up.

'Of course, there was nothing I could do to protect him. Mayele was part of the conspiracy. Mayele, my so-called brother knight, the messenger who often travelled between Chastel Blanc and Jerusalem. A man who undoubtedly,' he ignored Mayele's muttered curse, 'used such occasions to meet secretly with his fellow conspirators, especially the Lady Isabella.'

Isabella gazed back stony-eyed. De Payens peered at the window. The day was fading. He gestured at Hastang.

'Send one of your men outside to see that all is well.'

The coroner obeyed. De Payens waited for the serjeant to return and nod his reassurance.

'Count Raymond was murdered,' de Payens continued, 'and a massacre ensued, undoubtedly helped by you, Mayele. Berrington had chosen his intended victims: wealthy merchants, their coffers and caskets full of gold, silver and precious stones easily seized and secretly hidden away.'

'And the assassins?' Mayele asked.

'You know what happened to them. You hunted them down. Those three men you silenced before the church where I was sheltering? They were the assassins, used then killed before they could prattle.' De Payens stretched out his hand for a goblet brimming with wine, then remembered and drew back. 'Nothing of course runs smoothly. You, Berrington, fled Tripoli. You decided to take refuge in the Turkish-held town of Ascalon, where you hoped to prepare the next part of your plot.' De Payens shook his head. 'I don't know what that was, but you were busy. Meanwhile you, Lady Isabella, had already struck. You visited William Trussell. The old veteran had anxieties and suspicions of his own. He certainly doubted Walkyn's guilt. You, madam, have a midnight soul, black and hard, a true slayer. You probably fed him some noxious potion . . .'

Isabella simply stared at the goblet, and de Payens wondered if she'd intended him to die here. 'Meanwhile,' he cleared his throat, 'Berrington in Ascalon prepared his own story in readiness for his return to Jerusalem. How he had escaped Walkyn's murderous assault but been captured by desert wanderers, perhaps? Or forced to hide? Some fable for poor Tremelai that would, of course, precede a demand that Walkyn be pursued, even if it was to England.' De Payens stopped talking as Hastang's captain entered the hall. He stooped and whispered into the coroner's ear. Hastang, surprised, murmured back and the man left. The coroner glanced at de Payens, gesturing that it could wait. Isabella glanced in alarm at Berrington. Mayele shifted on his chair. De Payens caught a tension, a real fear. These warlocks were trapped; it was best to leave matters in God's hands and move to a conclusion. Judgement was waiting. He felt the ghosts cluster around him; all those murdered by these devil's assassins had come to witness that judgement.

# Chapter 14

The King caught a mild fever, sickened
and so departed this life.

'Nothing under God's sun goes as we wish,' de Payens
declared. 'You, Berrington, were plotting your next move
on the chessboard, only to have everything upset.
Baldwin III besieged Ascalon; Tremelai was there,
urging on the attack. I wonder if the Temple, with its
myriad of spies and legion of informers, had learned
how a Templar was in Ascalon. Did Tremelai know that?
Did he wonder if it was Walkyn, or perhaps Berrington,
who had mysteriously disappeared? The rest you know.

Ascalon fell, but Tremelai was killed. You, Berrington, emerged from the chaos, eager to carry on your mission by other means. An opportune moment! The Grand Master was dead, Trussell too. You could spin your tale, weave your lies. You had to leave for England. You were determined to bring Mayele and me with you. Mayele could keep me under your scrutiny, to ensure I suspected nothing about Tripoli and Hedad, and when the time was right, kill me. In your eyes I was a coney in the grass, a fool to be flattered by Isabella, patronised by Mayele and ordered about by you. My presence on the embassy to England would enhance your status. And if I was to die here, then it would be some unfortunate accident, or perhaps the work of the fugitive Walkyn.'

'Berrington said you should leave,' Mayele scoffed. 'You wanted to journey back to Outremer, you and the prying Genoese.'

'I was disgusted by Prince Eustace's raids,' de Payens countered. 'A matter of hot temper rather than cold resolve. Oh,' he gestured at Parmenio, 'the prying Genoese as you call him must have been a thorn in your side. You didn't know who he truly was – and why our masters had such confidence in him. I'm sure if an accident had befallen me he would have suffered a similar mishap. In the meantime, you could see I was not his true comrade. Parmenio was useful to you, a distraction for me, perhaps? True, you did want both of us to leave for Outremer, and why not? You had reached England. You had met with great success. You no longer needed either of us.' De Payens laughed abruptly. 'If we had left, I doubt we would have reached Dover alive. Your assassins would have seen to that.' His gaze drifted around the hall. He noticed the tapestries, the paintings, some coloured canvas nailed to a piece of wood. He could see no crucifix, nothing of the Church. He also wondered what Hastang's mercenaries had discovered in this temple of darkness.

'What de Payens said is true.' Parmenio spoke up. 'I heard rumours about a conspiracy in Tripoli, about a Templar being involved. I saw what happened in that city, and was so angry I almost did what you would have liked: struck at de Payens. On reflection, it was remarkable how certain merchants' houses were pillaged within a short while of Count Raymond's death. Of course that was planned.'

'Be that as it may,' de Payens continued, 'Montebard was only too willing to send envoys to the English king. Baiocis would also be eager to leave. On our journey you were cunning; nothing happened. We landed in England and the pursuit of the mysterious, elusive Walkyn began. You, Berrington, furnished us with a fable about Walkyn landing at Orwell in Essex.' He shook his head. 'Nonsense! You became busy. Baiocis was the first to die; he had to! God knows what he might know or suspect, what secret records he kept.'

'Edmund, Edmund!' Mayele tapped the table. 'You have missed one very important fact. You and I were sent to Hedad to question the caliph about the assassination of Count Raymond. Why would Tremelai do that if a Templar was suspected of being involved?'

'It was logical.' De Payens held Mayele's gaze. 'No one really knew who was responsible for the massacre in Tripoli. Tremelai still believed, indeed hoped, that he could lay the blame at the feet of the Assassins. After all, certain of their insignia, curved daggers, the red ribbons and the medallion, had been found. Of course, as Nisam said, such items can be purchased in any bazaar. Tremelai was also curious about the truth, and of course you would welcome that. There was nothing to lose and a great deal to gain by visiting Hedad.'

'Baiocis?' Hastang intervened. 'You were talking about Baiocis?'

'Oh yes, he was the first to die. He wasn't poisoned at the banquet but sometime before. He was clutching his belly from the very start. In all that confusion in the priory refectory, one of you poisoned his goblet to create the impression that the poisoning occurred then. In one swift, ruthless blow you had what you wanted: Baiocis dead, a place at the royal board, as well as control over the English Temple. Prince Eustace, Senlis and Murdac were just as easy to kill. You followed them into your old haunts in the eastern shires. By now you were using your secret wealth to contact other members of your coven, hire assassins and buy poisons. At the abbey, Prince Eustace's chamber overlooked the garden. One of you secretly entered through the window and smeared their goblets, a devastating blow against the crown: Stephen's heir and two of the king's most fervent supporters all murdered, the malicious work of Walkyn. Eustace and Senlis were wine-lovers; they drank swiftly. The second draught would clear all poison from their cups. Murdac of York was more temperate; his cup showed how it had been done. Eustace and Senlis died immediately; the archbishop didn't die, but he was weakened, marked down for death. Don't you remember, Berrington? You were so eager to remove that tray of cups and the flagon. You took it down to the infirmary. If Murdac had not been so moderate in his drinking, we might never have found the source of such dreadful poisonings.'

De Payens thrust away the goblet on the table. 'You continued your hunt. The king's second son, William? I am sure your coven had a hand in his accident outside Canterbury. You could organise such a mishap: all those messengers supposedly dispatched to the court, other Templar holdings or elsewhere, a marvellous device to communicate with members of your evil fraternity and plot further mischief, such as the attack on me in the forest.' He pointed at Isabella. 'As for you, fair of face and foul of heart, flirting with the king, sitting alone with him and, I am sure, poisoning his wine cup. What noxious potion did you feed him, a secret poison to rot his innards?' He glanced quickly as Parmenio stirred. He was not finished with the Genoese, not yet, but that would have to wait. 'The king will certainly die,' de Payens continued, 'in pain, great suffering, some malignancy in the gut or bowel, and then perhaps more civil war, which you can

310

exploit. Or were you satisfied, Berrington? Your new-found status as master of the English Temple would certainly allow you to continue your secret life. I have witnessed your work in London and Borley: young wenches, poor souls! God knows what horrors they experienced. You are immersed in such practices, addicted to your secret rites. I doubt if you can help yourself, be it in London or on your journey to Essex . . .'

Mayele began to clap, driving his hands together furiously. He sprang to his feet, the mocking applause echoing around the hall, and walked the length of the table. Hastang made to move, but de Payens made a sign to let it be. He suspected what Mayele intended, and welcomed it so as to give vent to his own rage. Mayele paused just before him and sat on the edge of the table.

'And what proof, the evidence for all this?' he jeered.

'Really, Judas-brother,' de Payens mocked back, 'is that what it's come to?' He shrugged. 'Proof enough. Walkyn is proof. A toper, a man given to wine and the joys of the flesh. Alienora was surprised at the proclamation issued against him. If he'd stood trial, others would have come forward to testify about his true character. So who is this Walkyn? Where is he? Can such a man really have the power and means to achieve what you three have done?' He tapped the table. 'Where is Walkyn, Mayele? Why did you kill those three men in Tripoli? And after the attack on me at Queenshithe, you and Isabella, as was your custom, were teasing me. You talked about my escape from that murderous assault in the woods outside the Abbey of St Edmund. You described my rescue. How did you know such details? I never told you. Which of you met with Baiocis before the banquet? Which of you poisoned that cup after Baiocis collapsed – when no one really cared to notice? And Isabella,' he stared down at the witch, 'how did you know which street I rode down as I left Jerusalem for Hedad? You actually mentioned the Streets of Chains. How could you know such a detail and remember it unless you were there, as you were, in your true guise as the witch Erictho, standing on the roof of that house glaring down at me? How would Walkyn know I was out in those woods, or journeying down to the Light in the Darkness at Queenshithe, or visiting Alienora? Strange: you three were always missing on such occasions. Moreover, who had the means, the knowledge, the wealth to hire assassins for such murderous assaults?'

'We were also attacked.' Mayele leaned down like a magister in a school confronting a clod-witted scholar.

'Lies!' De Payens smiled. 'What attack? Self-inflicted petty wounds? Pig's blood splashed on the floor of the guesthouse? Yet,' he spread his hands, 'not a drop of blood after that, no bloodstains up to the walls the assassins must have fled over. Stupid.' He pushed his face closer, 'You wanted to confuse me. Your arrogance had grown! Poor de Payens, he will accept whatever he is told. Well,' he smiled, 'you made other mistakes as well. Berrington underestimated Nisam at Hedad. As an act of deep friendship the caliph gave me a message, complex and hidden. I only understood it much later. It was enclosed in a verse about it being difficult to kick against the goad, followed by a question about who will guard the guards. He urged me to wake up, to be alert, to look at the Temple more closely. Above all he was urging me to reflect on someone who was on guard. Nisam, who sifts the gossip and the chatter of Outremer, did not believe your story. God knows why! Did he have you followed from Hedad? Did he make careful enquiries in Jerusalem about Walkyn's description, about yours? He had his messenger pigeons, his horses of the air. The Assassins pride themselves on their knowledge of other men's affairs. I have no proof, but I suspect Nisam learned the real truth about Walkyn and turned the entire story on its head. If Walkyn had been killed, who was this pretending to be him? It could be none other than the man who'd guarded Walkyn.' He sighed. 'As for evidence, we could search your belongings. We could put your hired assassins to torture. We could bribe and threaten.' He smiled thinly. 'All it will take is one confession, one loose thread, and your tapestry of lies would unravel. You thought you were safe. You wanted me out of the way; instead I'm here for revenge. One final matter.' De Payens glanced quickly at Parmenio. 'My prying Genoese friend has received information that Walkyn's remains may have been found.'

'Impossible!' Isabella screamed, and then paused, hands going to her mouth.

313

'You see,' de Payens smiled at Mayele, 'you see, Judas, how it will go?'

Mayele moved closer. 'I should have killed you, Edmund.' He leaned back as if to get up, then brought his right hand round so swiftly that no one could stop him, and struck de Payens across the mouth. 'There,' he smiled, 'a challenge! Come, little Edmund, you talk of evidence and proof. I challenge you to ordeal by battle. Let us settle this by the sword.'

De Payens felt his lip swell, blood seep into his mouth. His temper raged. He ignored Hastang's warning, Parmenio's shouted advice. His world was nothing but Mayele's taunting smile, the blood trickling over his tongue, hands desperate for his sword. He lunged to his feet and struck Mayele's cheek.

'À *l'outrance* – to the death!'

Hastang and Parmenio shouted caution. The coroner's comitatus brought up crossbows; others drew swords and daggers. Mayele was already across the chamber, taking down his war belt, unsheathing his sword, letting his cloak drop. Berrington and Isabella were also on their feet. Hastang shouted at them to sit down. They did so, Isabella smiling secretly to herself.

'Let it be.' De Payens drew his own sword. 'Trial by battle, ordeal by combat. If I lose, Hastang and Parmenio will leave?'

'Agreed!' Berrington taunted. 'Little Edmund, you have had your day in the sun.'

De Payens unclasped his cloak and let it fall. Mayele,

swift on his feet, came forward, both hands gripping the hilt of his sword as he turned slightly sideways. A consummate swordsman, a warrior confident of his own skill and strength, he lifted the blade in a mocking salute, then closed, his sword spinning like a farmer's flail, wicked, glittering arcs that de Payens blocked clumsily. Stepping back, he almost tripped over his own sword belt, which provoked a sharp laugh from Isabella. Mayele grinned. De Payens let his temper surge. He heard himself roaring defiance as he stepped back, shifting slightly, his blade snaking out as he swayed on his feet. He felt his hands grip the wide hilt, comfortable, sure. All he was concentrating on was shattering his opponent's defence. His blade scythed the air, twisting and turning, seeking an opening that would allow either point or edge to pierce or gash flesh. He was moving forward, the sweat streaming down his face. The glow of candlelight and the flare of cresset torch shimmered back through his fury. Mayele's face was drawn, chest heaving, his sword blows no longer fast and furious. De Payens was driving him back: the man who had mocked, patronised, betrayed and tried to kill him. His fury deepened. A voice screamed, '*Deus Vult! Deus Vult!*' Something hot splashed his face; he could no longer move forward, could do nothing except slice and cut. He felt a tug on his arm, hands pulling him away. He stopped, sword lowered, tip hard against the ground, and stared blindly at Hastang's mercenaries, who gazed fearfully back. Chest heaving, hot and sweat-drenched,

315

he was aware of Mayele sliding slowly down the wall. The gushing wounds in his opponent's right shoulder and the side of his neck stained the white plaster crimson. Blood bubbled between Mayele's lips. He slouched to the floor, eyelids flickering. Isabella was screaming; Berrington had tried to escape and was now held fast. Mayele, breath panting, lifted his head and glanced up at de Payens.

'I never knew,' his voice came as a croak, 'brother, I never knew. Forgive me, eh?'

'No.' De Payens moved forward and thrust the tip of his sword deep into the exposed neck. 'No,' he repeated watching the life dim in his enemy's eyes. 'But God might, so go to him.' He withdrew his sword, stepped back and watched Mayele die. Hastang clapped him on the shoulder.

'Berserkers,' the coroner whispered back, 'ancient warriors,' he explained, 'consumed by the fury of battle. I've heard of them, but until today never seen one.'

De Payens nodded and pointed his sword at Berrington and Isabella.

'God waits for them as well.'

'As he does for all of us,' Parmenio replied.

'And you?' de Payens muttered. 'You, Genoese?'

'Edmund, Edmund,' Hastang intervened, 'you'd best see this.'

The coroner ordered the prisoners to be kept fast and, accompanied by Parmenio, led the still sweating, still panting de Payens from the hall. Outside in the yard,

Berrington's six mercenaries stood disarmed, manacled together. Close by were the few servants who also had been hired. De Payens glanced at these; their faces betrayed them. He was sure they were all members of Berrington's coven, men and women who'd served with him during the glory days of Mandeville. The coroner urged him on across the bailey into a barn-like stone chamber. Torches flared to reveal a long, sombre room. Hastang led them across to where a raised flagstone was propped against the wall. One of his mercenaries stood on guard nearby, holding a cresset torch. At Hastang's orders he led them down narrow, steep steps into an ice-cold, airless dungeon. The man, gabbling a prayer, raised the torch. Five corpses, a man, a woman, two youths and a maid, hung by their necks from hooks driven into the roof beams, faces grotesque in their death agonies. A dreadful sight, arms and legs dangling, bodies turning slightly as the ropes creaked and twisted. De Payens pinched his nose at the foul smell. He touched the cheek of one of the corpses; it was hard, cold as ice.

'Who?' he whispered. 'Who are these?'

'I suspect,' Hastang murmured, covering his mouth and nose, 'that they must have been a family sheltering here in this deserted manor. The roads are crammed with such unfortunates.' He took his hand away from his mouth and swallowed hard. 'This manor,' he muttered, 'probably enjoys the same malevolent reputation as Borley; few local peasants would even dare come here. I suppose these wanderers did.'

'But why kill them?'

'Why not?' Hastang retorted. 'Berrington could not afford to let them leave. God knows what they found. Mayele would have enjoyed the killing. Edmund, what shall we do?'

The Templar stared at the corpses, all twisted and grotesque. Hastang repeated his question. De Payens just shook his head and, his body now cold with drying sweat, led the way back up the steps. At the top he stared at the flagstone, the great bolts and clasps that held it fast.

'They were probably killed after being held captive for a while,' he murmured. 'Perhaps they did find something down there or elsewhere.'

'Edmund, the prisoners?'

De Payens walked back into the hall. Berrington and Isabella, hands tied, sat slouched in chairs; Mayele's corpse, awash in its own blood, still slumped against the wall. De Payens had both prisoners searched. He did not speak to them. He refused to even look at Isabella, but ordered Mayele's corpse to be lifted and the prisoners brought out. Then he went back across the yard, ignoring Isabella's screams, Berrington's curses and a spate of questions from Hastang and Parmenio. In that eerie, sombre outhouse, he ordered Berrington and Isabella to be pushed down the steps, then Mayele's corpse was thrown in, bundled down like a sack of refuse.

'Go down!' de Payens instructed. 'Take two men, Master Coroner. Search the walls and floors; ensure there is no other entry.' He drew his sword, resting its blade across his shoulder. 'I am,' he whispered, 'senior knight of the English house of the Temple. I have the power.'

Hastang nodded. He beckoned at Parmenio and a few of his henchmen to follow. De Payens, sword still against his shoulder, stood guard at the top of the steps. He gazed at the other members of Hastang's retinue, who, though hardened by war, stared fearfully back at this man of blood. This place held the same creeping, chilling horror as Borley, an evil haunt to be cleansed by fire. Isabella was still screaming, begging, but de Payens thought of the bloodstain at Borley, those hapless corpses, that poor girl in the deserted church outside London, Murdac spitting and gasping in agony. He closed his eyes. Hastang and the others rejoined him. No other entrance could be found. De Payens ordered the flagstone to be lowered, and insisted on personally fixing the bolts in their clasps. He left two men on guard and went out into the yard, where he summoned the five servants, three men and two women. He walked past these, studying their faces, not liking what he saw there.

'Undoubtedly you served Berrington before.' He could not understand their rushed, desperate answers, but Parmenio and Hastang translated their protestations of innocence. De Payens studied them closely, his battle fury now ebbing. He felt a twinge of compassion, yet these were minions, retainers, servants of their dark, malignant lords.

'Strip!' he ordered.

Parmenio repeated the order.

All five prisoners did as they were told until they stood naked except for loincloths and the shabby cloaks de Payens offered the two women.

'Take them,' he ordered, 'and go!'

The five were pushed out through the gates, Hastang's mercenaries beating their buttocks with the flat of their swords.

'They can walk to the nearest village,' de Payens murmured, 'seek whatever shelter and consolation they can.'

'And these?' Hastang pointed to the six ruffians Berrington had hired in London, two of them nursing injuries.

'Take them back to London,' de Payens retorted. 'Examine them. Perhaps they can betray others, root out more of their coven.' He brought the flat of his sword down on one of the prisoner's shoulders. 'Find out who attacked me at Queenshithe. Were any of these in that bloody affray? Did they follow me to Alienora's and kill her as ordered by their masters? A poor woman horribly murdered simply because of what she might tell me. Or,' he lifted his sword, 'turn them over to the sheriff. Let him hang them!' He turned and walked back into the hall.

'You cannot stay here,' he warned Hastang. 'You and yours must not eat or drink anything here. Now, let's search the manor.'

It was dark before de Payens, now feeling tired, met

Parmenio and Hastang back in the solar. Despite the crackling fire, the dancing candle flames and the coloured tapestries, it was still a macabre place with its own hidden yet watchful evil. One of the guards reported how Isabella was still screaming and begging. De Payens replaced the guards with others, then, with the point of his sword, sifted amongst the possessions he and the others had collected from various chambers. He crouched down and picked up a small coffer crammed with pearls, diamonds and other precious stones. He lifted the pouches and purses stuffed with the gold and silver coins of Outremer. He examined the tray of pots and phials from Isabella's coffer; some were perfume, others exuded a noxious, baleful odour.

'Proof enough!' Parmenio knelt down beside him. 'No poor Templar knight could be so rich. This is what caused that hideous massacre in Tripoli.'

De Payens nodded and turned to the other artefacts: a black leather psalter, its yellowing pages full of strange symbols and incantations, a twisted cross, an ancient knife of obsidian stone, small carvings of winged, dragon-like creatures, amulets emblazoned with intricate carvings. He'd seen enough.

'No doubt,' Hastang whispered, 'my boys kept a little of the money for themselves.'

'They deserve it,' de Payens replied. 'Take the prisoners back to London, Master Coroner. Hand the treasure over to the next master of the Temple. Say it is a gift, a blood offering. Demand that masses be said.'

'And you?' Parmenio asked.

De Payens ignored the question as he picked up his sword. 'Stay at some tavern, the one we passed on the road into the valley. Use some of this treasure to pay, stint for nothing, enjoy yourselves and wait until I join you.'

'Which will be when?'

'You will know. I shall stand vigil here until the Berringtons are dead.'

'You were successful.' Parmenio smiled. 'The Holy Father, the Grand Master will be pleased. You truly are a warrior of God; also a clerk as sharp as any who serve in the Pope's secret chancery.'

'Am I?' De Payens smiled.

'Are you what?' Parmenio abruptly stepped back as de Payens brought his sword blade down to rest on the Genoese's shoulder, its sharp blood-encrusted edge almost brushing the side of Parmenio's neck.

'Am I really so successful?'

Hastang breathed in quickly. Parmenio made to move back. De Payens pressed down with his sword.

'So, I am the scholar being praised by his master. Yes?'

'What do you mean?'

'You clever Genoese! You followed the same path as I did and reached the same conclusion, but much sooner, much earlier, because you knew more than I did.'

'I . . . I . . .'

'Hush.' De Payens smiled. 'A matter of logic, Master

Parmenio. In your eyes I was a sword but one that would have to wait to be used. You are under orders from the Pope to hunt down malefactors, but you have other, more secret instructions.'

Parmenio blinked. He opened his mouth and breathed out noisily as de Payens pressed on the sword.

'Your secret orders brought you first to Outremer then here. Did our Grand Master Montebard really care about King Stephen?'

'Of course he did.'

'Did he, my friend? Or the Pope? Were they really concerned about Stephen and his arrogant, aggressive heir? Of course they wanted to see witches and warlocks sent to their just fate, but did they really care for Stephen or his son? After all, Henry Fitzempress is young and vigorous, a loyal son of Holy Mother Church. The powers in Rome and elsewhere want to end this savage, futile civil war. The bishops of England need to reclaim their own. The Temple is eager to expand. The papacy desires to see peace in a kingdom usually faithful and loyal to it. Holy Mother Church, in a word, both in England and Rome, wants peace, which will bring trade, money, revenues and a revival of learning. So think, my friend, as I have: who really cares if Stephen suddenly dies? If Eustace the drunk, the violent is silenced before he can wage his own civil war, beget an heir and pose a challenge? William, his younger brother, now injured and maimed, what threat can he now pose? Reflect, my friend. In the space of what, less than a year, Stephen is dying, Eustace is dead, William seriously injured. Murdac of York and Senlis of Northampton, Stephen's most loyal advisers, have also gone to their eternal reward. So no more division, no more strife, peace at last! The board has been swept clean. Young Henry Fitzempress can emerge and take all.'

'Are you implying . . . ?' Hastang asked.

'Yes, I am. Parmenio knew the truth but he lacked the proof, the firm evidence, but what did that matter? Let the warlocks do their worst. Let them, through their lust for revenge, bring about a situation others are secretly praying for. What is that phrase, Parmenio? How God keeps evil men close to his right hand so he can use them for his own secret purposes? In a word, that is what has happened. Berrington and his coven have cleared the board for you, and now that is done, they too can be killed.'

'You have proof of this?' Parmenio spluttered.

'Proof, my friend? Your face is proof enough! Go,' he lifted his sword, 'report back to your masters on how successful you have been. How you used the Templar to hunt down the sorcerers but not before they did exactly what your masters prayed for. I wonder how much the others knew of the truth: Tremelai, Montebard, Henry Fitzempress? Four people definitely do – you, me, Hastang and your master in Rome.'

'I didn't know at the beginning . . .'

'Oh no, of course you didn't, but what did it matter if it was Walkyn or Berrington? Let such people have their hour of mischief. My friend, by sheer logic and the passage of time you reached my conclusions a little earlier than I did. You were always suspicious of Mayele. Did you have your agents in Outremer and elsewhere search for the truth about Berrington and Isabella? About Walkyn? About what really happened in Jerusalem? Did they bring you such information in the murky corners of London taverns? And then you would tell them, your masters abroad, about how Stephen and all his house were finished. How Henry Fitzempress would come into his own and be grateful for the support of Holy Mother Church. How you would use this Templar, who could at last be trusted, to execute vengeance on a coven of murderous warlocks. You arrived in England to find no Walkyn, yet those hideous poisonings still took place. You probably began to suspect the truth after our stay at St Edmund's; it was just a matter of time and logic. Ah well! Let it ride.' De Payens sheathed his sword. 'Now it's time you were gone. Tomorrow, soon after dawn, your masters will be waiting.'

Coroner Hastang waited at the Tomb of Abraham, a spacious tavern out on the old Roman road that cut through the wild countryside to Lincoln. He manacled his prisoners in outhouses and feasted his comitatus, rewarding them with some of the plunder seized from Bruer manor. The mysterious Genoese, Parmenio, went his own way, leaving the tavern early, disappearing into the mist, gone like a thief in the night. Hastang entertained himself by listening to the macabre tales about the area, though the taverner became tight-lipped at any mention of Bruer. The coroner waited. He realised that the enigmatic Templar, the man with the far-seeing eyes, as he now thought of him, was maintaining a death watch at that desolate house. Hastang's retainers took turns to camp out at the mouth of the valley, watching what might happen. Mid-morning on the sixth day, two guards came galloping back to the tavern to report how the manor was burning like a farm-yard bonfire. By the time Hastang reached the mouth of the valley, he could see the flames roaring like the fires of hell, great flickering sheets, accompanied by gusts of black and grey smoke. A short while later, Edmund de Payens, dressed in his chain mail, helmet on, his great white Templar cloak with its emblazoned cross swirling about him, cantered along the trackway snaking down from the manor, a grim figure against the searing flames. He had apparently prepared for a long ride: the sumpter pony trailing behind him was stacked high with panniers and bundles. The Templar reined in, turning his destrier, and peered up at the greying clouds.

'Not yet full spring,' he murmured. 'Summer will be most welcome when it comes.'

'What happened?' Hastang asked.

'It's over, they are dead. The fire will consume the rest.' De Payens slouched on his horse, eyes smiling at Hastang. He stretched out a gauntleted hand, which Hastang clasped. 'Farewell, old friend.' De Payens squeezed the coroner's hand.

326

'You'll not come back to London? Your brothers at the Temple?'

'My brothers are not there, Hastang. I'll go back to the Abbey of St Edmund and seek my brothers amongst the forest folk.' He winked and let go of Hastang's hand. 'That's the only place I have ever really laughed out loud.'

'Your vows?'

'I'll keep my vows.' De Payens gestured back at the flames. 'Go now, it is finished. I will stay until this is over.'

Hastang made his final farewells and turned his horse, gesturing at his companions to follow. He rode off, not looking back until he heard his name called. De Payens, sword drawn, had moved his great war horse, making it rear up, iron-shod hooves ploughing the air. The Templar, cloak floating about him, raised his sword. '*Deus Vult*, old friend!' he cried. '*Deus Vult!*'

'Aye,' whispered Hastang, tears brimming in his eyes. 'God wills it, my friend, and may God have mercy on you.'

# Epilogue

Melrose Abbey, Scotland

Autumn 1314

Brother Benedict watched as Domina de Payens put down the manuscript, then turned as if to stroke the vellum parchments strewn over the writing table beside him.

'Is that how it ended?' the young monk asked.

'Perhaps,' the old woman whispered. 'You've read the letters, the memoranda, the chronicle of the monks at the Abbey of St Edmund? Some say that was written by de Payens himself.' She smiled. 'The good brothers certainly loved the stories, as did the forest folk.' She blinked quickly. 'Stories about a strange knight dressed in white who defended them against outlaws or any who tried to hurt them. Of the same knight appearing at tournaments to defend their rights or win purses of silver to better their lot.'

'But King Stephen, Tremelai, the Assassins, Count Raymond?'

'All true,' the old woman half whispered.

'And de Payens never returned to his order?'

'Oh, I think he did. He kept his vows, the paladin, the Poor Knight of Christ! He observed his oath to protect the weak and defend the holy. He fought the good fight. He kept faith, and at the end of our lives, how many of us will be able to say that?'

# Author's Note

Black magic, the pursuit of secret power, has been an obsession of human society in all cultures and at all times. Scholars realised the limitations to their knowledge and strove to pierce the veil in pursuit of fresh revelations. In the Middle Ages, black magic and political power often became intertwined. Allegations of witchcraft, for example, were levelled at a number of queens: Isabella of France (1327), Joanna of Navarre (1416) and of course Anne Boleyn. Kings of England have also been depicted as practitioners, the most famous being William Rufus, whose death by an arrow in the New Forest was, according to the anthropologist Margaret Murray, part of a sacrifice in an ancient rite. Great noble families did not escape the taint. In 1326 Hugh de Spenser, Edward II's chief minister and favourite, was the object of a black magic plot organised allegedly by the Prior of Coventry. De Spenser complained bitterly to the papacy, who wrote back tartly that he should say his prayers, reform his ways and put his trust in God. The great nobles of England tried Joan of Arc and burned her as a witch. Indeed, the English aristocracy were most adept at depicting their opponents as dabblers in the black arts; even Humphrey, Duke of Gloucester, uncle to Henry VI, was brought down by such an indictment.

Accordingly, it's hardly surprising that the Templars, when their day of judgement arrived, were also accused of practising witchcraft, an allegation that haunted the order throughout its two-hundred-year history. In 1307, when Philip IV launched his persecution of the Templars, sorcery and black magic figured prominently in the accusations levelled against them.

Nevertheless, even free of these allegations, the Templars were always regarded as suspicious. In Outremer they provoked both jealousy and apprehension for being quite prepared to negotiate and seek a rapprochement with the Muslim world. Such attitudes, coupled with secrecy and an innate talent for acquiring wealth, brought them into disrepute, and they were often accused of 'forming a kingdom within a kingdom'.

By 1152, the original concept of the 'Poor Knights' founded to help pilgrims and protect travellers to Jerusalem had been quickly subsumed into a magnificent fighting order with a warlike reputation second to none. The Templars made it very clear that they would never surrender. In fact they were as harsh to themselves as to any enemy. The chronicler William of Tyre recounts an anecdote about Templars who surrendered a castle being later hanged on a charge of cowardice.

Other sects and groups also flourished in the Middle East; none were so feared as the Assassins. They were as described in this novel, though it must be conceded that their victims were in the main not Franks, or even crusaders, but Islamic leaders who dared to oppose or cross them. William of Tyre, in his *History of Deeds*, describes how the Templars and the Assassins could be mortal enemies and stoop to murder in their feuds, but if circumstances changed were comfortable enough in doing business with each other.

The death of Count Raymond of Tripoli is as described in the novel. The true reason for his assassination has never been clarified, with allegations and accusations being hurled from all sides. His death did provoke a savage massacre, during which, according to William of Tyre, 'all those who were found to differ either in language or dress from the Latins' were 'put to the sword'. The chronicler believes that Count Raymond's killers were 'the Assassins', but the real victims of his death were the people of Tripoli.

The siege of Ascalon also happened as described here. The Templar Grand Master did lead that fatal, futile assault through the temporary breach in the walls. Tremelai and the others were cut off and annihilated; their gibbeted corpses only stiffened the resolve of Baldwin and the Frankish army. Ascalon surrendered on terms. For a while the Templar order was thrown into total disarray by the death of the Grand Master. No reason was given for Tremelai's foolish impetuosity. William of Tyre claims that it was due to the arrogance and greed of the Templars. I suggest another reason.

The civil war in England (1135–54) was bitter and savage, fuelled by the ambitions of the great lords. Geoffrey de Mandeville was chief amongst these. Historians have now tried to balance the heinous allegations of the chroniclers levelled against Mandeville. Nevertheless, certain accounts, such as that of the *Anglo-Saxon Chronicle*, do depict him as 'fearing neither God nor man'. Mandeville did wage war in the eastern shires, occupying and pillaging monasteries. He was killed as described in the novel, dying excommunicate, and for years his coffin hung eerily between heaven and earth in the Temple holding at Holborn. Eventually the papacy relented and allowed him honourable burial. The Templars' reception of Mandeville's corpse was a surprisingly religious act, and was probably part of a policy whereby the order, eager for acceptance in England, proved themselves amenable to both sides in the conflict. By 1153, the Templars did have a presence in England, under a master known as 'Boso'. Their house was in Holborn, and only later did they exchange that property for another, thus creating 'New Temple'.

The end to the civil war was both surprising and swift. Eustace, Stephen's son, collapsed 'choking' at St Edmund's Abbey after leading a ferocious raid throughout the surrounding countryside. Senlis of Northampton and Murdac of York, the king's close advisers, also died around the same time, as did others. Indeed, so many of Stephen's adherents died so swiftly and so opportunely that poison has been voiced as the cause by historians such as T. Callahan. David Crouch, however, in his scholarly work on King Stephen, dismisses this, arguing for 'quite a potent bacterial infection', judging by the number of prominent deaths in this one-year period. Nevertheless, the list of casualties amongst the royals during the period 1153–4 is most surprising. Stephen's second son William was seriously injured in an accident outside Canterbury; while Stephen himself, according to the chronicler Gervase of Canterbury, was 'seized of a bowel disorder accompanied by internal bleeding'. He died after a short illness at Dover on 25 October 1154, leaving the way free for Henry the Angevin, hale and hearty, to sweep to power.

Both Stephen and Mathilda did patronise the Templar order, which stayed neutral during the civil war. However, once Henry the Angevin became king, the order expanded rapidly. The crown and the great nobles were generous in their many grants. The Templars acquired land and status and were a powerful force until 1308, when Edward II eventually turned against them. The word 'temple' still figures prominently in English place-names.

Borley in Essex has always enjoyed a macabre reputation. The professional ghost-hunter Harry Price dubbed it 'the Most Haunted House in England'. The causes of the paranormal events described there have been discussed in many books and pamphlets. The possibility of the Templars having a manor there has been listed as another reason for such phenomena. Temple Bruer in Lincolnshire also has a sinister history. W. H. St John Hope wrote a learned article on the site in *Archaeologia* in 1908 (Vol.61). In this he mentions a previous article by a Rev. G. Oliver (published in 1837), which claims that secret vaults were found beneath the old Templar enclosure. In these 'lay quantities of cinders mixed with human bones'. The truth behind such a find has never been established.

Paul C Doherty
April 2009
www.paulcdoherty.com